ECHO
LOCATION

Linda Kay Silva

Bella
BOOKS
2011

Printed in the United States of America on acid-free paper
First Edition

Editor: Katherine V. Forrest
Cover designer: Linda Callaghan

ISBN 13: 978-1-59493-244-1

Acknowledgments

As I have settled into a new life in my old home, I have discovered new friends as well as old ones who have laughed with me, supported my writing, shared books, discussed movies, and even vacationed with me. As we age, we realize the quality of these friendships can be life-sustaining—they have the ability to lift us higher and fill us with joy. I am a very lucky woman to have such wonderful people in my life, and so I would like to take this page to thank them for helping me be a better writer, a better teacher, and a better person.

Fay and Karelia—Not only fellow writers and teachers, but two amazing women who change the lives of those they work with every day. You inspire everyone around you to greatness because you both are...amazingly great. Judge Styles and Professor World Why you rock.

Debbie and Donna—Donna is my Santa Claus. She brings me packages and goodies while sporting her brown shorts and beautiful smile. Everyone loves Donna, especially her lovely wife, Debbie, whose laughter is contagious. Thank you for laughing with us.

Joni and Dayna—What a treat you both are, and I am so glad we found you! We have loved laughing with you, talking about everything under the sun, and enjoying easy time in your splendid company. Meeting you both was the bonus of 2011! You totally rock.

My cousin Kristin—I can't imagine my life without you and your support. You listen, laugh, give hugs when needed, and you are always there for me. You mean more to me than you could ever know. Thank you so much for being more than my cousin...you are one of my best friends.

Billie Tzar—You are my workhorse, my go-to guy, my tech team, my cover artist, and my Renaissance Man. You make my life easier in so many ways. Thank you, for all that you do and all that you are.

Katherine V. Forest—I give her clay, she creates the Pieta. I give her coal, she hands back a diamond. Not just a fabulous editor, but also someone I include among my friends. Thank you for doing both so well.

My Aunt Cathy—You lend me your ear, your advice, and your loving support at a time when I truly need it. Thank you just isn't enough.

Kim Jacobs—You are, hands down, the best boss I have ever had...but the best part is you are also my friend. Thank you so much for that, and for hanging with me in DC. You make my job not feel like one. Thank you for all you do for me and those we teach.

Sandi—You have the fastest fingers to touch a keyboard and they help me write as much as I do. Thank you for unchaining me from my computers and being part of Team Storm.

Ellen—You are inspiring to others more than you realize... after all these years, it is great to be real friends. Thank you for being part of our family and for loving my girls as well as you do.

Dedication

This one goes to my girls...without whom, I wouldn't be who I am.

Lori—my girl, my love, my best friend—you give me the gift of time to do what I love most. You support my eccentricities (of which there are many), you make me laugh every day, you keep me fed and clothed, and you help me stay sane in an insane situation. I still get goose bumps whenever I look across a crowded room and see you. For a woman who has to put up with as much going on inside my Mega Mind as I have going, you handle it with great aplomb. You are more than the wind beneath my wings....you are the sun and the moon, the stars and the Milky Way. I do so love you.

Kelley—As I write this, you are somewhere in Swaziland helping people less fortunate than you. I am so incredibly proud of the woman you have grown into and the selfless path you have chosen. I miss you, and can't wait to go on safari with you. You have renewed my faith in your generation. I love you.

Sunnie—You are your own woman, strong, fiercely independent, and crazy as hell, and I love that about you. One of the greatest parts about raising you is that you aren't just my daughter, you are my friend. My life is better with you in it. I love you.

Lucy—Okay, so she's a dog. But she's the best dog in the world, and I adore her. She hangs out with me when I write, she cuddles me when Lori is out of town, she doesn't eat my bird when he flies on the ground in front of her, and she warms my heart every day. Everyone should have a Lucy!

About the Author

Linda Kay and her partner of 13 years have returned to her childhood home in the San Francisco Bay Area to care for her elderly father. There, she has reunited with old friends, met new ones, and fallen in love with her new Harley, Lucky. She belongs to a women's motorcycle club, plays on a tennis team, rescues turtles and tortoises, and travels around the world, having recently returned from Egypt. When she's not Professor Silva teaching Early American and British Literature at a Military University, she is busy working on the next novel of her Across Time Series and her new installment of this series. Linda Kay can be found on Facebook and YouTube under Linda Kay Silva, as well as Twitter under iamstorm. She welcomes (and responds to) all email at iamstorm@yahoo.com.

Finn slid across the ratty booth of our favorite greasy spoon. If truckers knew all the best places to eat, cops were second on that list. Marist Finn knew every great eatery in San Francisco, and had taken me to places I wouldn't have gone to if I were starving. They just looked plain scary. Where we were sitting looked pretty scary as well, with its tattered red vinyl seats and rusted license plates from nearly every state hanging on the wall like a jigsaw puzzle missing pieces. Were there no drivers in Rhode Island willing to part with their plates?

As Finn reached for a menu, she groaned. Her brown eyes looked tired, with dark bags under them. We had recently returned from New Orleans after Hurricane Katrina left her ugly imprint on a city that would never be the same—a city that had been the only home I had ever known. Both of us were pretty beaten up by what we had seen and experienced in the wake of a nightmare in one of the greatest cities in America. Having spent most of my teenage years there, I had many wonderful childhood memories of the Louisiana bayou, but now, many of my old haunts had been wiped out by the flood. Gone—just the cement foundations lying there like a ghost waiting to leave purgatory. We'd done as much as we could for those who had lost everything, but we came home exhausted, disillusioned and minus one of my best friends. Jacob Marley had given his life in the tangled chaos occurring on a nightly basis in the Ninth Ward and other hard-hit neighborhoods. We had come to help, and once there, needed as much help as we gave. I had returned home to San Francisco without my dear friend Jacob Marley, without completing a job that would probably take years to complete, and without the confidence or knowledge that my relationship with Finn was something that should continue.

No wonder she looked so tired.

"We need to talk," I told her, wishing this talk was going to be uplifting instead of a kick in the stomach.

"That never bodes well," Finn said, smiling softly. Her lips smiled, but her eyes did not.

Though we had only been home four days, we had spoken only once, and briefly at that. Everyone who had ever seen the aftermath of Katrina needed to decompress in their own way. For me, I came home, turned off my phones and crawled in bed for three days. When I woke, it all felt like a nightmare, but Jacob Marley was still dead, and my home destroyed.

"It's been impossible to get hold of you, Echo." Finn reached out and laid her hand on mine. "Makes me wonder if I've done something wrong."

I stared at her.

Wrong? I suppose accidentally seeing me and my friends using our paranormal powers could be categorized as *wrong*, but that wasn't *her* fault. Wrong place, wrong time, maybe, but Finn had done nothing less than save the life of my mentor—the woman who taught me how to harness and use my powers. Finn had possibly seen us using ours to defend ourselves from a man who would have destroyed us.

Finn *saw*. She'd never admitted it, but I knew.

I am an empath.

I feel people's emotions, their truths, and I knew she'd seen us.

I was born with the ability to read other people's emotions. I know when someone is lying and when they are embellishing the truth. I can read through layers of sadness, walls of protection and any amount of bullshit. I know when someone is experiencing violent tendencies, when they are physically ill and when they are keeping a secret. It has been both a blessing and curse, and at this moment, as I gazed into the beautiful eyes of my girlfriend of three months, it was a curse. She knew what was coming. She didn't need my empathic skills to read the sadness in my eyes. And I *was* sad. I had really started to believe maybe she was the one; that maybe I could share with her the largest skeleton in my closet...but she had seen something she wasn't meant to see— something that would change everything about us.

In downtown New Orleans, on a night filled with crazies and rioting, Finn had stumbled upon me and my supernatural family defending ourselves against an angry, ugly, mob. She saw something I'd been wrestling with divulging, and now, here it was, the elephant between us. I could no longer continue pretending to be normal. She *knew* I was not. She *saw*. Well...she didn't actually see *me* using my powers as an empath, but she saw me with my people as they used theirs. She might have also surmised that one of the reasons I was so good at my investigative reporter position at the *San Francisco Chronicle* was because I used my abilities to uncover the lies and deceit people emit every moment of every day. It's a very helpful power to have in my line of work, but not one I confess to having and not one I was ready to share with her.

She was a cop. It was her job to know when people were telling the truth and when they weren't. For the last three months, I had not been completely truthful with her. Well...I hadn't really been lying. I just committed lies by omission, which, in my book, was the same as lying. The choice I had been struggling with, whether or not to tell her what I was, was no longer mine to choose. All I could do at this point was deal with the fallout.

"You saw, didn't you?" I blurted. Normally, when I am in

public, I have psychic shields up so I don't go crazy feeling what everyone around me is feeling. Shields are the only forces protecting us from shorting our brains out. Too much input drives us insane, and unless a newbie psion is trained how to build shields, they will, most assuredly, go crazy from all of the static entering our brains.

I seldom have my shields down nor do I even lower them when I am with people I love. It's very invasive to know what someone is feeling at any given moment, and normally, I would rather they keep their private emotions private.

But not today.

Today, I needed to know exactly what was going on with her. I cared about Finn very much, but I knew in my heart I couldn't keep seeing her unless I was willing to be completely honest about who and what I was.

I just wasn't sure I could be that honest with *anyone* I was romantically involved with.

"Echo, I'm not entirely sure what I saw. It all happened so fast and it was dark and—"

She was lying, and my heart sank. "Finn—"

She held her hand up. "Okay, that's not true. I *did* see something, but—" She shook her head. "I'm pretty sure that what I think I saw cannot, in fact, really happen. I've been over this a thousand times in my head and I just don't know what to make of it. I was hoping you'd tell me."

So, there it was. Finn doubted her own vision, her own eyewitness account of supernaturals in action. My heart hurt for her. "What would you say if I told you that what you saw could, in fact, happen?"

She never took her eyes from mine; their intensity was palpable. "As far as I know, you've never lied to me, but that would be too much to believe even from you."

Officer Marist Finn was one of the best people I had ever met. She was honest, sincere, hardworking, loyal and not afraid of showing her emotions. At this moment, she didn't have to, because I knew she was afraid of losing me to something she couldn't even explain. It wasn't fair, but that was the way of the paranormal world. Like witches and other beings outside the norm, it wasn't safe for us to be known. Too many people would want to take advantage of a telepath. We would be turned into circus freaks first, and then some government agency would realize the power, the incredible bonus of having a telepath in their midst. We would be poked and prodded, examined like lab rats. In short, we would never be free.

Leaning back in the booth, I ran my hand through my short brown hair. I couldn't bear looking in her eyes. She wanted a truth I was not at liberty to tell. "The truth is...I am not at liberty to talk to you about what you saw. I can only tell you that you weren't seeing things and you aren't crazy."

She swallowed hard, but said nothing.

"But that's all I can say about it. I know it's not right, and I know it's hard to have a relationship with someone who has so many secrets...and that's...that's why I can't see you anymore."

She blinked a couple of times and then licked her lips slowly. "Let me get this straight. Because of what happened in New Orleans, you don't want to see me anymore."

It was one thing to tell your partner or a parent that you're a telekinetic who can move things with your mind, or a telepath, who can read thoughts, but a girlfriend didn't earn enough frequent flier miles to qualify as someone deserving of the greatest secret we all possessed. It was simply not a stable enough relationship yet to share something that could be used against us all if things went south. Most supernaturals, or supers, as we call ourselves, prefer not to share that information with anyone. It was just too big a risk, and so, we were, in a way, in the closet even from those we would most wish to share ourselves with.

Our collective safety happened because we were successful at flying under the radar of a society which seldom embraced anyone different from the norm. If people knew about us, our private lives would cease to exist. So as much as I adored Finn, we had come to that fork in the paranormal road and I had to take either the Tell Her path or the Leave Her path. I had decided before I came here that the latter was best for both of us. She was too nice to be dating someone she would never have the chance to really know.

"I...I just can't, Finn. This has run its course and—"

"We haven't even scratched the surface of us, Echo. I can't believe you can sit here and look me in the face and tell me you can't see me anymore because of something I *might* have seen."

Slowly sliding my hand out from under hers, I leaned across the table. "I am not who you think I am."

"I haven't even had the time to figure out who I think you are. Look, I know something big happened in New Orleans, but to be honest, I'm really not at all sure what it was. Now, you tell me we can't talk about it and that we're done."

Finn stood up. "Well, here's an idea. I don't *accept* that. It would be one thing if you could look me in the eye and tell me you were bored with me or that I have bad breath, or even that you met someone else, but this?" She stopped and sat back down. "Is that it? Did you meet someone in New Orleans or...or...did you start something up with one of those guys you were hanging out with?"

I had to throw my shields back up; the pain in her eyes was nothing compared to the pain she emitted. It bowled me over. "Guys? Uh, hello? I'm gay, and we weren't *hanging out*, Finn. We were helping people...*our* people. Can you accept that?"

She sat there and looked at me a long time before slowly shaking her head. "No...I don't accept it. I interview people all the time, Echo. I *know* a nonanswer when I hear it. If you're going to break up with me, at least respect me enough to be honest with me. I deserve that much."

"I...I wish I could."

She rose again and reached for her keys. "Then you can tell everyone the real reason we broke up: that *you* couldn't be honest with *me*. At least that I can accept."

I watched her walk out of the diner a very different woman than the one who entered. I felt like a total bitch, but there was nothing I could do. I couldn't very well say, "Yes, Finn, you saw someone throw a fireball. Yes, you saw a bunch of people attack us and then get melted like candles in a bonfire." Yeah. That would really cement us together forever.

Supernaturals like myself are able to move about in the normal world by remaining invisible, or, at least, by hiding our powers. If she knew the truth, not only would I be vulnerable, but so would everyone I knew and loved. Letting her go was something I had to do for all of us.

"Can I get you something?" the young red-headed waitress asked.

"Just a cup of coffee, thanks." As I waited for the coffee, I thought back to my time in New Orleans and the losses we suffered there.

My mentor, a Haitian super named Melika, had called us all back to the bayou after Katrina hit in order to put our skills to use helping our fellow Louisianans trapped during the subsequent flooding. Once there, we faced out-of-control mobs, toxic water and a foe who managed to kill our dear friend, Jacob Marley. We managed to subdue the mobs, maneuver through toxic bilge and eradicate our enemy. In doing so, we sacrificed Jacob's life, a young girl's soul and my relationship. It was no wonder I'd been feeling so depressed since we got home. I'd gone to New Orleans to help, and it had ended up costing me more than I could afford.

But when Melika calls, we come.

We come because without her, none of us would know how to control our powers, few of us would have even lived beyond the initial stages of learning, and some of us would have been caught in public doing things we shouldn't be doing in public, and possibly locked up forever. She was our mentor, teacher and mother. She alone had the ability to teach each of us how to survive our powers.

Puberty is when most of our powers kick in. For some of us, it's younger, and sometimes, there's a glimpse of our powers before we reach our teens, and when it happens, many of us become disoriented, confused or dead. When mine burst through, I nearly killed a boy, and was sent away from my fourteenth pair of foster parents to a psych ward in the Bay Area, where, luckily for me, Melika's son, Big George, spotted me.

Big George is called a spotter. A spotter's job is to spot supernaturals and get them to Melika before they can harm themselves or others. In the case of a young girl, we didn't manage to get to Cinder until after she had accidentally burned someone up. Cinder is a rare breed known as a pyrokinetic, or

PK. Our special community calls them fire starters, and the majority of young fire starters implode in a fiery mass before they even reach puberty.

Once any of us are spotted by my people, we're whisked away to the hinterlands of the bayou, where Melika and her right hand assistant, Tiponi Redhawk, spend upward of four years training us how to use our primary powers, our secondary powers if we have any and how to build up our psychic defenses. It took me almost a year to learn to build mine effectively.

Tip, our resident telepath, teaches us how to use our telepathy. Not all of us have it, and many, like me, experience it more like a radio wave that comes in strong sometimes and weak other times. It is always strong when Tip comes in because she was more than my teacher…she had been my lover. We have a long history together, and though I love her dearly, I stopped being *in love* with her a long time ago.

My being ten years her junior didn't keep her from pursuing me romantically once I left the bayou. She had always kept an eye out on me regardless of who I was dating, and back then, I seldom minded her overprotective nature or intrusive thoughts. There were times when I welcomed it, especially once I realized that her overprotectiveness was inherent in her genes. She came from a long line of warriors who were expected to protect those they loved.

Tip is a full-blooded Native American, and with this comes the kind of loyalty seldom found outside of tribes and ancient clans. She has a killer body with flawless, red skin most people fawn over once they stopped being intimidated by her. She turns heads, both male and female, wherever she goes, but she is unaffected by those stares. Tip is all business most of the time, which is one of the reasons I couldn't be with her anymore. It's not just that she isn't any fun. She can be on the rare occasion she lets her guard down. Her powers are so strong, they are invasive even when my shields are up. Unless I give it everything I have, I cannot keep her out of my mind. Or my life.

So I stopped trying.

Now, we're great friends who take care of the others from my "class." We hadn't managed to take care of Jacob, and were nursing that wound each in her own way. For me, I buried myself in my work. Tip...she roamed the world hunting other supers, looking for others to help, searching for a way to plug that hole Jacob once filled. I doubt any of us would ever truly get over that loss.

I dolefully finished my coffee and headed over to my best friend's place of work. Danica's computer business was called Savvy Software, and she'd owned it for several years now. Once an upstart software company, it was now a force that had come to the notice of such luminaries as lofty as Steve Jobs and Bill Gates.

Danica would be expecting me and my long face. After all, she was the one who told me it was time to end it with Finn. I could blame all of this on her. She felt I would be doing Finn a service by cutting her loose. Danica did not believe in pulling punches when it came to relationships. She should know—her relationships numbered in the dozens.

Flipping open my vidbook as I got in the car, I called her. A vidbook is a checkbook-size minicomputer with webcam and GPS tracking. Her company had vaulted to the top of the tech world once the technology was patented, making her richer than she'd ever dreamed of being.

Danica answered on the second ring and I smiled as her caramel-colored face appeared on the screen. She is an amazingly beautiful mixed race woman who, when not smiling or laughing, looks like she was ready to rip someone's face off. She looked that way now. "I've got rocky road and chocolate chip, Clark, so come on over."

Clark had been Danica's nickname for me since I was a cub reporter for the school newspaper in college. She loved the analogy that I had "super powers" and was a reporter like Superman. The nickname stuck, which was fine by me since my real name is Jane. Jane Doe. *Jane Doe* as in someone carried me for nine months then left me at the door of a hospital. At least, that was what I thought had happened. I don't have any memory of a life before the foster care homes. It was like I was born five years old and a ward of the state.

I was Jane when Danica and I first met, before my powers

kicked in. I changed it when I left a psych ward after being overcome by emotions I didn't understand. I understand them quite well now, and am no longer a plain Jane. The name Echo felt appropriate enough for the strange power I possess.

I nodded mutely, closed the vidbook, and turned my Bug in the direction of downtown. I knew breaking up with Finn would hurt, but coupled with my other recent losses, it did more than sting. It felt like someone had just poured salt into my wounds.

The tears were coming now, and I just let them flow.

When I opened the door to Danica's office, my sadness lifted for a moment. There she sat with two bowls heaped with ice cream, a bag of chocolate chip cookies from the bakery down the street and a liter of Coke.

There was no better best friend on the planet than Danica Johnson. Since we were fourteen years old, she had been walking beside me on this very special and almost unbelievable path. When we, by happenstance, attended a private school in Oakland, California, we were both outcasts for very different reasons. I had just moved to my fourteenth foster home and I knew *no one*, and Danica was a girl of mixed race whom neither side was willing to claim. Naturally, we gravitated toward each other, and our friendship took off right away. We were blood sisters in every sense of the word.

"You dumped her," she said softly, making her way around the large cherry wood desk in her nearly one thousand square foot office overlooking the bay. Danica's revenge over those who had thumbed their noses at her was to live well, and she managed to do better than that. When we graduated from Mills College, she had already developed a security software that made her rich, and Savvy Software was just a few notches away from being a Fortune 500 company. Earlier in her career, she'd hired a trio of tech heads fresh from Cal who developed everything from operating software to video games to apps. Savvy Software was already on the map…it was only a matter of time before it was the center of it.

"In the worst way imaginable," I said, flopping down on the ten thousand dollar butter yellow Italian leather sofa.

"On the cell phone?"

"No. I'm not that lame. I just told her that she didn't know me and I doubted she ever would."

Danica handed me a bowl and tucked her long legs beneath her while balancing her bowl on her knee. At six feet tall, she possessed all the right ingredients; brains, beauty, bravery. She had saved my life on more than one occasion and I was beginning to wonder when she had become my bodyguard. Not that I needed one. My overall powers are formidable, even though my primary powers are mostly empathic. Still, all the powers in the world couldn't protect my heart from being broken. Again.

"Bummer, Clark. What happened? Did you chicken out with the truth?"

Sighing, I shoved a spoonful of dark chocolate rocky road ice cream in my mouth. "I couldn't tell her the truth, and she didn't understand why not."

Danica moved her ice cream around the bowl as she searched for marshmallows. "You know, Clark, she's a good egg. *'Nihil peccat nisi quod nihil peccat.'* Her only fault is in not having any."

"She told me she wasn't going to give up that easily, and I *need* her to give up. I need her to walk away because I'm having a helluva time doing it myself. I don't have the strength."

Danica reached over and patted my leg. "I know, but still... you could have left her with some pride. Told her something she could at least digest. You could have salved the wound to her dignity. Bingo!" She found a marshmallow and ate it. "You had plenty of time to prepare for this. What happened?" Danica looked up from her bowl and I saw her face register the answer. "Oh, shit, Clark, you were really falling for her, weren't you?" She shook her head. She didn't need to be empathic to know the answer. "I should have known."

"She walked into the diner looking all yummy in her cop uniform. There was this little twinkle in her eye and..." As a tear escaped its perch on my eyelash, I nodded. "I didn't want to dump her."

Danica leaned over and scooped out a spoonful of my ice

cream. "Now I understand why you are so bummed. She meant more to you than you admitted to yourself."

"I can't help it, Dani. There's just so much I really like about her. She's fun. She's a great listener—"

"She's easy on the eyes."

I nodded and sighed heavily. It felt like an elephant was sitting on my heart. "This so sucks."

She fished out another marshmallow and popped it in her mouth. "If she hadn't seen you all fighting that mob back in New Orleans, you wouldn't be kicking her to the curb, would you?"

I shoveled more ice cream into my mouth and started eyeballing the cookies. "Nope. I'd be giving this more time to see where it was going. But I don't have that luxury now. She saw something, Dani. I am sure of it."

"You can still put the ball in her court. Tell her you're sure she has questions about what she saw that night, but if she wants to keep seeing you, she'll have to make sure she never brings it up again."

"And have this enormous secret between us?"

"Clark, every relationship is filled with secrets. It's part of the game. My dad never knew my mom hated the opera until she was on her death bed. She touched his face and said, 'Whatever you do, don't make your new wife go to the opera. It sucks.'" Danica laughed. "It was the first and last time I ever heard my mother use the word."

I reached for the cookie bag. "You really think everyone has secrets between them?"

"Hell yeah. Some are big, some are little, but all relationships have them. What do you think keeps all the daytime talk shows and soap operas afloat? We love to see what happens when people reveal their secrets. It's like personal roadkill. We can't look away no matter how much we want to."

I finished the first cookie and closed the bag. "Since when did you get so smart about relationships? It's not like you've been successful at any." Danica's longest relationship was about two nights and that was only because she had forgotten they had slept together the night before.

"Since I started taping *Oprah*. That sister knows what she's talking about. '*Sensus, non aetas, invenit sapientem.*' Good sense, not age, brings wisdom." Reaching for the cookies, Danica pulled one out of the bag and examined it. Studying food was one of the anomalies that made the kids tease her when we were kids. To this day, she never puts anything in her mouth without first examining it like a scientist looking through a microscope. "If you're going to go in that direction, you need to do it quickly, before the wound you dealt her becomes a scar." She rose and jammed the cookie in her mouth before offering her hand to me. "Had I known there was love at play here, I'd have given you different advice," she mumbled through her cookie.

"I don't think I realized it until I let her go. Then it hit me hard."

Swallowing the last of her cookie she said, "Then you need to go to the police station to see her before she goes off duty and starts drinking with her buddies, because believe you me they will not paint a pretty picture of you. That's what we do. It's human nature to vilify the dumper and offer sainthood to the dumpee."

Nodding, I handed her my empty bowl. "Will she even want to see me?"

"Look. Officer Hunky Pants is a cop. It's her job to read people. If she knows you at all, she knows you dumping her had nothing to do with how you feel about her. Tell her you have some secrets you want to talk to her about, but that you're just not ready to."

I nodded. "Thanks, I feel much better and fatter than I did before I got here."

"You can afford to eat a pork chop, Clark. Baby's got no front, no back, and barely any sides. You make a paper doll look fat."

I chuckled. "Thanks. I think."

"I mean it. You're too thin. All that damn heat and drama on the bayou melted the pounds away. Look at yourself." Danica steered me toward the full-length mirror behind the door.

I was several inches shorter than she was, but quite a few pounds lighter. She was curvaceous in all the right places and made Jessica Rabbit look like a rail. Still, Danica was right about my weight. I could afford to put on a few pounds. The bayou debacle had taken a lot out of me, and my clothes hung loosely as they might from a hanger. Even my normally wavy brown hair hung limply against my shoulders, almost as if it, too, was too tired to remain buoyant and bouncy. In short, I looked like crap on a stale cracker.

"See it now?"

"Paper-freakin'-doll," I said as Danica handed me the bag full of cookies. "It's a wonder Finn wants me at all."

"No kidding. Look, Clark, you haven't slowed down since you got back." Danica turned me around to face her. "I know what you're doing, Jane," she said softly, using my seldom-used first name. "You used to do it all the time in college, but working yourself to death to keep from feeling the loss only prolongs the inevitable. You know that."

"I'm not—"

"Yes you are. Jacob's gone. Tip has disappeared into the great nowhere, and your emotional sailboat is seriously listing in the water. You know, for an empath, you're pretty disconnected from your own emotions. I saw what Jacob's death did to you…to all of you, and yet, you're afraid if you slow down long enough, you'll feel his absence. Well, I hate to break it to you, but you're going to feel it no matter how long you try avoiding it."

If I wasn't feeling it before, I was beginning to feel it now, and tears quickly filled my eyes. Jacob and I had spent four years together on the bayou and he had taught me everything he knew about the majesty and wonder of that incredible place. We'd spent hours on the river just floating along telling each other the stories of our lives. I had been fascinated by the nature of his abilities as a necromancer. To converse with the dead was an incredible, if not altogether bizarre power, and Jacob had shared it all with me, from the time he heard his first spirit, to the many times he sat in graveyards listening to them. The fact that he hadn't gone completely nutters was a tribute to Melika's loving and skilled hand. She had saved a young necromancer from thinking he was insane and taught him how to block out their voices.

And now he was gone.

Wrapping my arms around Danica, I hugged her tightly. "Thank you," I whispered.

"You've lost enough for one year. Go downtown and see if maybe Officer Finn would be willing to play it your way. You love her, you silly goose. What have you got to lose?"

Pulling away, I wiped my eyes. "Mel always said it was our choice, but honestly, Dani, I don't know what to do. She's such a sweetheart, but what kind of relationship can we have if I always hide who I am from her?"

"If you don't know whether to tell her or not, then do what I always do."

"Have sex?"

She punched me. "No. Choose happiness. If that happens to involve sex, then good for you. Choose to be happy, Clark. I'll stand by any decision you make that involves happy, but I can't abide misery. Misery should be a choice you don't get to choose."

Everyone needs a best friend like Danica.

"What if she won't admit what she saw?"

"You'll know if she's lying or not. If she is then walk away and don't look back. If she isn't, then you can deal with it when the time is right. Either way, choose love, Clark. Always choose love. I'll be here most of the night if you want to swing back by and finish the ice cream."

I rose and looked around. "What are you working on?"

"The boys and I are working on a voice recognition program that has a ninety-seven percent accuracy rate in twenty-four major languages. We're also working on the bugs in the vidbook operating software. The second version is still in beta and there are some damn bugs we really need to work out. We're also working on a secret project I can't share with you."

I chuckled. She was always jerking my chain. "Nice. Busy bees."

"Always. In this business, one can't rest on one's laurels. You have to keep moving, keep producing, keep stepping forward. In the tech industry, what was cool today is in a junk pile tomorrow. Even Microsoft can't keep up, which means we little guys have the chance to come in and shake things up."

"And I know how much you like to do that."

Nodding, she started for the door. "Come by the Bat Cave

when you're done if you feel like the company. The boys would love to see you."

The boys were the three Cal grads who had been turned down by every major company in Silicon Valley and Seattle because they wanted to be hired as a package deal. Danica hired them on the spot, gave them office space the size of a small warehouse and all the electronic gadgets and toys they wanted. There were three desktops, nine laptops, three fifty-two inch HDTVs, assorted remote controlled cars, robots and dogs, a couple of Xboxes and PlayStations and more iPod parts than a Mac store. She paid them very well and they repaid her by developing things like the vidbook, a computerized cell phone/computer run by satellite with a nifty little GPS system that predated and outperformed all other cell phones and GPS systems on the market. That book had saved our bacon more than once.

"I'll stop by when I get the chance."

"They loved your article, by the way. They got together and made a newsletter they sent out to all their geeky tech-head friends. They're creating a fund to help purchase laptops for the schools that were flooded."

"Really?"

"Really. I can't believe how well-connected those three yahoos are. Bill Gates sent a hefty check, but asked that it remain anonymous. Jobs did the same thing. Those guys have donated a butt-load. The money is flying in, Clark, and it's all because of your article. You do good things, my friend."

"Well, I'm glad something good came from our trip down there. Sometimes, I wonder." Looking down, I shook my head. The loss of Jacob was a larger hole in my heart than I wanted to admit.

"Wonder no more. You call me one way or the other, okay? You're not alone, and you don't have to feel that loss by yourself."

I nodded. "Thanks."

"Oh, and Clark?"

"Yeah?"

"Eat a fucking pork chop."

I stood there amid the hustling and bustling police department wondering how anything ever got done with all the noise and chaos. Paper flew, phones rang, bad guys were handcuffed to benches or chairs, cops strode purposefully through it all, unscathed and unaffected. Chaos. Utter and complete chaos.

And the woman I had come to offer my heart to was creating an equal amount of chaos inside me. Across the room, sitting on the corner of the desk, Officer Finn was intensely engaged in a conversation with a woman who stood a little too close, laughed a little too hard, and touched her a little too often. From where I stood, she was flirtatious in a way that made me damn uncomfortable, and she was altogether too good looking for me to ignore. For Finn's part, she was too enraptured with this devil spawn to even notice I had come into the room. Hell, I could have waltzed in naked with my head on fire and she probably wouldn't have noticed.

I stood there, trying to keep my bright green emotions in check as I watched her engrossed in an animated conversation with a woman who wasn't only handsome, but almost six feet tall and built like a mugger's worst nightmare. She could bench press me without breaking a sweat. Her shoulder length brown hair was as animated as she was, and when she turned in my direction, I was struck by a pair of emerald green eyes that took my breath away. My own green eyes paled in comparison to hers. Not forest, not lime, not grass green, not teal, but deep emerald green—the kind that surveyed a room like a radar sweeping in its careful circular motion. They were stunning and they were framed by brown eyebrows that seemed to form question marks when she laughed.

I hated her.

No. I hated Finn. She couldn't *wait* a few days before zeroing in on a new squeeze? She was so obviously flirting with her in a way she had never flirted with me. I didn't have to lower my shield to feel this giant's charm oozing from her. Oozing like amber. Boy, had I misread Finn. What was I thinking? I had come all the way down here for this?

This was a huge mistake. I had thought Finn felt something more for me than she did. She had managed to fool an empath into thinking she really loved me. I thought we had something special...something...

Now, Finn was looking right at me. I wished my head really was on fire, just to...just to what? Get her attention away from the siren mesmerizing her? Yeah, that was the ticket. I needed to get out before I took a Zippo to my hair. Like a trapped animal, I looked for a way out. As busy as this place was, I had to be able to get to an exit before she could get to me. If only my legs would focus in and listen to me! I was standing there, rooted in place. I could be making an escape, but no, my legs were like two steel girders trapped in cement. All I could do was stand there like an idiot as Finn strode over to me with a dopey smile on her face. Jesus, the least she could do was look like she'd been caught!

"Miss me so soon?" she asked, sidestepping another cop who was moving faster than she was. "Did you actually come to your senses and realize you were dumping one of the hottest cops in the city?" She smiled at my confusion.

"I...uh—"

"You *are* here to see me, right?"

"No. Yes. I'm not really sure anymore." God, even my tongue had betrayed me.

"Look, I need to sign out...stay right here, okay?"

Yeah. Right. That's exactly what I was going to do with Lady Cat Eyes standing over there looking good enough to eat. My God, she was hot. And gay. Hot and gay and making a move on my cop? Oh hell no. I wasn't going down without a fight.

"*Okay?*" she asked once more.

I nodded mutely and took my eyes off the green-eyed usurper in order to look at Finn. "*Fine.*"

Cocking her head, she frowned as if trying to figure me out. "I'll be right back. If you leave, I'm coming after you with lights and sirens."

"I said fine."

She took two steps and then turned around. "I'm not kidding about the lights and siren."

I was so busy watching her walk away, I did not notice the

emerald girlfriend thief until she was right up on top of me. I mean literally towering over me.

"So, you're Echo Branson."

I stared up into those eyes, slightly intimidated by the penetrating green sizing me up. She had perfectly straight, ultra white teeth and a dimple on her left cheek when she smiled. She was as worthy an adversary as anyone could hope to never find. She oozed confidence and personal power.

"Yes, I am."

I almost jumped back when she extended her hand to me. This was a tricky one for sure. Cagey, even.

"I've read all your articles. You're a family favorite. We all read your work."

I hesitated slightly as I extended my hand to her. Oh, she was good, this one. Compliment the opponent to throw them off balance. She was more than cagey, but I wasn't born yesterday. "Oh, really? Which was your favorite?" Yeah, let her fumble around for some human interest story she read somewhere. Two could play this game.

"I loved the series on the organ harvesting and your experience with the Colombians was riveting and so factual. Most Americans refuse to believe that sort of horrific shit is alive and well in many countries. Trust me, I've seen it up close and personal and you nailed them. Great descriptions."

Okay, so maybe she *did* read my work. "You know about Colombians?" I can call a bluff as good as any.

She nodded as she retracted her hand. "Hell yes. I've had my own private run-ins with the Colombian cartel myself. I didn't win, either." She shook her head. "Not all of us came back."

Okay, now I was totally blindsided. Was she for real? Lowering my shields for a split second to see if she was bullshitting me, I was so stunned by the strength of her sorrow, I knew she wasn't kidding. This was no lure, no play, no caginess. She was actually still suffering the loss. This totally threw me off. "I'm...uh... wow. I've experienced the same kind of loss recently. Adventure gone bad, that sort of thing." I was losing the battle of hating her and that was really pissing me off. Could I be any weaker?

Her eyebrows spoke before her lips moved. "I'm sorry for

your loss. The Colombian cartel ought to be wiped off the face of the planet. Anyway, I just wanted you to know I think your investigative pieces are really well written and controversial, and I am all for rocking people's boats. I've rocked a few in my life."

I'll bet. Boats, worlds, beds, you name it, I'm sure she's rocked it.

Reaching into her back pocket, she pulled out a business card and handed it to me. "I've just moved to the city from down south and I'm trying to drum up some business. If you ever need someone to do those jobs you'd rather not tackle, give me a call."

I took the business card and read it:

For Your Eyes Only:
Discreet Detective Agency.
Let us be your eyes and ears.
Delta "Storm" Stevens.

Why was that name so familiar? I'd heard or seen it somewhere before. "You're a private eye?"

"Yeah. New city, new business, new life, I need new customers. Here. Take a few more to give to your friends and colleagues at the paper. Tell them we can find a sesame seed in the sands of Maui."

"We?" Maybe she had a real partner. Maybe her partner was a statuesque model who liked a lot of sex. Maybe...

"My partner and I."

I grinned and then stopped myself. I liked confident women, but this woman was beyond confident, bordering on...I don't know...arrogant? At least she was making it easier for me to hate her again even if she did have a partner. God, where had I heard that name before?

"Well, Echo, I've got a lot of work to do. It was really great meeting you. Finn raves on and on about you. Says you're incredible."

"She...did?"

Delta nodded. "She's pretty smitten. Keep coming out with those articles about New Orleans, too. The American public has a short memory and will soon forget those unfortunate people.

As long as you keep churning up the water, we'll be forced to remember."

I nodded, going back to almost liking her. "I will." As I watched her stride toward the door, I noticed a Latina woman standing by the door waiting for her. Delta said something to her and she looked in my direction. She didn't just look, though. It was almost as if she was reading me. Her eyes locked onto mine as if she was one of us, but I knew she wasn't. I picked up no paranormal energy in the room at all.

Who were these women?

As we locked eyes I knew there was something screaming *beware*. If green-eyed Delta Stevens was intimidating, it was nothing compared to the intensity of emotions from the Hispanic one. Everything about her said she could kick my ass into tomorrow.

"Missed me, didn't you?"

I turned and faced Finn who was grinning like a fool.

"You couldn't even wait a day before you started passing out your cop charm to the ladies? It's been what? Three, four hours, and you've already got someone else on the line? I can't believe I thought I loved you."

"Who are you...wait...you *love* me?"

"Oh please, Finn, don't even try to act like you're innocent. I *saw* you. You were flirting with her. Opening drooling all over her."

"Wait. You think—"

"It's not what I *think*, Finn, it's what I *saw*. It was a little disgusting the way you were Ms. Cock of the Walk and—"

"Her?" Finn looked toward the door and then tossed her head back and laughed. Loudly. "Oh, that's rich."

I started to walk away. "Laugh all you want. I know what I saw."

She grabbed my arm and turned me toward her. "You're jealous!"

"Don't be absurd. I just dumped you. Why would I be jealous?"

"I don't know, but by the looks of it, you're *really* jealous. You're getting all bent out of shape over a married woman."

"I am not! If you think—" I paused and processed what she just said. "Married?"

She nodded. "Happily. And for a long time."

"Don't even try messing with me, Finn, because I have my ways of finding out the truth."

Finn took me by the hand and pulled me into one of those little interrogation rooms. "I'm not messing with you, Echo," she said, closing the door behind her. "Delta and I were in the Academy together down in River Valley. Remember? I've told you tons of Storm stories."

Now I felt like an idiot. "That was *Storm* Stevens?"

She nodded. "In the flesh. I don't know what it was you think you saw, but she flirts with no one. Ever. She's happily married to a gorgeous woman who would tear out anyone's throat who came after Delta."

Relief flooded through me. Finn had regaled me with stories about the illustrious Delta "Storm" Stevens over dinner one night. Delta was a hero to Finn and she made no bones about how she looked up to her. "Storm Stevens...here in the city." I knew I'd heard that name before.

She nodded. "Moved to a town a few weeks ago and opened a PI business. She came down to give me a bunch of her cards to hand out trying to get some business. We really didn't have time to connect before I left for New Orleans." Her voice softened. "You know how that went."

I felt like such a boob. Rarely do I show my hand as visibly or as incorrectly as I had done just now. "She's...um...impressive."

Finn smiled. "Yes, she is, but enough about her. Have you come down here to undump me? To take me back?" Her boyish grin took the edge off her words. "I believe you said you loved me to a room full of people."

"No I didn't."

"We have video. Shall I—"

"I've come to lay a one-time-only deal on the table."

"Oooh, an offer." She stepped closer to me and rubbed her hands together. "I'm all ears."

I centered myself. "Finn, I don't know what, exactly, it is you saw in NOLA, but if you swear to never, ever bring it up, never talk about it to me or anyone else, never ask me one single question about it, then I'm willing to stay on the path you and I were on. It may be too much to ask, and you might think that someday in the future, I'll forget about this, but I won't. This is the only way I can do this and make it work."

"Not one question?"

"Not one. Not today, not tomorrow, not ever."

Finn pulled me to her and hugged me tightly. "I'll take it. It's a deal."

"You sure? I mean, think about it, Finn. You're a woman who seeks answers for a living. Mysteries are your bag. Don't answer too quickly, Deputy Dog. This goes against everything you're about. I don't want—"

"If the deal is still on the table, I'll take it. Otherwise, kiss me goodbye." Finn pulled me to her so that our foreheads touched. "Look. I know a good thing when I see it, and no matter what I saw, it wasn't worth losing you over."

I kissed her softly, feeling as if we had finally bridged the impasse. "Thank you."

"Don't thank me. Mama Finn didn't raise no dummy. Besides, I've gotten rather crazy about you, and like having you around."

"I like being around."

She leaned over and whispered, "You're really cute when you're jealous."

"I most certainly was not."

She laughed. "Whatever. Don't worry. Your secret is safe with me. All of them are safe with me."

I stared into her eyes, I smiled softly. Funny thing was...I believed her.

As I drove home, a mixture of relief, exhaustion and embarrassment swept over me. My green monster wasn't very pretty, and I wasn't very proud of it, but at least I reeled it in before I did anything stupid. Finn had never been anything but honest with me, and there I was, chastising her for flirting with a married friend? What kind of a girlfriend was I? I deserved to be embarrassed and feel stupid. I deserved another loss.

My thoughts drifted back to the night Jacob died. How was I ever going to get over that loss? Just when I thought I was really getting my life together—great job, great girlfriend, cool loft above a bakery, great friends, everything seemed to be shaken up like I was upside down in a snow globe. Death makes us re-evaluate what we thought we knew. It makes us look inward to see if what we are doing is what we should be doing. Death has a way of changing the picture we've been staring at and making us see something different. After watching one of my best friends die, I was beginning to wonder about my life; not just where I was going, but where I'd been.

It wasn't a new thought, by any stretch of the imagination. Kids who grow up in the foster care system are always wondering where we came from, why we weren't good enough to be kept, what life would have been like had we been truly loved. There are never-ending questions that tap on the door of our subconscious our entire lives. We want answers that rarely come, love that is rarely returned. We go through life never feeling good enough, as if we'll never quite measure up.

At twenty-eight years old, I had hoped those questions were a thing of my past. I thought my successes as a journalist had covered over my feelings of inadequacy. Tap. Tap. Tap. Echo Branson, where did you come from? Tap. Tap. Tap. Jane Doe, who are you, really? Like Mormons at the front door during dinner time, they irritated me so much, I didn't bother answering.

But since Jacob died, I'd found myself looking through the peephole. I am afraid of what might happen to me if I open the door even a crack; afraid they'll come in and start picking at scars long since healed. I don't need my scabs picked. I have no mother to put Band-Aids on, so I have no need to have the answers that will make me feel like I was swallowing broken glass. What I need is to get through this…get over it. I need to wait for the tapping to go away so I can resume pretending it doesn't matter to me.

Deep down, I know it does.

Just because I don't want it doesn't mean a thing. I'm not

looking for the mother I can't remember. I have Melika. I don't want a mother. What I want are answers. I'm an empath, for God's sake, I want to know where I got my powers from. I have so many questions about my powers, where they came from, where I may be going. I have so many questions, but I have no idea where to start even if I could.

There is a story in this, I know there is. There are thousands like me, like Britt Bevelaqua, who survived the revolving door of the foster system until she finally decided she could care for herself better than the system could. In the end, Britt busted me loose and she vanished into the real world. She'd tired of having her hopes dashed waiting for someone to love her. She was tired of the constant rejection and the walking on eggshells in the hopes that someone would keep her longer than a minute. I'd thought of Britt often in the last fourteen years. When I was at Mills College, I knew that every day I sat in a classroom, I moved further away from the life she lived. Britt was one of those wild girls who drove too fast, smoked too much and rode the edge too often. She had just wanted to be loved or be free. She settled for her freedom and I hoped she had found love.

I needed freedom as well: freedom from that annoying tapping. I needed to find some way of alleviating the constant questions about my origin. I had virtually no memory of my childhood earlier than when I was five years old, and from six to fourteen is pretty sketchy as well. I wanted to be free from wondering who my parents were and why they didn't want me. Melika had said to me during my last visit to the bayou that I couldn't really know where I was going until I knew where I'd been. That was her way of pushing me to answer the door, her way of giving me permission to root around in my past and try to find out who I might have been and who my parents were. She believed getting answers would settle my heart down and put my mind at ease. Sometimes, the worst is not knowing. Like many foster kids with abandonment issues, trust did not come easily to me. We always expect people to leave us, so we tend to enter every relationship with one foot already pointed toward the door. *Leave them before they leave you* was pretty much our slogan growing up. Britt was the first one I heard say that.

Poor Britt.

She had so much to offer and no place to give it. By the time she ran away, she was pretty streetwise and edgy, always suspicious of everyone and everything, never comfortable in her own skin. She had a good heart, but the older we got, the harder she became, until finally, when she left, she didn't have any room for tears.

I missed her terribly when she left. She had given me two twenty-dollar bills and told me not to use them until I really needed them. When I had been hospitalized in the psych unit, I knew I had to get out of there before I went crazy. Big George got me out of the hospital, but it was Britt who got me out of the state. One of the twenties she'd given me had her cell number on it, and true to her word, she got me out of there.

I hadn't seen her since and I doubted she was still alive.

Up until Katrina, the only people in my life who stayed were those I had spent time with in the bayou. And Danica, of course. Now, even my bayou buddy had left me, and it had unsettled me to no end. Now, I was back to square one. That's why I'd wanted to leave Finn earlier; it was that typical fight-or-flight response of a foster care kid. I just threw down my "it's best for the group" card so I wouldn't feel like I was moving backward.

I'm glad I retracted that toss. Maybe that showed some signs of maturation and growth. I didn't really want to leave her before she left me. I wanted to give us an honest fighting chance. So far, the only potential partner I had ever given an honest chance to was Tip, and I couldn't even make that work.

To be fair, Tip was ten years older and I wasn't the least bit prepared to be in a relationship with another super. Every little thing she did felt invasive, and I ended up acting like a paranoid little bitch. When I realized I was turning into someone I would never like, I broke it off in the hopes of salvaging our friendship. We had managed to do that, even though I knew she would always love me on a level I wasn't sure I could ever reach with anyone. As an empath, I was highly tuned in to other people's emotional state, but rarely did I scratch beneath the surface of my own.

Now, Tip and I were more like mother and father to the

younger supernaturals who came through Melika's home. I was learning how to become a spotter. I did not have any official duties as of yet, but spotting had been chosen for me based on my own powers. Tip was part cleaner, part trainer, part collector. She went around cleaning up "messes" left by other paranormals in an attempt to help us remain invisible. She also spent time working with the newbies on the bayou, and finally, she collected those psions needing to be rounded up, or "collected." Collecting was a difficult task because most of the time, the young supers did not know they needed to be saved. They might not have been ready to leave their homes and their families. They might be too young or too frightened. I thought collecting was the hardest job because suddenly, you have this young life in your hands and you're promising them a better life while not being able to tell them anything about it. Tip had spent many years teaching the newbies, getting them ready for the real world. Once my lover, she was now one of my dearest friends, and she was currently leaning against a rented Lexus SUV parked in front of my apartment.

I parked Ladybug, my '65 VW Bug, and raced over for a hug that lifted me off the ground. "Where in the hell have you been?" I demanded when she set me down. I hadn't heard from her in days.

"Here and there. I had some cleaning up to do with Jacob Marley's death, and then Melika has had us going all over the place looking for this elusive TK who apparently has pretty decent powers already."

"Us?" I followed Tip's gaze and saw a tall, thin blonde walking out of Luigi's bakery with a bag full of something yummy. "Bailey!"

Her eyes lit up when she saw me, and we both rushed into a bear hug that smashed the goodies in the bag between us.

"What a great surprise!" I said, pulling away and smiling into her clear blue eyes. "What are you doing hanging around such riff-raff?"

She laughed and the sound of it danced across the street. Bailey was tall, and screamed Southern California no matter where she was. Maybe it was the perpetual tan, maybe it was the sun-bleached hair, I wasn't sure. She was simply stunning both inside and out.

"I finally earned my wings, E. Melika is sending me out on my first collection! I get to collect my first TK here in California!" Bailey handed Tip the smooshed bag and made a shooing motion with her hands. "Tip has been lecturing me about the ins and outs of collecting since we left New York. Take me shopping and get me a decent mani-pedi or I might have to resort to murder."

I laughed. Tip could be more than a little intense. I smiled at her. Bailey cut quite a handsome figure in a skintight black crewneck sweater over khaki pants and Doc Marten shoes. The first time I saw Bailey and Tip together, that ugly green monster apparently holed up inside me came bursting out. I was a teensy bit jealous; not that I had any right to be, of course, but Bailey is young, bubbly, and has a wonderfully warm aura.

She is also a lesbian.

Needless to say, my monster retreated back to its dark cave waiting for its return today, when it helped me make a fool of myself with Finn and Storm Stevens.

"Oh God, Bailey, I remember all those tedious lectures about protecting the family and being careful, and making sure that—"

"...we changed names..."

"...and don't leave a trail..." Bailey and I laughed, falling together like two schoolgirls.

Tip could only shake her head. "I need to leave Bailey here with you, Echo. I don't want her flying solo on her first time out, but Mel wants me to check something weird that's happening in Santa Fe. You guys can do some at-home investigative work, but do not let her go out solo."

Bailey groaned. "I can handle this, Tip."

"I'm sure you can, but I want you to wait until I get back from Santa Fe."

"Rough assignment, that one, Tip. Call it what it is. You're leaving me on my own so you can go on your vacation."

Tip ignored her, turning her milk chocolate brown eyes to me. "Do you mind?"

"I'd be glad for the company." I smiled over at Bailey. "I need it more than I dare admit to myself."

Tip nodded. "That's what she said." I knew she wasn't referring to Bailey, but to Melika, whom we all were quite clear knew everything.

Tip took one step toward me and found Bailey's hand on her chest. "Step away, Chief. It's girl talk now. Good old, petty, catty, scratch-everyone's-eyes-out girl talk. You are now in a bossy-Indian-free zone, so step away."

Tip didn't move, but stared at me. Hard. I knew she was considering going around my considerable defenses to see if I was really okay, but wisely, she thought better of it. She knew how it angered me when she took liberties with her powers and pried open the lock to my mind. She had sworn to me she would not ever do it unless it was an emergency. This was not that.

"I'm fine, Tip," I said. "Don't look so worried. I'm not adjusting very well to life without him. There's this empty space where he used to be. I'm sure we're all feeling it. I'm sure every damn one of us is pissed off about it too. I'm jumping out of my skin with emotions. I don't need to lower my shields to know you feel the same way."

She looked away and nodded. "I do."

"That's why we're here," Bailey added softly. "Mel knows we're all not assimilating back into our own lives very well. The hole Jacob left in the fabric of our reality is bigger than any of us are used to feeling. She knows we need each other right now."

Tip looked back into my face, her eyes holding so much sorrow and regret. She had never lost one of us to a bad guy before; at least, not that I knew of. "Mel figured working was better than wallowing."

I nodded. That's pretty much what I was doing. Working, working, working. I hadn't thought of any other diversion except my job. I had written a five-part series on what was happening in New Orleans and how fucked up our government's reaction was to such a catastrophe.

"I'm not wallowing as much as I am overworking." I looked across the street as three alley cats made their way toward us; well, not us. They were coming to Bailey. Bailey's unique power was that of a Shaman. Her telepathic abilities were strictly with creatures of the animal kingdom, and thus, other supers referred to her as a creature. A creature can do more than communicate with animals. A creature also has empathic abilities with them, and attracts them to her with barely a thought. I have seen her direct animals to do things that Siegfried and Roy would have envied.

Being a Shaman was her secondary power. She was a powerful herbalist, an incredible healer, and someone you always wanted on your side during a fight. I had seen her powers with animals up close and in person, and I have to say I was really glad she was on my side.

"Mel's reasoning is seldom flawed," I said, reaching over and giving Tip's hand a quick squeeze. "So, what will you be doing in Santa Fe?"

Backing away, she forced a smile. "I need to heal my heart, and there's something strange going on at a reservation. I'm going to check it out and make sure it isn't anything paranormal."

"What do you mean *something is going on?*"

She shrugged. "I'll fill you in when I know more. After Santa Fe, looks like Mel might be sending me overseas for a collection. There's a lot going on out there. Anyway, in the meantime, you make sure Miss Bailey here doesn't try to collect that TK on her own. Our spotter said there's something hinky about the kid. He seems to be either lost or running away from home. She wasn't sure."

"How did she spot him?"

"Fluke, really. Spotter was on a motorcycle and saw our kid walking along the road. A bicyclist veered toward him and he pretty much chucked the bicyclist off the bike and into the closest hedge before taking off. She chased him for as long as she could, but he outran her."

"Where?"

"Near San Jose."

I nodded. "We have a spotter in San Jose?"

Tip grinned. "We're everywhere. Anyway, this kid might be getting ready to bust a move, so be careful. There are no wild boars in the city." Tip leaned over and kissed my cheek.

"You should have dumped her," she whispered before opening the driver's side door. "You guys have my cell. Take care of each other, and I'll see you in a week."

We watched her drive off, and then Bailey put her arm through mine and escorted me down the sidewalk. "Come on, E. I'm starving, and you have to tell me what happened between you and Officer Hunky. Tip wouldn't talk about it. She can be so damn frustrating at times."

"At times?"

"Okay, fine. All the time."

Laughing all the way to Spiro's, I couldn't have been happier to have Bailey with me. Mel, it seemed, really *did* know everything.

As I drove her back to her hotel, Bailey regaled me with tales of New York City and how she and Tip were two fish out of water. She said they felt like they were stuck in a cement cage breathing only smog and eating only fried foods. They had gone to New York to attend Jacob's funeral and clean up any lingering questions his family might have had. We had all wanted to go to Jacob's funeral, but his family did not know who we were and Melika was loath to draw suspicion to us. It was one of the major drawbacks of being different. We couldn't just appear without explanation. Once we left the bayou, each of us had set out on the task of fitting into the real world and having as regular a life as possible. That was a harder job when we were all together because the next thing you knew, one of us would push another one of us back without touching them, or light a finger on fire without thinking that someone else might be watching. It was simply harder to act normally when we were all together. It was sad, but that was the way it was. When we did all we could do for the good people of New Orleans, Zach retreated to Atlanta, I came home to the city by the bay, Tip cleaned up our mess, and Bailey, ever the nomad, roamed with her, learning everything she could from the master.

Melika was working with Cinder, the fire starter, who had

developed a special bond with Danica when we collected her. I hadn't yet met the other two. Cinder stayed not only because we needed her, but because her powers were still too unstable to release her into the world. She was one of the few fire starters who hadn't burned herself up before the age of sixteen. It was a good thing Cinder had stayed because we had needed her fire power more than ever.

Leaving her there…hell, leaving the bayou when it needed us most proved more difficult than I imagined, but Melika wanted all of us to return to our lives—to carry on. We had done a great deal to help, but now it was up to the Louisianans to help themselves.

Bailey and I ate lunch, had a few drinks, caught up on each other's lives and laughed our asses off. She had quickly become like a sister to me, and the friendship we had forged in the bayou was built on respect and admiration. I truly liked her. So did Danica.

After dropping Bailey off at her hotel, I headed back downtown to Danica's office complex overlooking the beautiful San Francisco Bay.

"I can tell just by looking at you it went well. Am I brilliant or am I a genius?"

"Can I buy a vowel?"

She walked over and practically sniffed the air around me. "Oh Christ, Clark, and here I was, thinking it was Finn who put that little bounce in your step. *She's* back, isn't she?"

Danica was no super, but her people instincts were impeccable. I'd never met anyone who could beat her. The smelling part was just part of her schtick that never ceased to amuse me. "How in the hell did you know that?"

She sat on the couch and pounded the space next to her. "I've known you a long time, Clark, and when that Indian is around, something happens to you. It's like…I don't know…you get more confident or something. It's spooky. Or creepy. Or maybe both. Come sit."

I sat next to her, the Italian leather couch creaking softly. "*You're* spooky, Dani. Yes, she's in town. Came with Bailey to collect a TK who's on the loose."

Danica stared at me. "She brought Bailey? She's not a collector, yet, is she?"

"Not yet. This is her first collection. Tip wanted to make sure it went well so she left her with me."

Danica shook her head. "They're an odd pair, don't you think?"

"Not really. They're more alike than you realize. All that animism between them makes a room pulse. I keep expecting fish or foul to walk in the room behind them."

"It's like there are these sparks that will never create a fire."

I looked at her. She was the least romantic person I had ever known. Ever. For as long as I'd known her, she'd been commitment phobic. When she slept with guys at her house, they had to leave when they were done. It didn't matter what time it was, what the weather was like, or how much she dug the guy. She had a very strict no sleepover policy that, as far as I knew, had never been violated.

"So, the Big Injun comes to town and suddenly, you're lighter on your feet? What's up with that? Please don't tell me—"

"Don't worry. She already left for Santa Fe. Drop-kicked Bailey to the curb to go put out another fire."

"Funny how Bailey's a part of you all now. Before Katrina, we'd never even heard of her. Now, here she is, hanging out with you and earning her collector's stripes." She looked away. "I guess Katrina changed us all, huh?"

The weight of Jacob Marley's death heavy on my heart, I nodded. "More than we realize. We're going to have to wait until the dust settles to see how this all works out for the country, but I have a feeling it's not going to be good for the American people."

"No doubt. Think Melika will want us back to help?"

I liked that Danica felt like one of us.

Family.

"If you need any help reeling in your problem TK, me and my leetle fren' are always at your disposal."

Danica had never had any problems pulling the trigger of her leetle fren', and had done so when we were in the Superdome in New Orleans. She had never had any qualms taking anyone out who threatened her. Or me. She just never looked back and I envied that about her.

"Keep your *leetle fren'* in its leetle holster, Billy Bob. We're collecting him, not putting him in a body bag."

Danica shrugged and looked at her nails. "I'm over that, Clark. I did what I had to do. You need to get over it as well. I know you're traumatized, but it's a dog-eat-dog world out there, and on that day, we were the bigger, better dogs." She shrugged again. "I don't carry their deaths around like baggage and you need to follow my lead on that one. Taking someone's life is a helluva lot easier than people think, and if it comes down to me or them…it's not even a question."

I always wondered about her steel façade, but after Katrina, after watching Danica coldly and without compunction or regret, blow a guy away, I knew it was no façade—it never had been. Self-preservation was in her blood. Dog-eat-dog? When it came to anyone taking Danica on, it was more dog-eat-hamster, with her being a mastiff.

"Whatever. I came by to thank you, Mighty Dog, for your brilliant genius about my romance. Finn agreed to play this one hundred percent my way. She won't ask me any questions about it and we'll pretend like it never happened."

"She's sweet. I only wish she could ring your bells as loudly as Tip does."

"Give that a rest, will you? I'm too damn tired to have my bells ringing. I'm just glad I was able to smooth things over with Finn. She really is a sweetheart, and I hated the idea that this ended before it even had the chance to grow."

Danica tucked her never-ending legs under her before turning to face me. "You could have thanked me on the phone. Why are you really here?"

I reached into my pocket and pulled out Delta Stevens' business card. "What would you say if I told you I think I'm ready to find out who my real parents were?"

Danica gazed down at the business card for a long time before looking up at me. "Why now? Don't get me wrong, Clark, I think it's a fab idea. I just wonder why now."

Staring out at sailboats dotting the bay, I shrugged. "It's

time. All my life I've wondered. I've questioned. I've dreamt about who they were and why they left me. I think…I think after losing Jacob Marley there are things I need to know. What do you think?"

"Honestly? I think you're ready. I think it's time you unload all that baggage and find out what happened and why you were left to fend for yourself. At the very least, you'll have some of your questions answered. For as long as I've known you, you've considered yourself an orphan. You don't remember anything about your childhood and have no clue why you can't remember. In short, you got nothin'. It's time you got something."

I nodded.

"Where'd you get the card?"

"She's a friend of Finn's. New in town."

"Her name looks familiar."

"That's what I thought too. She's looking to drum up some business and I think it might be worth a shot to hire her."

"Go for it. And if you need some money, you know the Bank of Danica is always open."

"Are private eyes expensive?"

Danica nodded. "Can be. It depends on how much we need them. If we use the boys to get background, it won't be so expensive, but don't worry about the cost, Clark. I mean it. I can't imagine my life without my mom. Hell, it was hard enough watching her die, but I can't even fathom what my life would have been like without her holding my hand." Danica shook her head sadly. "I'm surprised it's taken you so long to decide you were ready to hear the truth. I know Jacob's death rattled your cage, but I didn't know how much." She reached out and touched my hand. "But you're right. It's time."

Nodding, I rose and helped her to her feet. She unfolded like a cardboard doll. "Thanks. Can I get you dinner?"

"The guys and I ordered pizza. What you *can* do is tell me about this TK you're after. If I don't start thinking about something besides bits and bytes, I might go more insane than I already am."

"I think it's weird they want to meet for lunch," Danica said the next day as we drove to a wonderful little Italian bistro in Little Italy. "Who does lunch anymore? It's so twentieth century."

"Maybe they just want to see more of the city. Finn said they'd only been in town a few weeks."

"I put the boys on background duty. They've started in on your background at St. Ignatius to see what kind of kids they've taken in, where the majority of the kids came from, et-cetera. You know how those three nimrods adore you. The moment I told them what this was about, their little fingers started flying. They'll find out more in an hour than most people could in a month." She held up a hand to silence my next words. "Don't worry. They'll be discreet."

I *was* worried. Ever since I had made my mind up to hire Delta "Storm" Stevens and company, I had been plagued by what-ifs. What if we found out my parents had been mobsters? What if they gave me up because they were in jail? Or worse...what if they were...oh no...politicians? My mind had whirled around and around all night, wondering what people do when they find out who their birth parents are.

"Stop the monkey mind, Clark. You're doing the right thing. It's time. Mel has even told you it's time. There's a future out there waiting for you once you cut your past loose...regardless of what that past looks like."

"What if..." Here it was...my real issue. "What if my future is on the bayou?"

Danica slowly turned to me. "Is that what this is about? You don't think you could live on the bayou anymore?"

"It was tough as a teen. I can't imagine living there full time as an adult. Could you?"

Danica laughed. "Are you kidding me? I'd die in less than a week. I need culture. I need people. I need Starbucks!"

"You know what I mean."

"I do. You're afraid if Melika goes down, you're going to be the one to step into her place, huh? You think you're the Chosen One."

I nodded. "Aren't I? Who else is there?"

"Seems to me, Clark, there may be a lot more possibilities than you know. Look how Bailey appeared out of nowhere. There could be a hundred other people you don't know about who can step into that role—Bailey being one of them. The bayou is her domain. Shit, she's like a modern day Doctor Doolittle or something."

I looked out at the clear blue California sky. "She *is* pretty amazing."

"Pretty amazing? Convincing some wild boar to eat a man alive is more than pretty amazing, Clark. Bailey could live down there without batting an eye. But you? I mean, it was fun when you were growing up, but you live in the city now. You like all of the creature comforts while Bailey likes the creatures. It's no contest and Melika knows that. She'd never ask you to come back to a place you couldn't thrive in."

I drove for a few lights without saying anything. "I guess I got the impression from Mel she wants it to be me."

"You got the impression? You're a fucking empath, for Christ's sake, and that's the best you can do? You're fired. You have to stay here."

I turned to her when we came to a red light. "You'll miss me."

Danica stared straight ahead. "So?" Slowly, she turned. "When you were there during high school, I really missed you. I was barely able to keep myself out of fights, out of jail and in my class chair."

"That was then, Dani. You're all grown up now."

She barked out a laugh. "Oh really? Let's rewind, shall we? I spend most of my days playing on the computer while those three techies make me money hand-over-fist. I may appear to be the paragon of success, but the truth is, you're the one who keeps me grounded. You taught me how to save money, how to invest it wisely, and how to spread the wealth."

I reached over and patted her leg. I was fourteen when I when I went to the bayou and I had stayed there for four years. Throughout those four years, when most girls are at their self-absorbed worst, Danica never wavered in her friendship with me. Melika flew her out four times a year to visit, and we wrote constantly. Danica referred to me once as her living journal. She had been my only female companion the entire time I was on the bayou, and had been accepted as one of us. "Hopefully, I won't have to make that call for a long time."

"And when you do? What then? You need a plan, Clark. You never know when...when death might decide to creep up on you, you know?"

I shrugged. "Maybe you'd consider bringing the boys with you to New Orleans. I bet you could get a pretty cheap office space there now."

She visibly shuddered. "You have got to be insane, Clark. My precious half-and-half skin would curdle in that heat. No, I loved our times together when we were kids, but I need the climate of the city and, oh, gee, little things like electricity."

"I never knew you were so soft."

"Soft? You're kidding, right?"

"Yes. You're the butchest straight chick I know."

She grinned. "Thanks. Anyway, let's cross that bridge when we get there, okay? For now, let's just see if we can't find out who your parents were and why they decided to leave your cute little white ass as a ward of the state."

When we arrived at Rose Pistola, a trendy, somewhat pricey little bistro, I was starving.

"Is there anything I should know before we go in?" Danica asked.

"Like what?"

"Anything you don't want me to say? Anything you'd rather be kept hidden besides the obvious?"

I laughed. "As if I could stop you."

When we walked in, Delta Stevens and the Hispanic woman I'd seen at the police station were standing at the register. Delta was almost as tall as Danica, but her girth was in her shoulders, while Danica's was...well...not in her shoulders.

She was wearing a black leather jacket, white turtleneck and perfectly creased khaki pants. The Hispanic woman was wearing form-fitting jeans, a lavender sweater and a jean jacket with buttons resembling brooches.

"Delta. Good seeing you again," I said, turning to Dani. "This is my best friend in crime, Danica Johnson."

Danica and Delta shook hands and then Delta introduced us to Connie Rivera, *her* best friend. Connie Rivera had flawless caramel skin a shade lighter than Danica's and long black hair cascading over her shoulders. She was a handsome woman with riveting dark brown eyes that didn't just take us in, but sized us up, estimated without judgment, and computed everything from our age to our relationship. She had done the same thing to me at the station. Again, if I didn't know better, I would have thought she was one of us. Whatever she was ,was not something I had ever encountered in a natural.

When all of the introductions were over, we sat in a corner booth overlooking a beautiful courtyard filled with every possible color of bearded iris. It was stunning, and I thought of how much Bailey would love it.

"Echo tells me you guys have only been in town a few weeks," Danica began. "What brought you to our lovely neck of the woods?"

Delta folded her hands on the table and I noticed a platinum wedding band with several large diamonds embedded in it. One look over to Connie's hand and I had my answer about their relationship. No ring. "The short version goes like this: Con and I were cops in River Valley for many years. In one year, we lost Connie's lover, Gina, two of our best friends and our professional integrity all in one fell swoop." Delta looked to Connie who nodded.

"Harsh," Danica remarked.

Delta nodded. "Harsh is an understatement. The bad guys didn't win in the end, but they poked enough holes in our boat to make us reevaluate how we want to spend the rest of our days. We just decided life was too short to chase after criminals who were back on the streets before our shift was over." She shook her head. Disgust oozed from her. "Such a flawed system. Anyway, after Gina died, we tried to make a go of it, but our ship was listing too much. We needed a fresh start. We needed to take our girls and get the hell out of Dodge."

Was it coincidence she used the same phrases Danica and

I used? It was beginning to get under my skin. Who *were* these women?

"You have kids?" Danica asked, turning to Connie, who nodded.

"Don't ask her to show pictures, or we'll be here all afternoon." Delta shot a teasing grin over to Connie, who smiled back. Her quiet demeanor reminded me of Tip.

When Connie spoke, her voice was quiet, filled with pride. "I have a two-and-a-half-year-old daughter, Dakota, and Delta and Megan have a one-year-old terror, Phoenix."

Delta chuckled. "And then some."

These two women had been through the wringer together—their bond was obvious as if they were married. "Connie and I want more for our girls: more peace. Once you have kids, your outlook on life changes. Let someone else chase the bad guys for a while."

Danica nodded, staring at Connie as if trying to figure her out. "I'm sorry for your loss."

Connie smiled again. This woman wasn't just intense; she took in the world around her like a camera, saving everything she saw to a digital file in her brain. Delta may have been equally intense, but there was sharpness, a keenness about Connie that surpassed even Danica's brilliance. I wondered if Dani felt this as well.

"Thank you," Connie replied. "We are, only now, beginning to heal. Ninety-five percent of the time, cops end up picking up the pieces of broken lives after a crime's been committed. We seldom, if ever, actually prevent crimes from happening like they show on TV. After a while that can make you pretty bitter. When my daughter was born, I decided she deserved better than to have her remaining parent surround herself with the scum of the planet. I wanted more for her…and for me."

Delta nodded. "So, we left the force, traveled around awhile, and then decided there was no better or safer place for lesbians to raise kids than in the bosom of San Francisco."

"You got that right," Danica said, as if she was one of us. "We take care of our gays here."

Connie smiled at Danica, and that was when I realized what

a beautiful woman she really was when her eyes danced. Those dark brown eyes set deeply into her lighter skin were almost the exact same color as Danica's. As I studied her profile, I was pretty sure I detected some Native American in her.

"We did our homework, and decided we wanted to remain in California. So far, the girls seem to love it."

"Do you have pictures?" Danica asked, looking only at Connie.

I turned and stared at Danica. She was one of those women who handed a baby off like a football if someone pressed her to hold it. She had never been comfortable around little kids, so her question threw me off.

"More than any sane person would ever want to see, and I won't show you my phone photos," Delta said, opening her wallet and displaying a single photo across from her California driver's license. "The brunette is Dakota. That little ball of fire with the look of mischief in her eyes is mine and Megan's. We all call her Nickie."

They were beyond adorable. "They're gorgeous," I said, taking the photo from her and staring at it.

"And incredibly precocious. When we had them, we knew we didn't want to be those kind of parents who had kids and then shipped them off to day care, so the PI gig was the best way to manage the life we all wanted."

"Well, I sure hope it works out for you here," I said.

Delta grinned. "Thank you. Now, enough about us. Everything else you might wish to know about us and our methods is in here."

Connie slid a file folder to Danica, who did not open it. "Our credentials are nearly—"

"Finn vouches for you, so that's good enough for us," I added quickly.

Connie opened another folder and slid it over. "Good. Then here's..." She paused as the waiter came over. Connie ordered eggplant parmesan and Delta ordered a salmon and ricotta ravioli. Dani, true to her latest diet fad, ordered a salad.

"After you called me, Echo, Connie jumped on the computer to see what we could find out. There's a lot that can be had with a social security number and birthdates, but that's only the outline of the entire picture. Con will surely dig deeper than the obvious."

Danica leaned forward, her eyes locked onto Connie's. "You proficient with computers?"

Connie's lips curled slightly. "You might say that."

"Connie is the whiz kid of technology in the family. That's what she did for the PD: she poked around in cyberspace long before anyone called it the Internet." Delta drank from her Diet Pepsi before continuing. "What we found is a suspicious absence of any record of your existence prior to being admitted to Alta Bates."

Danica nodded. "Been there. Done that. There's nothing on her in any database anywhere."

Connie nodded. "There's next to nothing in any of the usual data banks I scoured. Of course, there are plenty more to go through, but so far—"

"You hacked into data banks?" Danica asked. I wished she would stop interrupting.

The twinkle in Connie's eye told me she was as proficient on a computer as the boys were. "The absence is what's suspicious. We live in an age when web and Internet presence is profound. Everyone can be found somewhere if you look hard enough."

"But not me," I said softly.

"Right. Not you." Delta opened the folder and pulled out a shiny black Mont Blanc pen from her pocket. "The more info you give us, the more we can return. No piece of information is too small. Write down where you went to grade school, junior high, high school. Maybe where you went to church or..." She paused and leaned across the table. "What is it?"

I stared blankly at the paper.

"She doesn't remember anything for most of her childhood," Dania explained. "There's almost a five-year block where she has no memory whatsoever."

Delta was staring at me with those riveting green eyes. "How many grammar schools did you attend?"

I shrugged. "Could have been eight or eighty. It would be impossible to say exactly. I didn't stay long in any one place. I guess I was a handful in my own right."

"But you were a ward of the state, correct?" Connie tapped her chin with a pencil. "And even with all of the Jane Does, we still should be able to find something about you. My guess is that your birthday is incorrect."

I started to protest, then stopped. "Wow. It never occurred to me that any of my personal information could be incorrect… but…now that I think about it, it does explain why Dani and her boys couldn't find anything."

Connie cocked her head at Dani. "You have kids?"

Danica barked out a laugh. "In a manner of speaking, yeah. But no, I employ three of the best technogeeks in the country, and they've come up with *nada*." She reached over and patted my leg. "Don't worry, Clark. That's what we're hiring them to find out."

"As you know," Connie continued, "the California Childcare System is very fallible. One misplaced number, one typo, and suddenly you're a year older and harder than hell to track down. The system is inherently bad, so I'm not at all surprised we couldn't find a match for you. The thing that bothers me most is the complete void. As if you'd been erased from the system. We need a starting point, Echo. Hell, even your file from Alta Bates is incomplete."

Danica practically levitated. "You broke into *hospital* records?"

Connie lowered her head as she looked left to right. "Getting around firewalls and other security systems is a little…shall we say hobby of mine." She glanced over at Delta, her eyes sparkling. "Very few systems can keep me out."

I heard the gauntlet thunk on the ground.

Danica's eyebrows raised and the look on her face was one I had never, ever seen. I had to turn toward her to get the full impact. She leaned over and said in a voice I did not recognize, "Ever hear of *The Echo*?"

Connie leaned back. "Tough bugger that one. Stymied me for nearly five hours before I found the Achilles. They all have one, you know. It's like the tiny ego of the creator just needs a teeny little door from which to peek at the monster they've created. But I managed to find it, all right."

I held my breath.

"Oh really? What's its Achilles?" Danica asked, but Delta put her hand up.

"Sorry, ladies, all that tech talk gives me a headache. Can we get back to the task at hand?"

Danica nodded. "Later, I would like to hear how you beat it, though."

"Anyway..." Delta cut back in once more. "If you could at least give us the last names of people who fostered you and any school names or organizations you remember, we can always work backward. It's possible one of them might remember something about you or even have paperwork from that time. Any little thing, Echo, any memory you can vaguely recall, needs to be written on that sheet. Maybe it would even help if you went back to your old neighborhoods. You were raised in the East Bay, right?"

I nodded. "In high school and junior high, but I could have been raised in Alaska for all I know or remember."

"Take your time then, and don't work so hard to remember. Just let them resurface as slowly as they need to."

Connie handed the same sheet to Danica. "And how far back did you say you two go?"

"Beginning of the eighth grade."

"Maybe you can fill one out as well. You might remember stories or info she might have told you along the way. Let your memories roam, but don't push it. When you're ready, we'll take it from there."

"In the meantime, we'll keep running Jane Does from around the time you think you were born."

"That could take some time," Danica said, pulling out her checkbook.

"What are you doing?" I asked.

"Hush, Clark. I didn't really come here for the emotional support as much as I came to make sure this was covered financially. You tend to turn into the world's worst tightwad when it comes to spending money on yourself." Ripping off a check, Danica handed it to Delta before I could stop her. "That ought to keep you on retainer long enough to get her the answers she needs."

I could tell by the look on Delta's face this retainer was a bit more than what she was used to. "Uh…Danica…"

Danica held her hand up. "This is important to her, which means it's important to me." She turned to me. "I have more money than God. In all the years we've known each other, you have never, not once, asked me for a penny. You drive that piece of crap car with manual windows, no air, and it doesn't even have a clock." She shook her head. "You and Bishop gave me time with my mother I would never have had; time I value every waking moment of every day; time I would never have had if you hadn't been who you are. I've waited fourteen years to be able to repay you for those last moments with my mother. Let me help you find yours."

When Danica first came to see me on the bayou, and I shared with her what I was and what that meant to my life, Bishop, Melika's mother, foresaw that Danica's mother was going to die from cancer while we were in college. That knowledge changed everything about our lives. Where we were once going to go to New York to college, we chose to go to Mills College in Oakland because it was closer to home, closer to her mother. Those last years Danica had with her mother were the best of her life, and when Judith died, I became Danica's family; me and my clan in the bayou.

I nodded slowly. "Thank you."

"We'll call you when we come up with something." Just then, our lunch arrived. "And you do the same. I have a feeling we'll be able to come up with something."

As I finished my first yummy mouthful of my ravioli, Connie looked over at Danica. "Did I hear you call her *Clark*?"

"I did."

"Clark—as in Clark Kent or Clark Gable?"

A grin slid onto Danica's face. "You're good."

Connie's eyes narrowed. "You would have to be in coma not to know there's something different about her…something… well…worthy of a nickname like Clark Kent."

Danica tossed her head back in laugh she normally reserved for bars and parties. "See, Clark? That's money already well spent. If these two can't find out who you are…then you don't exist."

"She still freaks me out," Danica said as we walked past Golden Gate Park after lunch. It was a gorgeous day in the city, with minimal fog and a bright, happy sun peering down at us. Sailboats glided across the bay, colorful kites flew high above, and the air was crisp and cool on my cheeks. We were on our way to see an old friend of mine who most people walked way around to avoid.

"All the places we've been and all the weird things we've seen, and Shirley freaks you out? You're weak."

Danica shrugged. "Totally. It's not her powers that are so scary, but that vacillation between sanity and insanity that gets under my skin. There's something about not knowing if she is going to snap right then and there I find disconcerting."

I nodded. The eccentric homeless woman we were going to see could welcome us with open arms or chase us around the block with an umbrella. It just depended on her mood.

Shirley was a precog; a clairvoyant who could see up and down the time spectrum at past, present and future events of a person's life. With the right item, she could scry with the best of them. Scrying is the ability to see something about a person by the object she or he was holding. She could see right into specific events of a person's life. There was only one problem with this: every time she used her powers, she lost a little more of her sanity. She wasn't crazy; she just went in and out of sanity. There's a difference.

"I'll leave you at that bench over there, then. I don't need you pissing her off."

"Are you nuts? I'm not missing out on the show! That crazy old bird is always worth a story or two. I said she freaked me out—that doesn't mean she scares me away. I'm in. I'm all in."

I smiled inwardly, not the least bit surprised. It would take more than a little insanity to scare Danica Johnson away. "Good. If I recall, the last time I left you on a park bench you let some guy pick you up and take you out to lunch and God only knows where else."

"How many times have I told you, he wasn't some guy? He was a forward for the Warriors and he had a really nice di—"

"And you think *Shirley* is nuts?"

Danica laughed and threaded her arm through mine. "I think we're all slightly off-center, don't you? Besides, we need someone who can help us bust down those steel bolted doors in your attic. I think it's just too damn weird you don't remember anything."

"Me, too. It was like I was born ten years old. I must have some sort of mental block, but still, there has to be something. Something."

"There has to be a reason, but don't you worry, Clark. I won't let anything bad happen to you. I'm right here and if any bogeyman pokes his head around the corner, I will blow his fucking head off."

"Comforting. Thanks."

When we got close enough to Shirley we could see her and her menagerie of animals: Cotton, a dalmatian with a black patch over one eye, Midnight, a black cat, and Emerald, a green parrot of some sort.

"What's with the homeless and their pets?" Danica muttered.

"They're homeless, not loveless." We slowed down so I could lower my shields and read Shirley's sanity level. Insanity screams an energy most naturals could hear if they paid any attention at all.

"She's good, okay," I said softly, resuming our approach. Like so many of us, Shirley's powers had driven her more than once to the brink of insanity; and whenever she hit the wall, she became extremely paranoid and suspected everyone of being the CIA or from the government trying to capture her. Her paranoia came in fits and starts. It was a frightening thing to experience, and I couldn't blame Danica for being apprehensive.

Cotton and Midnight raised their heads when they saw us coming.

"Shirley!" I said, leaning over to hug the old woman.

As usual, and as with most street people, she was wearing everything she owned: two plaid dresses, a pair of striped holey leggings peeking out from under the flannel-lined jeans I had given her, three pairs of socks, an expensive pair of high, tan Ugg boots my photographer, String Bean, had given her after she let him do a photo shoot of the animals. She was also wearing a couple of hand-knitted scarves, and a red hat similar to the sailor hat Gilligan wore.

Seeing me, she jumped to her feet and hugged me tightly. "Long time, missy! I've been reading all your articles when a spare paper pops up, and it appears you are having some kind of adventure, eh? Come. Sit." She turned and squinted at Danica. "Dani?"

Danica nodded. "How are you, Shirley?"

"Fine. Fine. Been better. Been a helluva lot worse. Come. Sit down. Make yourselves at home." She turned to me and grinned. "I see you brought your bodyguard."

I smiled, wondering if she knew precisely how accurate that statement was. "Never leave home without her." All three of us sat on the bench.

"What brings you gals out and about?"

"I need a favor, Shirl. A big one. I wouldn't even ask, but you're the only precog I know and—"

"Stop your hemming and hawing, girl, and spit it out." She winked her blue eye at me. Shirley had one green eye and one blue eye, and it seemed as if only one ever focused on you at a time. "Whatcha got, Echo? More lives to save? More daring adventures?"

"Actually, yeah, only the adventure I'm on is one where I am trying to figure out my own life."

"Ah. I see. You need to know something."

I nodded. "I do. I wouldn't normally come to you to ask this, but it's really important in the scheme of things. I...I think I might be the one to replace Melika when she retires, and—"

"Wait." Shirley held a hand up. "Are you certain of this?"

I shook my head. "Not entirely, no. It's just...she's hinted around, and when I think of all the others who might step in, I keep coming to the same conclusion."

"You are being groomed to be the next mentor."

I nodded.

"It's entirely possible, Echo. Someone is going to have to take her place, and the lineage has run dry. Other than Big George...and he's not really the mentoring type, her other boys are not interested. I've heard her daughter has no desire to leave Paris."

I cocked my head at her, surprised by just how much she knew about Melika and the rest of us.

Noticing my puzzlement, Shirley laughed. "I'm a precog, silly thing. I see things I don't want to see all the time. I've known of Melika's and George's existence long before I met you. What super doesn't? She's like a mythical hero to those of us who didn't have the luxury of meeting or being trained by her."

"I didn't realize—"

"There's a whole slew of us who had to raise ourselves, Echo—who had to fend off this insanity or the urge to just kill ourselves and be done with it. Melika gets to those she can, but there are many who fall through the cracks. What she has done...what she continues to do for us is priceless. Someday, her time will come to an end and someone else will need to step in and take over. If that someone is you, then whatever favor you have to ask is granted. I do not wish upon anyone the fate I have had to endure. The sheer madness that has taken over me at times; the paranoia, the going in and out of lucidity. Yes, my dear girl, if Melika has tapped you for her replacement, then it would be a pleasure to help you in any way I can." She snickered. "You're almost like royalty."

I smiled softly. "Hardly. I just...if it is going to be me, then there's a lot I need to know."

Shirley rubbed her hands together. "Then let's get started, shall we? What is it you think I can do for you?"

"I have virtually no recall of my life before the age of five. Nothing. Between the ages of five and ten, those memories are sketchy at best. Is it at all possible for you to read any memories I can't access?"

She licked her lips and tapped her chin. "You want me to try to read something that you, yourself, cannot?"

"Yes."

She thought some more as Midnight jumped into her lap and curled into a ball.

"Shirley, I know how you feel about using your powers, and I would never—"

"That is the least of my worries, child. I was thinking about what would be a fair exchange for my service."

"Name it," Danica added.

Shirley looked down at the dog. "There's something wrong with my Cotton. She hasn't been herself for days, and I am afraid she may have eaten something or been given something bad."

I nodded. "I noticed. Cotton's not usually so sluggish. Do you want me to take her to a vet?"

"That would be too much stress on her, I'm afraid. She's never been away from me. Not even for a minute."

I knelt down and petted the soft dog. She was the whitest dog I had ever seen. "Not feeling very well, girl?" I asked. I knew that getting a vet to come to the park would be nigh impossible and cost far more than I could afford.

"Bailey," Danica whispered, kneeling beside me to pet the dog. "She could find out in a heartbeat."

I turned and nodded. "Perfect." To Shirley I said, "Consider it done."

Shirley clapped her hands. Rising from the bench, she reached down and took both of my hands in hers. "Then, let us get started. The key is to make your mind a blank slate. Let the memories come and go as they wish. Let me connect with the past in my own way. I will not probe, as that is not an exact science. Too many thoughts, movies, books, article, dreams, et cetera have a tendency to appear to be memories when in reality they are only a disguise. Memories are tricky little buggers. They can play hide-and-seek with you for days, tickling, tantalizing, teasing and tormenting us until we reach down and rip them to the forefront of our minds. One cannot tread too softly where I am going to go, so hang on."

Nodding, I closed my eyes and envisioned a blank slate. I stood like this a long time before Shirley finally let go of my hands.

When I opened my eyes, she was frowning. "What? What is it? What did you see?"

She stared into my eyes a long time before slowly shaking her head. "That's just it. I should have seen a whole lot more. Whatever happened to you, whatever went on in your early childhood is buried so deeply, even I could not go there. It was as if—"

"As if what?"

Shirley shook her head. "As if your mind has been erased."

"Then...you didn't see anything?"

"Oh, I got something, all right, but that's what bothers me the most. It was only one thing. One tiny thing that may or may not be a memory at all. I looked and dug, careful not to linger in places that were not truly memories. As you know, a precog's greater strength lies in looking at the future. However, without much past to go on, even that was fuzzy around the edges, and I can't say for certain what I saw was, in fact, the future."

I waited, my heart pounding beneath my chest.

"There was only a name reaching through the darkness, Echo. Just a single name. I saw no pictures, felt no energy. Just a name: Mrs. Marshall."

"Mrs. Marshall?" I repeated dumbly. "Who is that?"

Shirley shrugged. "That's all I saw. The rest, I'm afraid, is up to you to find out. I wish I could be more help, but it is as if your memory was obliterated by your mind's defense mechanism."

"In short, she can't remember because her brain won't let her."

Shirley looked at me and shook her head. "Not really. A defense mechanism I would see. Repressed memories I would feel. I hate to say this, Echo, but you don't *have* any memories that I can find."

"I don't...have any?"

Shirley was still shaking her head. "I'm afraid not."

At ten o'clock the next morning, Bailey and I headed back to Golden Gate Park. She had slept very soundly in my guest bed, with my three-legged cat, Tripod, resting on her chest the entire night. I lowered my shields as Bailey slept and felt just how exhausted she really was, not just from traveling, but from Jacob Marley's death.

When we got to Shirley, I made the introductions, and I was amazed at how quickly Shirley warmed to her. Shirley was suspicious of everyone, even other paranormals, but not Bailey. She welcomed Bailey like I'd never seen her take to anyone. She immediately brought Bailey over to the grass where Cotton lay with her head on her paws.

"Let me take a walk over there with Cotton, and see if we can't find out what's got this cutie pie so depressed," Bailey said, her hand on Cotton's head.

"Depressed?" Shirley queried. "She's *depressed*?"

Bailey nodded as her hand fondled Cotton's ear. "This won't take very long."

We sat on the bench and watched as Bailey and Cotton walked about fifty yards away and then lay down on the grass together.

"She's a very powerful creature," Shirley said softly. "Cotton and Midnight perked their ears up long before I saw her coming."

"Bailey is amazing."

"You tend to attract those kinds of people to you, Echo. It is, perhaps, a greater gift than even your empathy."

I smiled softly. "Thank you."

"So, I imagine you are going to spend the day whirling about, trying to find out what Mrs. Marshall was to you."

"Danica's boys are all over it, but it's the proverbial needle. Any advice?"

"Yes, but none you'll heed."

I looked at her.

"Sometimes, the mind knows better than our hearts, and if it is protecting your heart from something too heinous for you to remember, it might be better left buried where it is. Do not underestimate the protective powers of the mind, Echo. There's a reason you don't remember."

I nodded. "I know. I need to know about me before I can even attempt to help those who are like me."

"Then it sounds like you've made your decision."

"Decision?"

"To step into Melika's shoes when the time comes."

"Oh no, no, no. No decisions made there. I just want to make sure I can actually *do it* when the time comes and if I am chosen. That has yet to be determined."

We watched silently as Bailey and Cotton wandered back over to us. "The old gal has what amounts to irritable bowel syndrome. She just needs a little medication and she should be good to go."

"Medication? What kind?"

Bailey grinned. "The kind I can whip up in two minutes and two seconds. You just hang on, Shirley, and I'll have Cotton wagging her long tail in no time." To me she said, "I am going in search of ingredients, E. I'll be back in a few."

When Bailey left, Cotton put her head on Shirley's lap.

"See what I mean? You're the perfect person to do what Melika does. You have all the right people to help you train and assist the next generation of supernaturals."

"I don't know, Shirley. I can't see myself moving to the bayou and living out there without electricity, without all of the modern conveniences we have. I love this city. I love my life here."

"Who says you have to stay on the bayou?"

"I...uh..." I blinked. "Well, for one, it's safer. No one can really see us from there, and—" My mind started racing with the possibilities.

She grinned. "All you have to do is protect them from prying eyes, correct?"

I nodded.

"There are many places you could go in order to make that happen. You simply need the right piece of property, and there are scads of private homes here in the Bay Area."

"I couldn't ever afford anything like that."

"You couldn't...but Danica could. Could and would, just to keep you near. Her bond with you is an unbreakable one. As tough as she acts, that girl would be lost without you."

I looked askance at her. "You saw something, didn't you?"

Chuckling, she shook her head. "What I saw, my dear, I saw with my own two eyes. That girl is bound to you in ways that might rival even a man's affection. She cares for you, heart and soul, and would think nothing of investing in a place for you to do what you need to do in order to keep you in her daily life. You know, the one thing you never got to see was how she longed for you when you were in the bayou. You might ask her about it some time."

"You saw all that with just your own two eyes?"

She smiled into my face, eyes sparkling mischievously. "More or less."

When Bailey came back, she had a brownish mixture on a large maple leaf. After feeding it to Cotton, she sat down with the dog and massaged her belly. "She's already feeling better, Shirley." Handing the rest of the goop to Shirley, Bailey instructed her to give her some more before bedtime. "That ought to fix her right up."

Standing, Bailey brushed off her shorts while Cotton leapt to her feet, tail wagging. "Told you…we guarantee a tail wag with every visit."

Shirley rose and hugged Cotton to her. "I can't thank you enough, Miss Bailey. My critters…they mean everything to me."

Bailey nodded. "I know they do. Cotton is about the sweetest dog I have ever met. She is very happy and content. I'd make sure you fed her a higher quality of dog food, though, just to make sure that isn't the reason for her condition."

Shirley nodded and I walked over to hug her. "Thanks for the idea about where to live."

I slipped two twenty-dollar bills into her hand. She had never taken money from me before, and was getting ready to resist, when I whispered, "It's for Cotton's food. Get the good stuff."

When she pulled away, there were tears in her eyes. "Go on, now, before you get this old bag of bones a bawlin'."

When we got in the car, Bailey rolled her window down and hung her head out like a dog. "I've known wolves and dogs with two different colored eyes, but not many people. I tell you what, you do not want to mess with an animal when you find one with two different colored eyes. They will rend you limb from limb."

"No kidding."

"If she's a precog, why didn't you ask her the whereabouts of our roaming TK?"

"I've asked enough favors of her already. Every time she does a reading, she loses a small piece of herself. Besides, what's the deal with this kid, anyway? Not many supers can give Tip the slip. What happened?"

"I have no idea. We were in Silicon Valley when the little bastard saw me and bolted. I mean, that kid can run."

"Makes you wonder what he's running from."

She pulled her head back into the car and slouched down in the seat. "Hell if I know. He was probably pickpocketing someone or doing something he ought not to be doing with his nubile powers. You know how they are—especially if they are male TKs. They go all Rambo on you and start thinking they're some kind of superhero." She sighed. "This kid has some awesome powers, E. Our spotter followed him after the bike incident and saw him in San Jose using his skills to stop a mugging. By the time we got there, he was long gone and hanging in some little rich burg in the East Bay called Blackbird or..."

"Blackhawk?"

"Yeah. That's it."

"Why did he go there?"

"I don't know, but he didn't stay long. He must have gotten the funds he needed to get to the city."

Blackhawk is an area in the East Bay where the *nouveau riche* live in monster mansions behind big gates in fear from people of a lower income bracket. Anyone managing to get in there on foot would find open homes ready to be pilfered and plundered. The people in Blackhawk lived under a false sense of security, so when their security systems were off, their doors were always unlocked. Our boy might know that...or he might have gone home to plunder the cookie jar.

"If he gets out of the state, we'll never find him."

I turned left on Masonic. As we made our silent way over the Bay Bridge and then through the Caldecott Tunnel, I couldn't stop thinking about this Mrs. Marshall. How could that be the only name Shirley could come up with?

Delta and Connie had thought the same thing. After we got back from Shirley's I had dropped Danica at the office and called Delta. I gave her the miniscule piece of information, she promised to get back to me within twenty-four hours. She had made it well under her own deadline.

"There were a lot of ways Connie and I wanted to go with this," Delta told me when I picked up my cell. "But we're leaning toward teacher."

"Teacher?"

"Yeah. By Con's calculations, you would have had anywhere between twelve and fifty teachers before middle school. This includes, of course, art, PE and music teachers as well as librarians, cafeteria workers and playground supervisors. Education was still a female-dominated career back then, and we figured someone could have made an impact on little Echo."

"Jane. I was Jane back then. I didn't change my name until I left Alta Bates." I took a breath. "Sounds like a wise direction. I never realized how many teachers a foster kid could have over the course of a dozen years. It makes sense but I have to wonder why one teacher's name stands out. I appreciate the update."

Leaving the computer geniuses to do their thing, I had grabbed Bailey and decided I needed to help her catch her wandering TK. She was going to do it anyway, just to prove to Tip she could. I just couldn't let her go out there on her own.

"Where, exactly, are we going?" I asked Bailey.

"Walnut Creek BART. Tip thinks he's going to try to get into the city and the easiest way to do that is on the Bay Area Rapid Transit. It's easier to blend in in the city. He might also be trying to get to the airport. Another spotter saw him near the McDonald's in Walnut Creek earlier this morning. If we're lucky, we'll get there before he does."

I studied Bailey as she looked out the passenger window. "What's really going on?"

Sighing loudly, she turned to me. "Tip bet me the kid would head to the city and I disagreed. *I* think he is purposely leading us on a wild goose chase."

"For what purpose? You never made contact with him, right? Why would he be afraid of you?"

She shrugged. "Maybe he's empathic as well."

Pulling into the Walnut Creek BART, I found a parking place Ladybug could squeeze into between two overbearing Hummers. "You think he's running from you or someone else?"

"It's hard to explain, Echo, but I can smell a fear in that kid as pungent as a skunk stink."

"You don't think he was afraid of Tip?"

She shook her head. "No, it's more than that. He's terrified of something."

"So we're going to patrol the BART stations in the hopes that he shows up?" I was afraid her collecting days would soon be over if this was how she was going to approach it.

"I'm not a complete boob, E. The kid is running. He made it to Blackhawk. The best way for him to get away from whatever is chasing him is by plane. Now, he didn't go to the San Jose airport, probably because he was afraid whoever it was would be watching for him there. That means he might be trying to get to either the Oakland airport or SFO. Either way, BART is the easiest way to get there; lots of crowds, easy to get on and off."

"Good thinking. Tip would be proud."

"She will only be proud if I can catch this brat. You know how she is…totally results oriented. That's the reason you need to take over when Mel retires. Hell, she'd chase every last one of us away. We *need* you at the helm, E."

I blinked several times, but said nothing.

"Oh come on. We all know it's *you* Melika wants to succeed her, not Tip. She does not have the patience to teach the younger ones. Tip is good at what she does, but let's face it. She's a lousy teacher. You're the obvious choice. If it ever came down to a vote, you'd win hands down."

I couldn't have felt further from the obvious choice than I did at that moment. "Well, Mel's a long way from retirement, so let's not worry about that right now, and I'm not ready."

"Luckily for you, you don't have to be ready. Just be *getting* ready. Don't worry, though. You can stay in your denial for as long as you need to. When it comes time to wake you from it,

I'll be right there. Now, let's catch this kid so I can shove Tip's money up her tight ass."

We stationed ourselves near the ticket machines, but not where he could see us. This looked to be a very long stakeout, and I wished I had brought a comfortable chair and snacks or something.

It turned out to be a much shorter wait than I anticipated. A tall, thin teenager with beach boy blond bangs and baggie jeans snuck up to the ticket machine. I say snuck up because his paranoia entered the BART station before he did. This emotion has a taste to it that perked me right up. Bailey hadn't exaggerated about his fear being palpable. This was one frightened pup.

"That's him," Bailey said.

"Yep." I read that he was more suspicious than afraid, and he was operating on some level of deceit. He was not what he appeared to be. "Wait. He's...this isn't right. There's something else happening with him." Something else played around the edges of his energy.

Looking around, he quickly put his money in the machine and bought a ticket. "Wait...don't grab him yet." This wasn't in the game plan, and like a trained super, he sensed something wasn't right and stopped just as he reached for his ticket.

Before I could stop her, Bailey jumped out in front of him. "I just want to talk to you," she said, putting her hands in the air as if she were surrendering.

The boy thrust both his hands toward her, knocking her a good ten feet against the wall behind her. Then, he took off toward the parking lot with me in hot pursuit, pissed off that I hadn't worn the right shoes. I was a pretty fast runner, but he was younger and more desperate than I, and it was obvious I wasn't going to catch him.

"Wait! We're on your side!"

The kid stopped and whirled around. I had learned enough from Tip and Zach to know what was coming next, so I threw out a defensive force field of my own to counteract the blast he instinctively threw toward me. When his energy caromed off it, the look on his face was priceless. He might have been a telekinetic, but he was unschooled and undisciplined in how to effectively use his powers. He reacted more like a baby rattler and used the majority of his powers in his first two tosses. He was toast.

Seeing the ineffectiveness of his power rattled him even more, so he took off running again, with me in pursuit. Tired and clearly incapable of beating him in a foot race, I stopped, put my hands around either side of my mouth, and yelled, "We're just trying to help you!"

And then he disappeared down the street.

When I turned to go back and check on Bailey, I nearly knocked her down. She had caught up to me.

"You okay?"

"Little fucker throws quite a punch," she said, looking up at the sky.

I knew what she was looking for; an eagle or a hawk, or maybe even a crow. As a Shaman, she was one with nature and part of the earth. Bailey had several unique powers, one of which was the ability to transfer her consciousness into that of her totem animals. It was a skill handed down through the ages in dozens of different cultures, from Native Americans to Aborigines, to people in Amazonia. I'd seen her do it once, and it was the most impressive thing I had ever seen.

"Damn it," she said. The sky was empty. "God damned city."

"That's okay. You don't have to worry about him leaving the state."

"Why not?"

"I picked up some emotions I couldn't place until I threw up my shield. You were right about him being suspicious and paranoid, but there was something else. He isn't looting or planning to make some big escape."

Bailey stopped looking at the sky and zeroed in on me. "No? Then what the hell is he up to?"

I sighed. "Revenge."

Danica and I met Connie and Delta at their office and I

have to say, I was impressed by their operation; lots of high-tech gadgetry that brought Danica's eyes to life like a dieter seeing a fountain of chocolate. She practically swooned.

"Nice," Danica murmured, looking down at an array of Mac laptops the size of a textbook and thinner than an address book.

Connie grinned. "We try to stay one step ahead of the rest of the world."

I stepped away as they blathered on in their secret computer lingo no one but techies understand.

"Let's both leave the geeks alone for now," Delta said. "It's been awhile since Connie's had anyone to play with. I hope she doesn't bore Danica to death with all that technobabble."

I smiled. Danica had not yet said anything to Connie about the fact that she was the creator of The Echo—the security program Connie had somehow managed to skirt around. I wondered how that would go.

"Please, have a seat, Echo. Can I get you something to drink? Coffee? Soda?"

I shook my head. "I'm fine, really. Thanks."

"Well, if you don't mind, I'll have a cup of coffee."

I grinned. "Old habits?"

"You have no idea." Delta grinned at me before turning to a gorgeous blonde who practically floated into the room. She was slightly taller than Delta, and walked like a runway model. She carried in her well-manicured hands a tray with a coffee carafe and four mugs. Her blue eyes caught Delta's and smiled.

"Taylor came by and took the girls so I can get some shopping done and run a few errands," she said, trailing one of her perfectly manicured fingernails across the back of Delta's neck. "There's this great looking farmers' market I want to try out." The woman deposited the tray on the desk and extended her hand to me. "I'm Megan, Delta's better half."

I shook her hand firmly and marveled at how tall she was: tall and absolutely gorgeous. Every movement she made was fluid, like water running down the front of a window pane. I read her quickly and saw she was a woman comfortable in her own skin who was madly in love with her other half. Their bond rang my bells like few things ever had.

"Nice meeting you. I'm Echo, and that's Danica."

Megan waved to Danica, who barely looked up and waved back before putting her head back together with Connie over some upturned laptop they were toying with. "Thanks so much for the business," she said to me. "These two were driving even the little ones crazy. They're both like working dogs; they need work or they start digging up the yard and tearing up all the furniture."

I grinned. I warmed to her instantly. She was down-to-earth and open, and I suspected she was the air balancing Delta's watery Storm. "From what I can tell," I said, accepting a mug of coffee from her, "they're pretty good at what they do."

Megan laughed. "Oh, they're much better than pretty good, and they haven't even started yet." She handed Danica a mug and came back to get the tray. "If they can't find out what you need to know, then nobody can. Give them time, be patient, and try not to roll your eyes when they get on a verbal roll. The two of them together can make a person want to smack them over the head."

"I'll keep that in mind."

Delta chuckled as she took Megan's hand and kissed the back of it.

Megan smiled a thousand watter to her lover before turning back to me. "You do that," she told me. She leaned over to me. "There's no one better than these two, Echo. I guarantee it."

I watched her walk away, feeling as if everything I was doing was the right thing.

Delta set her mug down and opened a file. "Okay, Echo, here's what we've got so far." She pulled a list from the file. "There are a couple dozen Mrs. Marshalls who taught around the time you were in school. We broadened the parameters of the search because we weren't sure of the date of your birth. Connie and I operate on facts, not supposition. Until we have factual data, we can only make conjectures."

I sighed and nodded. The idea that even my birth date might be wrong was unsettling.

"We have four kindergarten teachers, three grammar school teachers and six middle school teachers in the Bay Area around the time you might have been in kindergarten. We've narrowed it down to an area within this map here." She pulled out a map with yellow highlights dotting it. "Which takes three of these women out of the mix."

Connie and Danica joined us at the desk.

"But that doesn't mean one of them couldn't be our gal. Or none of them. She could be dead, remarried, any number of things. Hell, she may not be a teacher anymore or maybe she was never a teacher, or—"

"We're checking on other things as well," Connie interjected. "Churches, synagogues, Girl Scout leaders, that sort of thing. We've got our computers working overtime to come up with all the Marshalls in the state. We'll start here and then move outward if we have to."

Danica nodded. "My guys are on the same thought patterns. They're plugging in every Marshall marriage in the northern part of the state. It's broad, and there are a ton of Marshalls to go through, but we won't leave any stones unturned."

I studied the list, willing a memory, any memory to rise like cream to the surface, but nothing came. "That sounds like a solid plan of attack, but like the proverbial needle."

"Delta and I specialize in finding needles, Echo," Connie said softly. "Trust us."

Delta nodded. "Connie and I thought we'd go to the East Bay and visit a few of the grammar schools there."

I nodded. "Some of this legwork needs to be done by me. I'm doing a story on this and it will be more powerful if I am actually doing it. I'll take the grammar school list and let me see what I can find out."

Delta nodded before sipping her coffee. "You take the East Bay then, and Con and I will take the South Bay, San Francisco, and everything on this side of the bridges."

"Perfect."

Delta handed me the file. "This is yours. We duplicated everything so we're all on the same page. If your Mrs. Marshall is alive, we'll find her."

The first five schools yielded nothing, except a learning curve. We were able to figure out by the second school we needed to be more specific about our request. We needed something people seldom give, and that was the truth. The older administrative assistants were sympathetic and hopped about trying to help us, while the younger ones were a little less...enthusiastic. It seemed like getting our hands on a yearbook was going to take an act of Congress. But with my powers, and Danica's persuasive techniques, we managed to wrangle half a dozen yearbooks out of their hands. None of them had a Mrs. Marshall or a little Jane Doe.

The sixth school was Green Valley School in Danville: a quaint upper middle-class burg in the heart of the East Bay surrounded by the foothills of Mount Diablo. It was the kind of place that should have been named Pleasantville or Happy Valley something as serene. A Mrs. Marshall had taught kindergarten there around the time I would have been five. Unlike the other schools, the staff at Green Valley was very helpful and handed us armloads of yearbooks. Standing at the front desk, we began flipping through the books staring down at a sea of smiling faces. How could I not remember one tiny thing about kindergarten?

After the third yearbook, Danica sighed. "After a while, all these little white faces start looking alike."

I couldn't disagree. In Oakland and Berkeley, at least there were a variety of kids of color. In this higher-end community, twenty-something years ago, there was nothing but a sea of white, freckled faces of kids named Johnny and Bobbie, Suzie and Leslie.

"After this, I'm going to need a ghetto fix," Danica whispered. "Only one little black kid in the whole class, and look at how stinkin' cute she is. She's the cutest one in the class. Say one thing for my people. Nobody but nobody has prettier babies."

I smiled as I stared at little Marcy Davis, and then, my smile froze. Looking back at me like the happiest kid in the world was a photo of a kid who had to be me. At least, I was pretty sure it was me. I had a pixie cut showing a bite mark I sported on my ear.

Absentmindedly, my hand reached up to my ear. I had been

told when I was eleven that a dog had bitten my ear when I was just a little kid. I had no recollection of that, either.

If I had any doubt she was me, it vanished when Danica's slender index finger came over my shoulder and lightly brushed the scar. "That's you, Clark," she murmured softly, sitting in the chair next to me. "I could tell that silly little grin a mile away. And look…there's your scar."

I was frozen. It really *was* me with my little pixie cut and goofy grin staring back at the camera. Blinking several times and feeling this huge sense of loss, I sat down hard next to her. "If only I could remember. If only she could speak to me."

"Oh shit," Danica groaned, covering the photo.

I kept blinking. "What?" I looked down the page to where her finger was, and I saw the reason for her expletive. There in bold type was my given name.

"Charlotte Hayward." My voice sounded strange to me, as if coming from someone else's mouth. "My name used to be…" I swallowed hard and covered my mouth. "Charlotte."

We sat there in silence, both of us staring at a little girl who was me and not me. There I was, looking like a normal kid, wearing a pink and white top and smiling like I hadn't a care in the world. It felt like I was staring at any little girl in kindergarten. There was no attachment to the picture at all.

Having a *real* name meant only one thing.

"If I had a name…" Turning to Danica, I blinked back tears that came too fast to hold back. "I didn't start out as a Jane Doe. I didn't start out as a kid with no parents. I—" Shaking my head, I let the tears fall. "I had parents."

"I…shit, Clark, I don't know what to say." Danica shook her head and pulled me to her with one arm. "Shit."

I barely nodded and impatiently wiped the tears away before they could fall. Tears that fell carried too much emotion in them and made it harder to recover, and I needed to recover.

"Is everything all right?" the secretary wanted to know.

"Yes. She's fine," Danica replied, looking at me. "Right?"

Swallowing hard, I stared at the photo of Charlotte. She looked so incredibly happy. How could I not remember? "We got what we came for, yes. Thank you."

"At least we have a last name to go on now."

I nodded again, finally letting myself breathe. "Charlotte." I rolled the name around in my mouth like a taster does wine. "*Someone* named me Charlotte." I blinked back more tears. "Someone loved me once. So what happened that I became Jane Doe?"

Danica whistled. "Jesus, Clark. Everything you've always believed about your life isn't true. You weren't born a Jane Doe. Someone—"

"Gave me up."

Danica motioned to the secretary and asked her if we could make a photocopy. Then she asked for a glass of water. The secretary took the album to the Xerox machine, and Danica handed me a plastic cup of water. "I don't need you going weak on me in here, Clark, but you look like you're going down. You're whiter than normal."

I nodded and rose, taking the water. "I feel like someone really big just kicked me in the stomach."

"Hang in there. We're going to get all the answers you need. We won't stop until every fucking question is answered. I promise."

We got to the car and sat there quietly for a few moments as I stared down at the photo. "I feel sorry for her," I said at last. "I feel like something is creeping up on her that is going to change her life forever and I can't stop it."

"Charlotte?"

I nodded. "She had such bright eyes, but there was something else behind them."

"I see it too. Maybe that's why you don't remember. Maybe bad things were going on…things we'd rather not talk about."

I nodded again. "Maybe."

"You still want to know?"

"More than ever. Dani, *something* happened to make that little girl forget. And it hurts my heart to think of all she must have lost."

Danica patted my shoulder. "Don't you worry, Clark. Whatever it was, we're going to find it. I swear."

As I drove back across the bridge, Danica called and asked Connie and Delta to meet us at Danica's office, downstairs in the lobby. When the four of us got in the elevator, I pulled out the Xeroxed copy of little Charlotte Hayward.

"Meet Charlotte Hayward," I said, handing the photo to Delta.

She looked at the photo, then at me, then back to the photo again before handing it to Connie. "I can see the resemblance for sure. You both have that bite mark on your right ear, but those eyes...they are the same as they were back then."

Connie took the photo and studied it without looking at me. "Yeah, this is her. Look at the shape of the ear, and how that one hangs just a little lower. Look here at the shape of the chin. If you want," she looked up at me now, "I can get a programmer to age this for you and we can see for sure."

I shook my head. "That scar says it all. That's me, Connie. I may not remember, but I know."

"Your name gives us a lot to go on, Echo. We'll have answers for you sooner than you think."

Danica nodded. "My guys are already on it."

"We're not looking for Charlotte Hayward, Danica. We'll be searching for the parents and siblings of her. This way we can cover all our bases."

Delta nodded. "Someone in California has records of when Charlotte was up for adoption. St. Ignatius owes you some answers, and we're not stopping until someone coughs them up."

I sighed, feeling my emotions purge from my body like vapor from a hot sidewalk. Someone had stopped loving little Charlotte Hayward. Someone had left her somewhere and never returned.

When the elevator dinged and we got off on the top floor, Connie took two steps and stopped as she stared at the sign. "Savvy Software? You work for Savvy Software?"

Danica chuckled. "Sort of. I *am* Savvy Software. This is my company."

Connie stared, slack-jawed. "*You're* D. Johnson?"

She nodded. "It's still a man's world out there, so I stuck with the gender neutral first initial."

Impressed, Connie nodded in appreciation. "Smart. Like most of your products. Your voice recognition software will revolutionize the industry. You might single-handedly replace the need for a keyboard."

"That's the plan." Danica motioned for us all to follow her. "I am also the creator of The Echo you seemed to have broken into."

Connie shook her head. "Well, aren't you full of surprises?"

"You have no idea." Opening the door to the Bat Cave, she stepped aside and Connie walked in like a kid walks into a toy store. The three boys waved to us, and Roger came over and made all of the introductions.

"You said you needed more computer power, Ms. Rivera," Danica said. "Well, here it is. One hundred-fold."

I stared at Danica. I couldn't tell if she was showing off, issuing a challenge, or what, but no one else seemed to notice. I mean, *Ms. Rivera*? What was up with that?

"We'll take good care of her, boss," Roger said, straightening his wrinkled shirt. There were three different stains on his shirt. Roger was the head geek who took care of the boys in the Bat Cave, and there wasn't a better IT man alive.

Danica shook her head. "The hell you will. I'll show her around." To me, she said, "We'll be out in a little while, Clark. You guys can use the computers in my office if you want to start rooting around, or you can stay here and play with the boys."

Connie grabbed Danica's hand and started for one of the laptops.

"Oh my God." Connie murmured. "Is that the beta of the PR94?"

"You *know* about the PR94?" Danica asked as they both sat down in chairs and wheeled over to the laptop oblivious to everything else. There's a reason they are called geeks.

I closed the door behind them and took Delta into Danica's office.

"Looks like Con has finally met her match." Delta walked

around the office, arms behind her back, surveying with the calculating eyes of a cop. She read the room like a book, storing tiny pieces of information somewhere in that steel trap of hers.

"She sure has. Danica is nothing short of a genius."

Delta sat on the edge of the couch, not like she was uncomfortable, but as if she couldn't really light anywhere until she got a feel for her surroundings. I was pretty sure Bailey would read this woman much like a creature: a caged panther pacing back and forth. Delta Stevens was an incredibly perceptive natural—far superior to regular normals. I would have to pay closer attention to this woman and see the extent of her own personal magic.

"Con will have names of every Hayward within a hundred-mile radius of that school neighborhood. She'll check tax records, property records, births and deaths, Social Security, and any other government agency she can break into."

"She's that good?" I sat on the dark leather chair across from the red leather couch Delta was perched on.

"No. She's better than good. I've never met anyone like her. She gets in, gets out and leaves no trail. The things she knows about hacking would make our government very nervous."

I felt a familiar tingling at the base of my skull. Tip.

"Hey kiddo. You guys lost that TK again?"

"I'm busy."

"I know. Look, I really need you to help Bailey on this. I don't want her to fail her first time out. She'll lose confidence."

"Then you shouldn't have left her alone."

"I didn't leave her alone. I left her with you."

"And I'm busy!"

"When aren't you? Look, it's really important for her. She needs to get him collected."

"I understand that."

"And the kid is powerful. Stronger than I realized."

"I'm doing my best. Now go away so I can do my life."

"Okay. You okay?"

"Bye, Tip."

Damn her. She knew I wasn't okay. That was why she popped in. She *knew*. I refused to let her pull me back into her life. It was time for me to move on.

Delta was looking at me, waiting for me to answer a question I didn't hear. I was just getting ready to be embarrassed when my cell rang.

I looked at the caller ID. Finn. Of course. Was it raining women right now or what?

"It's Finn. I can let it go."

"No, no, go ahead. I'm going to check on Connie. If I don't sit on her, she'll fall in a wormhole or something."

I smiled. "From *our* background check on *you*, it appears *she's* the one always bailing *you* out of trouble."

Delta laughed. "As much as I would like to deny that nasty little rumor, it's true. I see someone has been doing their homework. Good."

I shrugged. "Finn's told me stories."

She grinned. "She lies. You can tell her that, too." She was still laughing when she walked out of the office.

"Hi there," I said into the cell, forcing the cheeriest voice from my mouth.

"Hey stranger. Is your cell broken?"

"I'm sorry. I'm just finishing up a big story and I'm on a pretty strict deadline. I'm also working on something really big…something personally big. How are you?"

"Busy. Bored. Missing you. You're not avoiding me, are you?"

"Don't be silly. Our schedules are just off. How does your lunch schedule look tomorrow?"

"I have a firearms test in the morning. How about two?"

"I have an interview. Dinner?"

"I'm teaching at the Academy."

There was a long pause of frustration on both ends.

"I can clear up time on Sunday, how about you?"

I looked down at the calendar on my vidbook. "I'll try. I'm on this pretty fast-paced story, so I can't promise anything." I motioned for Delta to come back in. "I'll call you later. Or you call me. Whatever." I hung up. Damn Tip. Her appearance always threw a wet blanket over the smoldering embers of my love life.

"You okay?" Delta asked as sat back on the couch now. It was as if she'd finally gotten the lay of the land and was able to relax. "You don't look so hot."

"Finn and I just can't seem to make our schedules mesh. It's frustrating. How did you and Megan do it?"

"It wasn't easy at first. Being a cop wasn't what I did for a living. It was *who* I was. You eat, sleep and breathe that job or you'll end up cashing it in at the end of a shift. It takes no quarter. I'd say ninety-nine percent of our arguments centered around my commitment to my job over my commitment to our relationship."

"Ouch."

She shrugged. "Yeah, that didn't go over very well with her. We used to butt heads all the time and then…well…I almost lost her and that was enough to make me realize I'd rather be with her than anywhere else in the world. I got the wakeup call that time and have been wide-eyed ever since."

"So you just quit?"

Delta shook her head. "Actually, no. I didn't quit until we lost Connie's wife, Gina. By then, I knew it was time to be done. I had lost so many people I cared about. It's not a job, Echo. It's a lifestyle, and not an easy one for partners who always feel a little on the outside of the blue inner circle. If cops aren't careful, they begin developing a *we versus them* mentality, and our partners aren't ever sure which side they fall on. If you're really thinking about hanging in there with Finn, you ought to talk to Megan. She's a pro at figuring out how to maneuver through the emotional maze of being a cop's partner."

"I might just take you up on that."

She grinned. "You really like Finn, huh?"

I nodded. "I do. She's a great person."

"Yes, she is, but you still need to pay attention to the warning signs that scream *Warning! Main priority is the badge and gun!* It happens to all of us at one time or another, and if we're not reeled in quickly, we fall down the rabbit hole. Don't let that happen to Finn if you can help it."

I had been so busy climbing up out of my own rabbit hole, I hadn't been paying much attention to where she was in all of this. "I'll keep that in mind."

The office door flew open and Danica and Connie came waltzing through it.

"We have too many Haywards right now, so I put the boys

on it. We should be able to narrow things down pretty quickly from here."

"What we found, though, is pretty exciting." Connie handed me a slip of paper. "We think we found your Mrs. Marshall, but her name is Mrs. Olsen now, and she's still teaching."

Danica stood next to Connie beaming. "She's teaching sixth grade at Walnut Creek Intermediate."

I almost shot out of my chair. Walnut Creek was a stone's throw from Green Valley School—a couple of towns over. Once a small city filled with oak trees, it, too, had become an overpriced, overinflated version of its once quaint self.

"You and Storm check her out. Dani and I are going to stay with the boys and keep working on the paper trail to see if we can't find the Haywards who used to live in Danville."

Delta was already up and moving toward the door, jacket in hand. "We're on it. Stay out of trouble, Chief. I know how you and multiple computers do things that aren't quite...kosher."

"She's got a lot of illegal things to teach me," Danica whispered to me. She sounded like the girl I went to college with, and if I didn't know better, I'd think Dani had a little techno crush. "And I have a few things up my sleeve to teach her."

With those parting words, Delta and I were on the Bay Bridge making our way back to the East Bay in search of a little girl who had died a long, long time ago.

When we pulled up to Walnut Creek Intermediate, school was just letting out. I'd had no problem sitting in the red convertible 1965 Mustang Delta drove. It was pristine and restored to perfection, all the way down to original Pony seats. This car had a navigation system built into it, but other than that, it screamed retro.

I jumped out, Xerox in hand. I had no delusions this woman would remember me more than twenty years after she had been my teacher. I mean, how many students had she seen in those years and how much had we all changed?

"If you consider thirty kids in a class over twenty years ago, you're talking six, seven hundred kids, Echo, so don't expect her to remember you."

I stopped walking and stared at her. I hadn't said anything out loud; merely, thought about it. How was it she always seemed to be half a step ahead of me? Was there something I kept missing?

"Don't be nervous," she continued, again, pegging my emotional state to the wall.

"You read people very well, Delta."

She shrugged. "Call it a gift. I relied heavily on that talent when I was a cop, which didn't always bode well for me. Cops want solid, concrete facts, and too often, I flew by the seat of my pants, on my gut instinct. It was more often a problem than not."

When we finally got to room 222, Mrs. Olsen was hanging maps of Asia on the walls. The classroom was a typical middle school room and smelled of glue, dry erase markers and paint. Filled with artwork the kids had done, there were maps of Asia drawn by them hanging on the far wall.

When Mrs. Olsen turned around, she was much younger than I expected, and my hopes were dashed that she couldn't be the right woman.

"Excuse us, Mrs. Olsen, but do you have a moment?" Delta asked.

She smiled. "Certainly. Won't you have a seat? You're not parents of mine, are you?" She sat down and I realized that from far away, she appeared younger than she was. Crow's feet tickled the edges of her eyes and there was a wizened look about her mouth. On closer inspection, she could very well have been my kindergarten teacher.

"No, ma'am, we're not."

"How can I help you?"

Sliding the Xerox copy over to her, I braced myself and asked, "I don't expect you to remember me, Mrs. Olsen, but I was in your kindergarten class when your name was Mrs. Marshall. I'm trying to find out—"

Typical teacher, she held her hand up to silence me. She stared at the photo a long time, and then lowered it to look at me. She was choosing her words carefully. "I've been teaching a long time, and I know what Father Time does to my little faces. Still, I don't quite know how *you* could be this little girl."

I leaned forward. Lowering my shields, I realized at once that she did, in fact, recognize me. "You really recognize me, don't you?"

She studied the photo a moment before looking at me. "That is not what I said. I recognize this little girl, yes, but I don't know how you could be her." She stared at the photo again and slowly shook her head before handing it back to me. "The resemblance is obvious, though."

Delta leaned forward as well. "Why can't she have been this little girl, Mrs. Olsen?"

Mrs. Olsen took a quick intake of breath. "Because that little girl died a long time ago."

The room went completely still, and all I could hear was my heart pounding in my head. Time had been put on pause, allowing me a moment to catch up to words I hadn't ever expected to hear. My tongue suddenly felt like a lead block in my mouth. I was lucky I had brought Delta because I was dead in the water. Right now, it was all I could do to stay in the chair. My body felt like pudding oozing out the sides of the chair.

"Dead?" Delta reached for my hand. "Something *happened* to this little girl that made you think she was dead?"

Mrs. Olsen wrung her hands, and suddenly, she looked much older. "My, yes. It was awful too. I'll never forget that day as long as I live." She sighed. "Such a sweet little girl too." Glancing up at me, she wasn't sure where to go from here.

I had to really focus on her lips to hear what she was saying next because I could hear nothing above the banging of my heart.

Delta gave my hand a squeeze. "Do you remember what happened to her?"

"Oh yes. It was such a tragedy. That little girl burned to death in a house fire." She leaned back in her chair, wearing the mask of remembrance. "Horrible, horrible thing, that fire. Burned so hot and so fast, it took the house and everything in it to the ground within minutes. The firemen had no time to contain it because it burned down so fast." She sighed and shook her head sadly. "They said she never made it out."

"They?"

I could sense Delta's disciplined urgency. Like a cat with a mouse, she skillfully prodded Mrs. Olsen without alarming her or making her uncomfortable. Delta must have sensed my utter distress, because she kept her hand firmly on mine.

"Who said she never made it out? Her parents or the fire department?"

She looked at me and then back to Delta. "Neither. As I recall it, I was told by the principal. I don't know who told him. The papers simply said that she was killed in a house fire that may or may not have been intentionally set."

I thought I was going to faint. This was more than I could bear, and I would have stood up to pace, but Delta's firm grip on my hand told me to stay put.

"What happened to her parents?" Delta asked.

She looked at Delta and then leaned forward to look at me, her eyes zeroing in on my ear. "Where did you get that scar?"

I instinctively reached up to touch the crescent-shaped scar on my ear. "I was bitten."

The blood drained from her face. "Charlotte had the same such mark from a dog bite as well. She—" She stopped and stared at me, her hand covering her mouth. "It can't be, and yet, here you are with the exact same bite mark on your ear. You...you really are Charlotte, aren't you?"

I swallowed hard, hoping my tongue would finally work. "That's why we're here. I have no memory of my childhood, and we're trying to find out who I was and what happened to me."

She fanned herself with the Asia maps. "Oh my. Well...from the looks of it, you were Charlotte Hayward, but I have no idea how you could have survived that fire. They found your body in the house. The fire burned too fast for you to escape it. You don't remember any of that?"

I shook my head. "I don't. I was raised in foster care my whole life."

"Foster care?" She shook her head, confused. "But why? Your parents weren't killed in that fire."

I took that like a punch in the stomach. All the air rushed from me. "Excuse me?"

Mrs. Olsen returned to wringing her hands. "Oh my. I am so sorry. This is all a little awkward for me."

Delta nodded. "That's okay, ma'am, she said, her cop demeanor clearly rising to the surface. "Take your time. Just tell us whatever it is you can remember."

"Your parents...they weren't killed in the fire." She paused and thought a moment. "Well, now, that doesn't make any sense, does it?"

"None of this is making any sense, Mrs. Olsen. The state home that Echo...that...uh...Charlotte spent her childhood in has her listed as coming in as a Jane Doe. Parentless Jane Doe."

Mrs. Olsen sat back as if slapped. "Don't be ridiculous. If you really *are* Charlotte, then...what happened in that fire? Who took you to foster care? Where are your parents? I'm afraid I don't understand at all." She pulled her sweater around her shoulders protectively. "Your parents...do they know? Of course they know." She looked up. "Right?"

"That's what we're trying to find out." Delta pulled a small pad from her pocket. "And anything you can tell us to help locate them would be wonderful."

Mrs. Olsen reached over and laid her hand on my leg. "You were such a sweet little girl." Pulling the copy to her, she studied it a moment. "Your best friend's name was Marcy Something. I've forgotten her last name, but the two of you always took nap time together. That's her. Right here. I would have to chide you for giggling at nap time, the two of you were such magpies. That little girl was inconsolable for weeks after you...after the fire. Cried for two weeks during nap time. I just let her cry, poor thing."

I was feeling like the poor thing now. It was so utterly strange to hear about your own life and death from the lips of a stranger; to have someone turn the pages of a biography you have no recollection of was an odd, odd place to be.

"You wouldn't happen to know where this Marcy might have ended up, do you?"

Mrs. Olsen shook her head. "All I can tell you is that little Marcy adored Charlotte...uh...you. Charlotte was the only student who didn't think Marcy was different. If I recall, I think you didn't even know Marcy was black. Someone had called her a name and made her cry once, and you...well...let's say I had to send you home for punching little Bergen Hunt in the nose."

Delta prodded her on. "You have a great memory, Mrs. Olsen."

"Not so much these days; not since they started overloading my classes. I remember my first couple of classes because it's a sink-or-swim situation when you get your first class. You know next to nothing when you first start teaching, but I remember you were a feisty little thing, always ready to defend the less fortunate; not that Marcy was, of course. I'm sure it wasn't easy growing up in such a homogeneous environment. She just adored you after that." Mrs. Olsen shook her head slowly. "I just don't understand how you could have been raised in foster care. Your parents simply doted on you. They came to the parent-teacher meetings."

"What happened after the fire?"

"That house smoldered and left a burning stench in the air for days until they removed all of the rubble."

"What do you think happened to her parents?"

Mrs. Olsen blinked several times before answering, and I sensed how she carefully chose her next words. "I never saw them again. The grandmother came by to collect Charlotte's things. I couldn't get much out of her. She was so distraught, of course. Mr. Hayward had his mother take everything with your name on it. She spent about a half an hour looking through things and staring at work you had done. It was awful. She was so incredibly heartbroken. We all were."

I sat there. Stunned. I had a grandmother? A real, flesh-and-blood grandmother; not the one I used to lay in bed dreaming about when Britt and I would discuss getting the hell out of the home.

Delta pressed on. "What about the house? Did they rebuild the house?"

"They razed the house and built a retirement home on the land. That happens a lot around here now."

I was still back on the grandmother piece. "Wait. Please." I held up a hand. "My grandmother—"

"Oh my, but that woman was so sad, as we all were, of course." She sighed and rose, signaling, as most teachers do, an end to the meeting. "I wish I could tell you more, but that's about all I can remember. You've grown into a beautiful woman, Charlotte, and I am incredibly curious about how all of this came to be. Obviously, you did not die in that fire, but what, exactly, did happen?"

"We're going to find answers to all those questions," Delta replied, also standing. She handed Mrs. Olsen her card. "If you can think of anything else, no matter how unimportant you think it might be, please don't hesitate to contact me."

Mrs. Olsen took the card, but did not look at it. Instead, she reached down and took my hand. "I know it is probably no consolation to you, but I am most happy to see that you did not die in that fire."

I rose and handed her one of my business cards too. This one, she looked at, her expression changing to bewilderment. "You're...not Charlotte anymore?"

"Mrs. Olsen, we weren't kidding. I really *am* listed as a Jane Doe in the state records. Don't you find that odd considering my parents were alive? Why would they have just left me to the state?" I didn't wait for her to answer. "I'm looking for answers as to how this could ever have happened."

"You're Echo Branson, *the reporter.*"

I smiled, suddenly energized by the simple spoken truth; because that's who I *really* was; not Charlotte Hayward, a little girl whose death was obviously feigned—not Jane Doe waiting to be adopted. I was Echo Branson, a person of some merit, not some thrown away kid. "I am."

"I love your articles. Is that why you are doing all of this now? Are you writing a story?"

I nodded. "I am now."

"Good. Your pieces about Katrina and New Orleans were riveting."

"Thank you."

"Would you call me if you find out anything? I am a big mystery reader and this certainly qualifies as one, don't you think?"

"Absolutely. Thank you so much for your time, Mrs. Olsen... and for your wonderful memory."

Delta and I walked in silence to the Mustang. She opened my door and said, "I'll call Con and Dani and tell them what we got. Why don't you just put your head back and let it all sink in for a bit? I can't pretend to know how you're feeling, but the look in your eyes speaks volumes."

I appreciated Delta's sensitivity, but I wasn't at all sure how I was feeling. Varied emotions banged around each other like bingo balls. I was dizzy from it all and had a hard time catching my breath. To be an empath and have such little control over your own emotions was disconcerting. I needed to meditate, to get it all together, but I just couldn't. In a panic like this, I was tempted to call out for Tip, but that would ruin everything. She would get to me in a heartbeat, and I didn't need any more complications.

While Delta relayed the tale of Mrs. Olsen over the phone, I looked out at the passing scenery of the verdant East Bay. My parents had given me up after a house fire and reported I had died? If that were true, where were they now? How could they just walk away? Why didn't they come back?

Closing my eyes, I built as strong a wall as I could around me. I didn't need Tip feeling my angst and despair. Of course, who was I kidding? *I* didn't want to feel my angst and despair. With too many questions and not enough answers, I wrapped myself in a cocoon of sleep the entire way home.

After a long bath and leftovers I wasn't completely sure I should risk eating, I sat on the couch with my three-legged cat, Tripod, in my lap trying to calm a mind racing at the speed of light. Danica wanted to come over, but I needed time alone. I needed to think more carefully, to take a deep breath and understand this was a process that was going to take time. The answers weren't going to just jump into my lap. I needed...well... needed a lot of things, but mostly, I needed my "mom."

When Melika answered, I started right in. "Did you know?"

"Does that matter?"

My heart sank. "Of course it matters! How could you know I wasn't some abandoned little baby and not tell me? How could you let me wonder all this time?" Now the tears came, hot, hard, angry tears, not just for me, but for little Charlotte, lost and left at an orphanage with not a shred of memory to her name.

"Calm down, my dear. Striking out at those who love you is not the way you want to go."

"Did. You. Know?"

I heard her sigh. "Of your early years, I'm afraid I know nothing. When you first came to us, I had Tip poke around inside your head, and though she cannot locate memories, she *does* have the ability to feel remnants of emotions. Your thoughts and those remnants rarely went beyond your seventh grade year. We both had a feeling there was some sort of trauma in your life disconnecting you from your past, but what that was, we could never ascertain. You have my word on that."

"But you *did* know something."

"I had no facts, Echo, no. I knew it was time for you to find out. You're at a place in your life when you're ready to handle the truth; whatever that truth is. Beyond that, my dear, I know as little as you do. Now take a deep breath and calm yourself. The emotions bubbling over can be counterproductive. Do not push away those who can help because of your anger and frustration." She paused here for effect. "Welcome to your truth."

"I don't *feel* ready. I feel like I had my teeth kicked in and I have no idea where to go with these emotions. Mel...they *left* me! They left me in a fucking orphanage!"

"I understand that. I really do, but you wanted the truth, and it is seldom our friend in the beginning. The truth is all any of us require but are seldom ready for. Trust me, my dear. You *are* ready. It is time. This doesn't mean it's going to be easy. It just means it's time for you to explore what all of this means to you now."

"Is it time because it's something you think I need to know for me, or time because of some other reason you're not sharing?"

She laughed softly. "It is not like you to speak in such a

circular and hidden fashion, Echo. What is it you really want to know?"

"Are you retiring?"

Her laughter was a bit more audible this time. "Where on earth did you get that idea? I have healed nicely from our little encounter. Besides, The Others are the ones who determine when that time is. When I find out, you'll be one of the first to know. But this isn't about me, Echo, it's about you and the journey you are on. You need to move forward with confidence, and that's hard to do when you're constantly looking back, wondering who you are. I know you're afraid. I would be too. Suddenly, there are things you never knew, things you never thought *could* be true. It's only natural to be afraid of the unknown...even if that unknown already happened."

Gently pushing Tripod from my lap, I started pacing. "My parents were alive when they *gave me up*. Gave me up as a fucking Jane Doe!" The tears came again. "What kind of people do that?"

"Do you have all the facts yet?"

I hesitated. "Not really." I wiped my eyes with a kitchen towel.

"Then don't jump to conclusions. You do not have enough information yet before you start flailing wildly about. Don't get all balled up over this and forget that your present life needs tending to as well. Don't neglect that which is far more important and has yet to be lived. Anger is a poor substitution for real emotions. You know that."

I nodded. "I do. I'm trying not to let it build inside me, but it's hard. It seems like the more answers I get, the more questions I have."

"But don't you see? That's how life should be! Most people don't get that. They get an answer and stop learning and stop growing. Not you. You must keep learning and growing because you have a destiny to fulfill."

I sighed loudly. "Yes, ma'am."

"You are going to be fine. That much I can tell you. Do you trust me?"

I nodded. "I do."

"Then trust that this is a new path and a new process, and you are going to be fine at the end of it all. I'm not saying it won't hurt, but you *will* come out in one piece. I promise you that." She sighed wearily and I could feel her shields drop a little. "Now, tell me about this TK who keeps getting away. What's the problem?"

"He thinks we're after him."

"You are."

"No, this is different. He's *terrified* of being caught."

"What does Tip say?"

"What else? Bring him in. Mel, I need a better bead on this kid before he gets out of the state. There's a whole lotta something I don't know."

"I'll have one of my more experienced spotters find him for you. Tip is busy on another assignment and can't cut loose. We will find your boy and get right back to you, okay? In the meantime, go easy on yourself and this parent piece. Take time to assess your feelings. If I know you, and I do, you've already started to shove your emotions into a corner somewhere. *Feel* the emotions, Echo. *That's* how you grow. Take your time putting the puzzle pieces together."

"How do you know it's a puzzle?"

"Bishop. She once told me your past was going to catch up to you one day and you'd have the hardest decision of your life to make. That was all she said, and we never spoke of it again. That is all you need. Trust me. Trust Bishop."

I nodded again, slightly embarrassed that I was so self-absorbed I hadn't asked about her. "How is she?"

"Recovering slowly. At her age, every little physical ailment is painful. Her plan was to stay with The Others until she's strong enough to return to the city, but I don't see that happening in the near future and neither does she. It's going to take some time to get the city back together, and they don't want her down in it while they do. I'll pass your love to her."

"Thank you. And thanks for listening. I was freaking out."

"That's normal. Everything you're experiencing is normal."

I grinned. "For once in my life, I'm normal? No wonder I'm freaking. Normal sucks."

She laughed. "It can. We're always here for you when you need us. Take care of yourself while you are on that path, and collect that TK."

"Yes, ma'am."

Hanging up, I flopped down on the bed, her words still ringing in my ears. I picked up the phone to call Finn, and her voice mail picked up. I didn't leave a message, but I did hear Delta's voice reminding me about the nature of being a cop's partner.

Did I really want a woman who expected me home at a certain hour? Did I want or even need consistency or predictability in my life? When had my life ever really been that way? Not even out on the bayou was there anything remotely predictable about any day—hell, any hour.

When I was getting ready to fly to New Orleans, Finn's singular response had been to remind me not to drink the water. She did not question the sanity of going into a flooded area that was in a state of emergency. She did not question my decision to go do a story in the middle of all that disaster of looting and civil unrest. She allowed me to lead my life the way I allowed her to lead hers.

What kind of life were we leading if we never spent time together outside a tattered diner?

I stared at the phone and willed Finn to call me. I needed her to be here for me, but I didn't have the words to ask for it. I wondered if I ever would.

The phone rang. I picked it right up. "Hi there."

"You okay, darlin'?"

Tip.

I burst into tears. For the first five minutes I cried into the phone telling her everything I'd learned at the school. I told her all about our search and what we had uncovered. She listened patiently, softly telling me over and over that I was okay. Her voice was like two arms holding me to her.

"Tip, if you know the truth about any of this, please, please tell me."

"Darlin', the truth is exactly as Mel said it was. Something is buried deep within you and it's so deep, not even Bishop could extract it. No one knows anything beyond that. I swear."

I wiped my face with the sleeve of my sweatshirt. "Thank you."

"None needed. It's what we do. You may be seeing Finn, darlin,' but I will love you always, and all you ever need to do is call me and I'll be there. I just figured you needed a good cry and that's easier to do over the phone."

Swallowing back my sadness, I nodded. "Thank you." Collecting myself, I inhaled deeply and forged ahead into the present, doing exactly what Mel said I would do. "We're bringing your TK in shortly. Just give Bailey some time."

"Not that important right now Echo, really. Take some time to—"

"He doesn't have the luxury of time, Tip. I need to find him as soon as possible."

"Mel told me she has another spotter on it, so you should be able to get the jump on him. She'll call when she locates him. It won't take long."

"How come we don't even know this kid's name?"

"Came outta nowhere. A freak incidence made him reveal his powers. Then, he went on the run. That's about all we have. Reeling him in is important for his safety as well as ours."

"If it's that important, what are *you* doing?"

"Top secret stuff. If I told you, I'd have to kill you. You know how Sedona, Santa Fe and Nome all have those dead spots in them where psychic energy is sort of disrupted?"

"I do."

"I'm checking a few things out. I'll tell you more when I know more. Look, you need me, you know what to do. I'll come in a heartbeat. And Echo? I can be here for you and not ruin anything you are trying to build with Finn. I promise. I'm your friend. I'm here to help you through this. Trust me."

Only one problem with that request: I did. I think I trusted her almost as much as I trusted Dani. Tip would not stand in my way with Finn. It just wasn't in her nature.

When we hung up, I felt slightly better than before. I tried calling Danica to see if she would meet me for a drink, but she wasn't picking up.

With Tripod on my bed and my laptop on my lap, I started my next piece about kids raised in state homes. Two hours later, when I was too exhausted to read one more blog, I closed my laptop and my heavy eyelids followed shortly thereafter.

The next morning after two cups of coffee and a round of cleaning, I headed off to Danica's. She seldom answered her phone in the morning until after she had a gallon of caffeine, so I stopped by Starbucks on my way over and grabbed some java and few yummy, fattening, tasty treats I knew she'd adore.

Pulling into the cul-de-sac, I parked in the empty driveway that extended all the way around to the back of the house. Danica must have used the car service to get home. We both felt that non-drivers ought to stay out of a city like San Francisco, where there are impossible hills and hairpin turns even an Indy driver couldn't maneuver.

As I got out, I stretched and breathed in the crisp morning air. I'd slept poorly, my dreams invaded by images of little girls playing on the playground laughing with a fire burning brightly in the background. I woke up with a tear-stained pillow.

I needed my best friend, who was missing in action.

Danica's house was enormous by anyone's standards. She had purchased two houses and remodeled them into one giant, but splendidly designed house like something out of *Architectural Digest*. The house was nearly seven thousand square feet, but the inside still managed to have a quaint and homey feel like the house she had grown up in. No longer Victorian (which pissed off some of the neighbors), it had been shaped by Danica into something more sleek and modern—all silver and glass: very industrial. It stood out of place, but Dani didn't care; she never had, so why start now? Out of place was how Danica Johnson had spent the majority of her life and it didn't appear likely she would change.

When Danica had had the house built, she'd paid for it with cash. When she drove up in a Jaguar, the neighbors all peeked out their windows to see what that "crazy black woman" was doing driving that kind of car. The wheels of equality turn ever so slowly, even in the 'burbs of California.

Ringing the doorbell, I waved at the surveillance camera. She had them all over the property, and I wondered who monitored them all. I peeked in the bag at the goodies I'd brought. They were too good for me to keep my hands off of, so I pinched a bite while I waited. It was taking Danica longer to open than usual, and I was getting ready to fish around in my bag for my vidbook when the door opened. Barely.

"Clark. You're up early," she said through the crack.

"I didn't sleep very well last night after all the things Delta and I found out from Mrs. Marshall. I tried calling you last night, but—" I waited for her to open the door. She didn't open it any further.

"I know. I'm sorry. I...uh...got really busy. You okay? You don't look so hot."

I pushed open the door she was hiding behind and stood in the enormous foyer handing her the coffee. The marble floor was a stunning black and white that reflected the shiny silver and glass. Long, winding staircases of dark cherry adorned both sides of the foyer. "Yesterday was way more than I was ready for. I—"

"Clark—"

"I don't know what to think. I have a *grandmother*, Dani. Well, I don't know if she is still alive, but—"

"Clark!" Danica practically barked in my face.

I paused for a second and then I heard it...or him. Someone was in the kitchen grinding coffee. "Oh God, Dani, I am so sorry. It's just—" I hesitated as I looked into her eyes. Something was wrong. This was my best friend who did *not* do sleepovers and yet, there was someone in her kitchen? No wonder she hadn't answered my calls. She was...

"Clark—"

I couldn't help myself. For the first time in my empathic life, I had to look with my eyes to see if what I was feeling from her was correct. Sure enough, as I peeked around the corner, there stood Connie Rivera with her back to me wearing Danica's robe and pouring ground coffee into the machine.

Slamming my hand over my mouth, I grabbed Danica's hand and yanked her into the study off the foyer. "Oh. My. God! Please don't...this isn't...you're not...you didn't! You *did*!" I stared at her incredulously. "Say something, goddamn it!"

Danica avoided my gaze and shrugged. "I would, but you seem to be in the throes of sputtering and spitting. Speechlessness becomes you."

I paced back and forth, tossing the goodies out of the bag and onto the large cherry wood desk. "This *cannot* be happening. Please tell me she just came over to make breakfast and—"

"Keep your voice down, will you?" Crossing her arms, Danica leaned against the twelve-foot bookshelf shaking her head.

How in the hell did I not see this coming?

"Okay. Okay," I panted. "I'm calm. I'm good." I wasn't. I don't know why. I mean, Danica had probably slept with more women than I had.

"Bullshit. You can't even ask the question. If you can't say the words, Clark, we cannot have this conversation."

"I don't *want* to have this conversation."

"Fine." Danica turned for the door and I reached out to stop her.

"Wait. Okay. Wait a minute. Let me catch my breath. I can do this."

"There's nothing to *do*, Clark. We don't have to have this conversation right now. Clearly, you're upset."

"Oh yes we do. Like I can just walk out of here and not know...not know...what is it I don't *know*, Dani?"

She moved closer to me and lowered her voice. "What is it you want to know, Clark? Ask the questions and I'll give you the answers."

I lowered my voice. "What's going on here? I mean, I don't give a shit who you sleep with. I'm just...surprised, that's all. I thought we shared everything."

"We do. What surprises you? That I had sex with a woman or that I'm letting her cook in my designer kitchen?" Danica smiled. "God, Clark, you have always been such a Puritan. We had sex. Say it."

"No."

"Say lesbian sex."

"Stop it."

She laughed. "Come on. Be a big grown-up girl and say it after me."

"I'm going to hurt you."

Throwing her arms around me, Danica hugged me tightly. "Such a prude. Come on. Ask me. Did I have *lesbian* sex with that hot Mexican *chica* out there?"

I tried to pull away, but she held on.

"Say it."

"Fine. Did you…have you…you know…" I lowered my voice again. "Have…sex with her?"

"No."

I felt my body nearly crumple with relief, though I am not sure why.

"We had fucking *awesome*, bed-shaking, earthquake-making sex!"

I pulled away and glared at her, mouth agape.

"What's the matter, Clark? What is crawling under your skin so much that you'd make a big deal out of this? It's not like she's my first or tenth woman."

"I know that. It's just…you have *no idea* what you're getting yourself into, Dani."

"Yes I do. I'm getting into her undies."

I groaned and paced across the floor. "You haven't the faintest idea of what lesbians are like. We don't *have* meaningless sex! We mate for life. Hell, she's probably already called for a U-Haul."

"You did not just say mate for life."

"It's true. This isn't stranger sex. This is people-we-know-and-work-with sex."

Danica shook her head. "Clark, *nothing* mates for life, and besides, this isn't mating on any level. It's fucking. There's a difference."

I let out an exasperated sigh. "Does *she* know that?"

A tense silence hung between us, broken only by Danica's widening grin and soft chuckle. "Apparently, she does. I haven't had sex that great in years. That woman sure knows her way around the pus—"

"Stop!" I put my hands over my ears like a five year old. "Way too much information."

Danica laughed out loud and threw both her arms around me. "I love you more than life itself, but you have *got* to join the rest of us in the twenty-first century. Even teenagers have friends with benefits. Sex is a recreational activity, like bowling or tennis. It's not—"

"Friends with benefits? Is that what you call this?"

"I call it two women enjoying each other's killer bodies. She is built like a brick sh—"

I pulled away from her. "What happened to your no sleepover policy?"

"It's a no sleepover policy with *men*. It's a slumber party with women. There's a difference. A big difference, really."

My eyebrows rose. "Oh yes. That clears things up. I really see the difference now. Thanks. Appreciate it." I shook my head. "You shouldn't mix business with pleasure. It's not healthy."

"I'm not. *You* hired them. They work for you. I just pay the bills."

"You could really complicate matters, you know? What happens if she falls in love with you? What then?"

Danica shook her head, the smile falling from her face. "She's already in love."

"Oh God. With you?"

"No. With her lover, the one who died. Look, she made it perfectly clear: her mind is available days and her body at nights, but her heart, not so much. There is nothing wrong with two people enjoying a mutual physical attraction to each other. No harm, no foul and no promises. You should try it sometime."

I looked at her; her dancing eyes were lit with energy even the dead could feel, and suddenly I felt a little envious of her carefree attitude and easy-going lifestyle. Danica, who never let anyone get close enough to her heart was not the love-'em-but-still-leave-'em sort of woman. I had never seen her commit to anyone. She was as commitment-phobic as an eighty-year-old bachelor, and though her commitment to me was unwavering, she had never ventured beyond that to something deeper and more meaningful with someone else.

"I can't. I...I'm not interested in...that. And I didn't know... you never told me—"

"That I swing both ways? Double dip? Play on both teams? You know of my female dalliances at Mills."

I did. "If the roles were reversed..."

"I wouldn't *still* be standing in your house lecturing you about the straight lifestyle while your bed buddy cooked breakfast in your kitchen. That's the difference between us, Clark. I trust you know what you're doing with your life. I don't always second-guess you."

"I trust you. I also trust that Delta Stevens is one *very* scary woman, and I don't imagine she'll cotton very well to anyone who hurts Connie. I don't know if you noticed, but they're—"

"Like us?"

I nodded. "Worse. They're like us, but they carry guns and kick the shit out of people. Did you not *read* their bios the boys pulled for us? People *die* when these two get pissed off."

"Okay, so they have bigger guns than we do. So what? I'm not afraid."

"You should be. I pulled up some articles about their little... adventures. Did you know they've been to Colombia?"

"You've been to Paris. What's the point?"

"The point is, Delta is like some sort of feminist icon. She has a flippin' fan club online with clippings of all these police exploits she and Connie participated in. She's like a latter-day Xena. They're a force to be reckoned with and I'd rather stay on their good side."

"The point, Clark?"

"The point, you boob, is you're playing in Delta's backyard with *her* toys. You break it and she's going to kick your ass so hard, you'll be a hunchback. They are out of our league, Dani. Way out. Is *that* point clear enough?"

Danica nodded. "Roger that. Look. If you're so worried, talk to her."

"To whom?"

"To Delta. She knows."

I stared at her. "What do you mean *she knows*? She knows *what*?"

"She saw what was going on and had some concerns. I let her know I wasn't looking for anything complicated. Believe me, she was going to make sure I was *very* clear about the way Connie needed to be treated. I passed muster and here we are. Enjoying the fruits of our labor, so to speak."

I blinked several times and shook my head. How had I missed this? What kind of empath missed something this huge?

"So, before the bed gets too cold, can I ask you why you are here?"

"Oh. No." I waved it away like a bad smell. "It's not important. Go back to your...breakfast. We'll get on this after you've—"

"Finished my bacon? Cracked a few eggs? Dunked my doughnut—"

I shoved her and she would have hit the door, except that Connie had just started to open it.

"Oh. I'm sorry," she said, catching Danica before she hit the floor. "I just wanted you to know I made enough for three."

I didn't need to hear Danica's words to know that staying was not an option. "No...uh, thank you, Connie. I think I've done enough...I mean—"

When Connie stepped into the room, the smell of bacon followed her. "Echo, I'm sure you're worried. Unlike my sisters-in-arms, there isn't a U-haul lurking around the corner. I have a life and a daughter to take care of. I am not looking for anything long-lasting, permanent or serious. If I were, I'm a purebred lesbian and Danica's not even gay. Never the twain shall meet on that score. She's a fan of the big salami while I prefer the Swiss cheese."

I don't remember what I muttered on my way out, but I'm sure it was unintelligible. I practically peeled rubber as I jammed Ladybug into a gear I wasn't sure existed.

As I took the first corner on two wheels, my cell rang. I pulled over to get it, recognizing I was in a state of shock or something; more like uncomfortable in my own skin. "Hello?"

"Echo?" It was Delta. "Connie thought you might like to meet me for coffee in say, half an hour? I'm near the paper."

"She just called you, didn't she?"

Delta chuckled. "Coffee or no?"

"See you in fifteen or twenty."

"Whoa. Get out! You actually delivered Connie's baby with a *Bowie* knife?" I had been listening to Delta's stories through one and a half cups of coffee and was feeling much better than when I had left Danica's.

"Yeah. I'd gone down to Colombia to get Megan out of a jam, and it ended up costing us Connie's lover and Sal's best friend. Neither of them will ever fully recover."

"What about you? How do you get over something like that?"

"You never really fully recover from a loss like that. As much as Connie adores Dakota, the baby will always remind her of the love who isn't sitting at the table with us anymore. That may change, and if and when it does, everyone who touches Con's life is just a momentary blip on her love radar. Blips can come and go, but they may *not* do any damage. That was what I needed you to know. Don't go getting all flustered about Danica."

"Blip?"

Delta nodded. "Connie Rivera is an easy woman to fall in love with, whether you're gay or straight, man or woman. And no matter how distant your best friend may be emotionally, Connie can melt the heart of a polar bear. Keep an eye out on Danica, Echo. It happens all the time. She's a pretty special lady."

I looked squarely into those emerald eyes and read the thinly veiled threat. "Ever happen to you?"

Delta's left eyebrow shot into a question mark. "As hard as it is to explain, it's even harder to understand. Megan is my wife, my lover and my partner. I would give my life for her in an instant. But Connie is my soul mate, my business partner and my best friend. We are as intertwined as two people can be without sharing our bodies."

"And Megan is okay with this?"

Delta grinned and one deep dimple showed. Damn she was a good-looking woman. "Megan is a remarkable woman in her own right, and is secure in our relationship. She knows how important Connie is to me and understands we are a package deal. Much like you both." Delta leaned forward. "I've made a living watching people, making educated guesses about them, about their habits and their lifestyle. Know what I see? Here's my street-wise educated guess. I'll bet Danica hasn't had a *real* relationship since you've known her. She sleeps with a lot of people but is attached to no one. Well, no one save you. She may not sleep with you, but she would lay down her life for you. Probably already has. She would risk everything, including jail, to make sure you remain safe." She grinned. "Probably already has." Dimple showed. "How'm I doing so far?"

I nodded, thinking of her pulling that trigger in the Superdome, of having my back in the Tenderloin, of always being there for me.

Delta continued. "*You* are her primary relationship. *You* are her sounding board, her secret sharer, her partner in crime. She may fulfill her physical needs elsewhere, but you...you are the most important person to her. That's what I mean by package deal. You two, like me and Connie, are a pair. Anyone coming into that has to pass inspection. So, yeah, I get why you reacted that way this morning. I might have reacted the same way. There's a *reason* they call me Storm."

I had never thought of it that way—never saw us so intertwined before. But of course we were. Why else had Melika allowed Danica to come to the bayou all those years ago? She was the only natural I knew who had *ever* been given carte blanche to come to the river. Melika *knew*.

Delta smiled knowingly. "Look, we really like you both, and would love nothing more than to help you find out who you are. You guys are good people, and trust me...I've seen enough to know. Just be sure you keep a pulse on Danica's emotional radar where Connie is concerned. Make sure she doesn't fall in love with someone she can't have."

Something twisted in my gut and I leaned forward. Danica wasn't the only one of us from the 'hood. "Okay, I can't say that you're wrong. I would be lying if I said you pegged her wrong, but there's a lot more to her than meets the eye." I leaned over even more. "Now let me tell *you* something since we are sharing.

Danica Johnson *always* gets what she wants. You think it was easy for a black woman to mix it up in the white male-dominated world of the computer industry? Danica makes pit bulls and piranhas look toothless. And when she decides to go after something, neither hell nor high water can stand in her way, so if *anyone* ought to watch out for their best friend, it ought to be *you*."

I did not take my eyes off Delta's. The slight change in the emerald color said she was enjoying this. She was the kind of woman who respected women with backbones. This was one woman who preferred her adversary to have more than a bark, and when it came to Danica, I bypassed bark and went right for the throat.

Leaning back, she lifted her coffee mug that had Storm Warning on the side. "May the best friend win."

I lifted my mug and clinked it to hers.

"Now that that's out of the way, let's get back to the business of finding your parents."

"I've got a bead on our TK," Bailey said through the phone. "I thought for sure he was long gone, but that second spotter managed to find him back in the Valley."

"Where?"

"Cupertino."

I jotted this down. "He's backtracking. Why?"

"No idea. Could be trying to get more money. Maybe he thinks he's thrown us off his trail. I don't know. I have the address. You want me to go it alone?"

"No way. Tip would kill me. I've got about an hour's worth of work. I'll meet you back at the apartment."

I stared down at the yellow notepad I'd been using to clear my thoughts. My editor wanted to see me about my last article and I had tons of phone messages to return, which I did in record time. You have to love voice mail and text messaging.

After checking in with my editor and getting suggestions, I was on my way out to get a few supplies for Tripod when Bailey called and told me if we moved fast, we might be able to nab our elusive quarry in San Jose, a relatively short ride from the city, depending, of course, on time of day and traffic.

"Wanna talk about it?" Bailey asked as we maneuvered through relatively light traffic.

I never should have put my toe in that water, and now it was too late to back out. "Would you sleep with a straight woman you weren't…you know…involved with?"

"Involved, huh? E, you know we lesbians don't *do* involved. We get in, we commit, we make promises we can't keep, we get out, we have goodbye sex, become friends, and call it a day."

"But you've done it with straight women?"

"Oh. Straights? Sure. Once or twice."

"And what happened?"

"They both wanted more, but I am not into bringing someone out of the closet. Let me tell you, the coming out process may be different for each of us, but no one gets away unscathed." She turned back to me. "Oh no. Don't tell me—"

"No! It's not me."

We drove in silence until Bailey reached over and nudged me with her fist. "Gay-straight relationships rarely work out."

I nodded.

"Is that all? You're awfully pensive today."

"For now." I told her all about the investigation into my parents and how that had really taken hold of my attention. "Let's just catch this kid so I can get back to my life investigation."

She nodded. "The spotter has been giving me updates every fifteen on my cell. We'll get him."

I nodded. "What's he's up to? Makes all my bells and whistles go off that he's returning to where he was first spotted, you know? It doesn't make any sense."

"Yeah, it's weird. I thought for sure he was headed to the city. He was getting the hell out of Dodge. I think he's trying to give us the slip."

"Us, or someone else. If there's someone else in this picture, I want to know."

"Yeah, that could complicate things, huh?"

"I've been thinking. He had the perfect opportunity to strike out at us, to deliver a few damaging blows, but he didn't. He ran.

He ran because he's afraid, but not necessarily of us." I got on Interstate 880 toward San Jose and punched Ladybug enough to meld into traffic. "We might need cleaners."

"I'll let Tip know."

Shaking my head, I kept my eyes moving from mirror to mirror. "Not yet. She's itching for a reason to come back here. I'd rather not give her one."

We listened to music and sang to the '80s one-hit wonders the rest of the way. Bailey was easy time and I found myself really enjoying her company.

Her phone rang to ABBA's *Dancing Queen*.

"There's Roxanne." Bailey flipped open her vidbook and listened. "Uh-huh. Got it. Magic Comics on the corner of Eighth and…" She paused and listened. "Excellent. Thanks." To me she said, "He's at this comic book store. Just got there. We might have a good shot."

A good shot hit me about fifteen minutes later, when the kid blasted us back against a Dumpster right outside the comic book store.

"God. Damn. It," Bailey growled, helping me to my feet. He had come out of the store carrying a brown bag, and when he saw us, he blasted us before we could get a single syllable out. "We are catching that little fucker today, E. You go that way. I'll go around that side. If he so much as twitches, blast him."

Before I could say anything, Bailey took off in a sprint that looked silver medalist Olympic good. Shaking the cobwebs from my head, and ignoring the throbbing in my back, I ran, not nearly as fast, in the other direction. I was achy tired, and getting pissed off. That was twice now I'd let this runt slam me with his powers. It wasn't going to happen again.

We were in an unincorporated area of San Jose, the outskirts of a town more barrio than Silicon Valley. Houses were further apart here, the streets a little darker, and there were less places for the little prick to hide. I knew we were going to get him tonight. I just didn't know how.

Bailey did.

As I came wheezing around the corner, the kid saw me and raised his hand. Ready for him this time, I threw my strongest shield up and out, deflecting the energy he pushed at me so it bounced harmlessly into the air. His reaction confirmed my belief that he hadn't been running from us. He genuinely appeared confused about us being supers. "How—"

"We're here to help you," I said, as he started backing away. I kept my shields up.

"Bullshit." Turning on a dime, he started to run back the way he came. It occurred to me Bailey did not have the same ability to create a shield like the one I had thrown up. As strong as he was, he could really hurt her.

Slightly lowering my defenses, I started after him. Suddenly, he skidded to a halt and turned to run back toward me, a mask of fear pressing into his face. His fear almost knocked me over. He was so scared, he ran smack into the center of my shield and bounced off, landing square on his back, his breath making a whooshing sound as it left his body.

I looked up just in time to see what it was that had scared him so.

Rounding the corner were six of the mangiest dogs I had ever seen, all snarling with teeth bared. They were coming right at me. For a second I thought we were both toast, until I remembered one of Bailey's primary powers was her ability to communicate with animals. This gave her a whole host of allies from which to draw, and whenever she called them, they answered immediately. Somehow, between getting smacked against a Dumpster and now, she'd called on her private cavalry and here they came. I had to hand it to her—her powers trumped mine any day.

Releasing my shield, I bent over the kid and slammed a second shield into his chest, pinning him to the ground. "You *ever* use your powers against me again, boy, and I'll let those dogs use you for a play toy. Understand?"

His eyes were wide and he nodded vigorously as the six dogs sniffed him, sensing he was being held by a force they didn't understand. Two were rottweilers, two were pit bulls and the others were of unknown origin. Only two had collars.

"Easy, E." Bailey walked briskly around the corner, and all six dogs immediately sat.

"Backup was a smart call," I said, looking up at her.

She nodded. "The kid's wearing two hundred dollar Nikes. He'd have outrun us again and that wasn't happening." Bailey lightly touched the top of the rottweilers' heads as she knelt next to our TK. "Okay, here's the deal: we came to help you get to a place where you can learn how to properly utilize this new power of yours. You have a couple of choices here. You can go with us without causing any problems, or become more acquainted with my friends here until we can find a way to ship you out of here. It's your call."

As she spoke, I lowered my shields so I could read his response. The little idiot was actually thinking about making a run for it.

Before he could make his move, I walked behind him and knocked him in the head with the only psychic offensive weapon I possessed. He sagged back to the ground, unconscious.

"What did you do that for?" Bailey asked, astonished. I rarely use offensive powers.

"He was getting ready to bolt."

She tsked and shook her head. "What a fool."

"Not a fool, Bailey. He's scared. Whatever he's afraid of terrifies him big time. To risk being torn apart by these dogs says something. I could feel his fear even if I weren't empathic."

She shrugged. "Do we care? Let's wrap him up and ship him out of here. He's strong, E. Maybe even stronger than Zack. He needs what Melika can do for him."

I stared down at him. "I agree...but something has this kid seriously nutted up. We need to find out what that is before we ship him off to Melika. I don't want someone following him there."

"Let's get him back to your place and see if he won't tell us what the hell is going on."

"Good idea, because something's not right here."

Boy was that an understatement. *Something* was a thing neither Bailey nor I were even remotely ready to deal with.

We managed to get him to my place before he fully regained

consciousness. He wavered in and out once I passed over the bridge, but he never really came to until we got to the city. I had tried contacting Tip to let her know we had finally been successful in corralling the kid, but she didn't answer either Bailey's cell calls nor my mental ones.

That, in itself, was strange.

We made one stop along the way and that was to purchase some cable ties. It was a brilliant idea I'd love to take credit for, but won't.

"You're going to make a really good collector," I whispered to Bailey. "I would never have thought about tying his hands until after he'd pummeled me one more time."

"Sure you would have. You know, E, you just don't give yourself enough credit. I saw how you were leaning over him. You were tired of getting knocked around too. Well, when we get him upstairs, I'm doing the same to his feet and gagging the little fucker. Cooper won't be yelling his fool head off until *after* he hears us out."

"Cooper? Where'd you get his name?"

"Spotter's a telepath. She pulled it from him." She finished with his hands and came back to the passenger seat. "I know he's scared. We all were, but that doesn't mean you can go off half-cocked. He needs to fucking listen."

"How will you do that?"

"Can I borrow Tripod?"

"Sure."

"Good. Once we get him to listen to reason, we're going to find out what it is he's so damn afraid of."

"You want me to stay?"

She shook her head. "I'd like to say yes, but I need to do this on my own. Go about your agenda for a while and leave him to me. He's not going anywhere now."

We dragged him up to the apartment and secured him to the American rocker in my family room.

I drove over to Delta's office. On my way, I tried Finn one more time. She hadn't returned my earlier messages nor had she called. Seems none of my women were around when I needed them.

On the fifth ring, I was getting ready to hang up, when she answered. "Finn here."

"Oh. Hi. It's me. You busy?"

"Busier than I want to be. Sorry I haven't gotten back to you, but things are a little crazy here." Her voice carried that strained sound it gets whenever there's something she wants to say, but can't really talk about it. She was keeping something from me, but it was probably for my own good. The stories she had told me about kids being raped and prostitutes getting cut up were more than I ever really wanted to know. I just wondered…how does one share her life with a cop when you don't really want to hear about her day and she doesn't really want to tell you about it?

"What's going on, Finn?"

"I'm…uh…working undercover. I can't really talk about it now. Just don't worry. We'll talk about it in a few days, okay?"

It wasn't okay, but what choice did I have?

When we hung up, I kept hearing Delta's words swimming through my mind. I wasn't bothered Finn was busy, but suddenly, I realized what it was like to be on the other side of a secret.

It didn't feel so good.

When I got to Delta's office, she and Connie were both at their computers. I was a little nervous about seeing Connie again, and couldn't stop thinking of her in Dani's robe standing at the stove.

"How's it going?"

"We located some Hayward families in the area who claimed kids on their tax returns."

I blinked several times before I said anything. "What? You were able to access IRS records?"

Connie shrugged. "We ran the name, dates and locations and came up with a couple of possibilities."

My heart raced. "Haywards? You found more than one?"

Connie nodded and consulted her papers. "We checked out each of them and narrowed down the possibility to one family. Working forward, we have a family named Hayward who claimed two children in nineteen eighty-two and three, but stopped sending in returns after eighty-four. There is literally nothing from them in the database after that."

"Except this one." Delta handed me a slip of paper with a woman's name and address on it. "Could be your grandmother... could be a nobody, but she lives in the Bay Area. She's worth checking out."

"Where?"

Delta consulted her notes. "Alamo."

I felt a little dizzy. Alamo was the town bordering Danville. Was I looking at my grandmother's name? "I can't believe she could be that close and I never knew it."

"You want us to do the legwork and check her out?"

I shook my head. "I'd like to go."

Delta shot Connie a look. "We thought you'd say that. We'll keep digging to see if there is any other connection than just the Hayward name. We're curious about the family that stopped turning in tax forms in nineteen eighty-four, but we can't just focus on them."

I nodded. "Gotcha. Any ideas about the best way to approach this Mrs. Hayward?"

"We think you ought to go right up to her doorstep and rattle her cage. Don't call, don't write, don't e-mail. You can't give people a chance to put on a mask or weave a web of lies. You want the truth, you gotta go straight at her."

"You want me to rattle the cage of an old woman I've never met?"

Delta nodded. "Look, Echo, Connie and I have kicked the asses of quite a few bad guys using the element of surprise. Take our word for it. It's the best way."

"Surprise an old woman? She's hardly a bad guy."

Connie stood closer to me. "Something happened to you when you were a kid, and someone knows what that was. Those people have been sitting on their secret for a long time, so you can't give them the opportunity to cover anything up or dissemble in any way."

Delta nodded. "You're a good reader of people, Echo. You'll know. Watch her pupils. Don't take your eyes off hers. She'll tell you everything you need to know without saying a word."

Little did they know. Folding up the paper, I put it in my purse. "If that's how you think I ought to handle this, then I will. I trust you both know what you're doing." My gaze traveled over to Connie. "I trust you with more than just my past. I am trusting you with my present and everyone in it."

Connie's gaze held mine and never wavered. "You have my word that we'll take good care of both."

With slip in hand, and hope in my heart, I got back in Ladybug and headed back across the Bay Bridge to face a past I never knew existed.

Alamo is a gorgeous upper-middle-class town full of grand oak trees with a quaint downtown area which had seen little change in the last four decades. The big brown horse on top of the feed and grain store on the corner perpetually needed a paint job, and there was now a Starbucks on the main street, but other than that, when writers write about bedroom communities, Alamo is what springs to my mind.

As I drove down the two-lane main street, I felt a memory desperately trying to push its way up, much like a weed does through a small fissure in the cement. I knew enough to leave it alone, hoping it could find its way to the light without me.

I took a right into an older, well-established neighborhood with towering oaks and their sturdy allies, eucalyptus trees.

Another right took me to homes which used to be a modest sixteen to eighteen hundred square feet, but had now been remodeled to double and triple that size. The only house that hadn't been updated was the brown and white one I pulled up to.

The 1940s rancher had a front yard meticulously cared for, no doubt, by a landscaping company that trimmed the hedges and kept the boulders in the Japanese Zen Garden in the same meticulous order. A tiny pond bubbled off to one side of the garden near the front door, which was painted in the new feng shui color of roasted red pepper. The woman behind that door might be older, but she was definitely not dated by her house.

Steadying my nerves, I pressed the doorbell. A slight smile played at the corners of my mouth as I thought about Delta's admonition about looking at the woman's eyes. I would know the moment I saw her if she recognized me or not. It would be like a trumpet playing in my ear; I would *know*. There would be no hiding it, no dissembling, no chance of covering it up. The one thing people cannot hide from an empath of my caliber is the truth.

When the door swung open and that old woman looked at me, the trumpets blared recognition. She knew who I was the moment she saw me.

She stared at me a moment and then shook her head as if she had had an entire conversation with herself in the space of time it had taken to look at me.

But she did more than look.

She *saw*.

Shaking her head again, she opened the door wider. "I always said you were too smart for your own good." She looked both ways before quickly ushering me inside.

I picked up a slight sense of fear and trepidation as I walked past her. She not only knew who I was, but she was afraid of that knowledge…afraid of something about me.

"You know who I am, don't you?"

Closing the door, she moved by me into the kitchen. I followed her, not pausing to look around me. Of all the scenarios I'd run through in my mind, this instant recognition hadn't made the list.

"It's risky business you showing up here like this. I gotta say, though, I'd given up on you quite a while ago. Figured you'd never remember." She grabbed a teapot and filled it with water, not looking at me. I sat on the stool at the counter, wondering if any memories of her or this kitchen would break the surface.

"So you do know."

She chuckled softly. "Of course I know, silly, but mind your manners, Charlie. I know you have a lot of questions, and I'll get to them all in good time. Let me make us a nice pot of tea and then I'll answer as many questions as I can, but please be patient." She turned from me and pulled the blinds down on the kitchen window. Yes, it was fear, all right, but she was also very happy to see me.

She was white-headed. Not gray, completely white; and she kept her hair in a stylish bob. Fit for her age, which I estimated to be around sixty-five, she wore a contemporary lavender sweat suit and exuded an energy of someone who loves life.

After setting the pot on the stove, she turned to face me. Her energy changed instantly to sorrow, regret and tenderness, all of which she was trying to suppress. She didn't *want* to feel what she was feeling, but she couldn't help herself.

Kind blue eyes studied my face like blind fingers reading Braille. "My God, you look like your mother."

I locked eyes with her. "I wouldn't know."

She nodded slowly and leaned on the kitchen counter. "I don't suppose you do." She looked at me with her head tilted to one side. "Please forgive me. It's just...you turned out to be so beautiful. You have the same intense eyes as—"

"You called me Charlie."

She grinned sadly. "So much you don't know. You were one of those kids who couldn't pronounce your own name when you were little, so you named yourself."

Ironic, then, that I named myself again when I was fourteen. "It's not my name now."

The teapot whistled. "I don't imagine it is." She turned from me and poured the water into matching mugs. "Have you been looking long?"

"No. I've never been ready for the truth, but I'm ready now."

"Cream or sugar?"

"Both, thank you." I waited for her to sit across from me, but she chose to stand and lean against the counter, steam from her mug rising to steam her glasses.

"So, where would you like to begin?"

Wrapping my hands around the mug, I chose from my rehearsed script carefully. "Are you my grandmother?"

"Yes, I am."

My stomach flipped and I swallowed hard. "And I used to be Charlotte Hayward."

"Yes, you did." Her clear blue eyes were steady and unblinking. She was telling me just the truth I was asking—no more, no less.

I wouldn't say her responses were as rehearsed as my questions, as much as it was just...a long time coming. She had been ready for me.

I decided on a different, less emotional tack. "What happened to the house I used to live in?"

"It burned to the ground."

"But I wasn't in it like everyone thought."

She looked out at the backyard. "No. You were not. You were never in danger." She put her hands around mine on the mug. I felt the softness of her emotions, the love she could no longer hold back. "I am so terribly sorry, Charlie. I've had a long time to practice this talk, but...I stopped practicing a ways back and I'm a little rusty. After so much time went by, I...I never really expected to see you again."

I nodded. Questions began mounting in her, and she couldn't stop herself from asking the most important one. "Have you... have you noticed anything...*different* about yourself?"

My heart went Mach 5. She *knew*. She really knew. As happy as this should have made me, I wasn't feeling particularly gracious at this moment. I wasn't about to give myself up to a woman I'd just met, regardless of who she'd once been to me.

"Different? Like how?" I felt her struggling with the truth, with how much to divulge, with whether or not she should even go down that path. She wondered how much I knew.

Shaking her head, she looked away, tears in her eyes. "She was so sure...she said she'd seen..." She impatiently wiped tears away. "What a waste. What a horrible, horrible waste."

I let some time go by as she wiped her eyes and struggled with her version of the truth. She may be my grandmother by blood, but she was a stranger to me, and I felt no compunction to help her with that truth. I imagined it was getting heavier by the second.

Leaning forward, I looked into a kind face, a face that was, at this moment, struggling with the truth of me. I was still bound by the code of the bayou not to reveal who or what I was...even to a woman who was my long-lost granny. There was too much at stake. "Mrs. Hayward, there's a lot that's different about me. What, specifically, are you referring to?"

She blinked back more tears and inhaled deeply. "I can't...it's not my place, Charlie. You either are or you're..."

"Not. Not what, Mrs. Hayward? What is it you think I might be?"

She blinked at me. "Nothing. Just the rambling of an old woman who thought you might...be different."

"I am."

"You are...what? A telepath? A telekinetic? What did you become, Charlie?"

"I'm an empath." The words flew from my mouth before I could stop them, and her energy immediately registered in my head: She knew what I was talking about. She was not surprised...only...relieved. What an odd response.

"How long have you known?"

"That I was different?"

Slight nod.

"Since I was fourteen."

She nodded as understanding fell over her. She knew about puberty and the onset of our abilities. She was not surprised that I had them—not surprised at all. "Is that why you're here, Charlie? Have you come to sort that out after all these years?"

Her use of that nickname was a bit disconcerting. "No. Not really. I've spent the last fourteen years of my life learning how to control it, how to understand it, how to live with what I am. I am crystal clear about *what* I am. What I came here for is to find out *who* I am and where I came from."

Mrs. Hayward looked me in the eyes and I sensed a sadness buried deep within her. "I see. So, you dug deep enough to uncover my name?" She shook her head. "As happy as I am to see you, coming here was a mistake, Charlie."

Now, *that* one hurt. "A mistake? Is that why you closed the blinds? Why you peered outside to see if anyone was watching you? *Who* would be watching you, Mrs. Hayward? What are you so afraid of?"

Wrapping her arms around herself as if she were cold, Mrs. Hayward looked so very sad. "That, I'm afraid, is not my story to tell, and please, call me Jig. My friends call me Jig."

I felt a tingle at the base of my skull, but ignored it. "Jig?"

She grinned. "I suppose it's too much to ask for Grams or Granny, so I'll settle for Jig, after Hemingway's character in—"

"*Hills Like White Elephants.* I have a degree in English." I sipped my tea. It was mint. "Okay, then. If that's not your story to tell, are my parents alive to tell it?" I wasn't going to play word games with her. She was acting skittish enough as it was and I needed information from her before her fear got the best of her.

"That's jumping to the middle. Let's back up and I can tell you all I promised I would." She poured more sugar into her tea and stirred it. "You say you've been learning to control your powers for the last fourteen years, but what about before that?"

"Before that? Before that, I barely remember a damn thing. I have very little memory from my childhood, and I am beginning to suspect that the memories I do have are not quite accurate."

She nodded thoughtfully. "I see. Well then, let's begin at the beginning, shall we?" Inhaling deeply, she steadied her nerves and looked me straight in the eye. "I wondered if I would ever have the chance to tell you all of this. It's been a heavy burden I have carried around for far too long, and I am happy to finally be rid of it. Just know, though, Charlie, that telling you all of this is a little like playing hot potato. And that potato is scorching."

"I'll take my chances."

Nodding again, she sipped her tea. "It is not a tale I am fond of telling, but it is part of your personal truth—a truth you are prepared to hear. Your parents were genetic engineers working for the National Security Agency back in the day when they could both work. They made good money, loved their jobs, did what they were told to do, but, as with so many of our top secret programs, things started sliding sideways on them, got out of control. Suddenly, they were assigned to work in a top secret unit to research why mutant genes seemed to be popping up in our society."

Mutant genes. Melika had referred to those when I was being trained. *She* believed something had changed our DNA and our genetic makeup was responsible for the powers we had. She didn't go into much scientific detail; suffice it to say, *she* believed we used a different part of our brains than naturals did and it had nothing to do with DNA or mutant gene gobbledygook. "Go on."

"Your mother was transferred to the lab to work on a project to isolate those genes they felt were responsible for paranormal powers." She stopped and shook her head. "Everything changed when they started working on that goddamned project. Everything. One minute, they were two lab rats punching a time clock, the next...they were planning the great escape."

"Great escape? What happened?"

"The NSA believed in psionics way back when it was just something written in science fiction novels. They believed they could isolate the gene responsible for our powers. If that happened—"

"They could create us." The thought sent chills down my spine as the words tumbled from my lips.

"Or find you through blood tests."

I reflected back on all the warnings Melika imposed on us about telling people what we were. Slowly, everything began to fall into place.

"The NSA managed to locate and snag a real telepath. A powerful one. They brought him in, ran test after test, and offered him a lucrative position if he could find others. He was more than willing to collect a paycheck for pointing the rest of you out. What we didn't know at the time, was that less than a year after the Genesys Project began, *you* would begin showing signs yourself."

"How old was I?"

"The first time, you had just turned five."

"What did I do?"

Jig shook her head. "It was the strangest thing, really. Your mom walked in and saw you reaching for something on your desk and it...it came to you. She thought she was seeing things at first, but then, it happened more and more."

I frowned. "But that's telekinesis, and I don't have that particular power."

"Maybe not now, but you did back then. Scared the holy Jesus out of her."

"Because she knew I was going to be a problem?"

"Because she was afraid the telepath for the NSA would eventually know she harbored her own supernatural daughter.

She was afraid he would read her mind and they would haul you in for all sorts of tests."

"For this Genesys Project."

"Yes." She sipped her tea and shuddered. "She saw the horrible tests those other kids were put through, and she wasn't about to let them get their hands on you. She feared every moment of every day they went in to work. This telepath was more than just strong—he was mean. Angry. He hated supernaturals and regular folk alike and didn't care who he hurt.

"One day, he was staring hard at her, like he *knew* she had a secret or something. It freaked her out something awful. That evening, she and your father decided there was only one way to make sure the government didn't get to you."

My eyes filled with tears. "So they killed me."

She nodded and looked away. "I'm so sorry, Charlie. I know it seems extreme, and I can't imagine how you're feeling at this moment, but she was scared and desperate to save your life."

"They couldn't have just quit?"

Jig chuffed and shook her head. "Being on the Special Ops programs in the NSA is like being a part of the Mob; you don't simply quit. You don't get to just up and walk away, especially after everything they had seen and done. Those tests amounted to torture to those poor children. They weren't going to let your parents just walk away, and they were anxious to get you as far away from the NSA and Genesys as possible."

Wiping my eyes, I nodded. So many lies. So many stories. All to keep me from becoming part of some freak show. Years of anger melted away from little Jane Doe inside me. I *had* been loved enough that they made the ultimate sacrifice.

Sighing, shaking her head, she stared down into her mug, tears hanging off her eyelashes "They knew they had to wipe out your existence. They had to erase you from the grid. That was the second worst day of my life...saying goodbye to my little Charlie girl." Her eyes filled with tears she let fall as she looked back up at me. Her pain was palpable. "That day...was awful. Tore my heart out, it did." Wiping her eyes, she grabbed a Kleenex and blew her nose.

"So they faked my death by burning the house down and

claiming I was in it? How did that work without a body?"

She nodded and reached for another Kleenex. "It was the quickest way they could think of to get you out of harm's way. Your father had access to the NSA morgue for his lab work and your mother had just finished examining a little girl who had…" She shook her head and then blew her nose. "Who had spontaneously combusted."

"A fire starter."

Jig nodded and looked into my eyes again. "The poor little thing couldn't handle the pressure of the tests and just burst into flames. There wasn't much left of her once they got the fire out."

"So they used her body in place of mine."

Jig nodded, waves of sadness hitting me like waves crashing into a shore. "Yes. Your mother figured at least the girl's death wouldn't be in vain; that maybe she could save you. So they put her in your room and set the house on fire."

"How could they not have gotten caught?"

"Your parents were incredibly bright people, Charlie. Getting caught was neither a fear nor an option."

I noticed her use of the past tense, but said nothing.

"The NSA was in bed with just about every covert operation in this country and even other countries, so your parents' scheme had to be as simple as it was elaborate. Once they set the house on fire, your father took you to a psionic who he had helped escape. This woman helped you forget much of your childhood. From what I understand, she wiped it out."

My eyes grew wide. I'd heard of erasers but had never met one. "Wait. He helped someone escape?"

Sipping her tea, she nodded. "The mental anguish those tests put children through turned most of them into vegetables. They were human guinea pigs treated no better than the poor souls Mengele operated on during the Holocaust." She paused and shook her head "This…this paranormal promised to help your parents if they would just leave one door unlocked. Your father did and he escaped."

"They never caught him?"

Jig looked away. "I'm afraid they did. Shortly after he met

with you. That telepath found him and led the NSA right to him, but not before he had worked his magic on you." Jig stared off for a moment before returning her eyes to mine. "I have to say, I never expected it would be so permanent or so widespread in your memory, but apparently, whatever he had done to you worked." She waved it away. "I'm sure you've been mad at them your whole life, but you have to understand they did everything they could to protect their family. It was not easy to get out of a covert government organization that had too many *accidental* deaths among the employees who actually *did* manage to get out. If they couldn't get out, then they were going to get *you* out. To keep you out, they had to erase your memory of them, of your life, of all of it."

I swallowed hard. "I was erased."

She nodded. "Yes. Otherwise, you could tell people who you were and where you lived, and you'd be in danger all over again. You were just a little girl, and they couldn't afford you accidentally telling someone who you were. Your father worked magic to wipe your slate clean. He hired a lot of top-notch people to destroy any paper trail of you. Your parents gave up everything to make sure you disappeared off the grid."

My heart hurt for poor little Charlie, who must have been scared to death when all of this was happening. To be a happy kindergarten kid one moment and then not even know who you are the next must have been frightening. I blinked quickly to allay the tears. "So, they burned the house down, erased her memory, and then dropped her off at some shelter?"

Jig reached out and set her hand on top of mine. "Not *her*, Charlie. *You*. Your mother was sure the telepath had honed in on her and knew she was keeping some sort of secret. Time was of the essence and they couldn't have just left the country. Where would they go? Taking their family on the run for the rest of their lives wasn't an option. They wanted to save your life. You had to be dead if you were ever going to have a normal life...and by normal, I mean not being a lab rat."

"So they dropped me off at a shelter and then what? Started life all over again? Moved on without me?" The hot tears fell...not for me...but for her...for Charlie. For a little girl left at an orphanage not knowing who she was or why she was left behind.

Handing me the box of tissues, Jig patted my arm. "I wish it had been that easy, Charlie. Don't ever forget who your parents were dealing with here. Your mother and father knew they had to do much more than feign your death. They needed to get *out* so they could protect *your* secret as well as their own lives. To do that, your mother..." Jig blinked away her own tears. "She made it appear your death pushed her over the edge, and she admitted herself into a psych ward. She felt it was the safest place for her to be and the most believable response to having lost her child. She had been interviewed by several NSA agents after she was admitted, of course, but under a doctor's supervision. That damned telepath was not allowed in, so she could fool them into believing the truth your parents had created."

"All of this was to keep the telepath from me?"

"Yes. I'm sure you've been angry with her most of your life for giving you up, but what you could never understand was just how much of her own life she gave up to protect you and keep you safe from an agency that would have used you up and taken all of your freedom away."

I thought I might throw up. Of all the stories I had told myself about my family when I was a child, nothing compared to this horror story. "How long did she stay in there?"

Jig finished her tea and set the mug in the sink. "In the psych ward? Nine years."

"What?" My mouth hung open like a broken gate. "*Nine* years?"

Turning back to me, she nodded. "She had to. Only when the director who hired her died, did she feel she could get out. So, she stayed. She wanted to make sure you were happy, so she kept as close an eye on you as possible, even from the inside of a padded cell."

"From the psych ward."

Jig barely grinned. "She had her eyes and ears."

"You."

She nodded. "That's how I was able to recognize you straightaway. I would watch you from a distance at school, check up on the houses you stayed in. The problem was, you never stayed long and we wondered if maybe it was because of your powers. Three times, I called the Child Protective Services on the foster parents when I felt they were not treating you right."

This rocked me. "Really? You mean—"

"You weren't always given back because of something *you* did or didn't do, Charlie. Sometimes you were relinquished because we refused to have you in a home that was less than fair with you." She shrugged. "It was the best we could do."

I shook my head. It was inconceivable to me that my mother had given up nine years of her life to protect me. My heart hurt from the thought of it. It hurt for all the years of misplaced anger toward a woman who surrendered her own life for mine. "I'm so sorry, Jig."

Jig reached across the counter and caressed my cheek. "My daughter-in-law had a strong will, Charlie. She was going to save you at all cost. The best I could do was keep an eye out on her daughter, my granddaughter. If we could have done anything else but foster care, we would have. We just didn't have the time and we were pretty certain the NSA kept tabs on all employees, past and present."

I ran my hands through my hair and felt a tingle at the base of my neck. Tip was checking in. I ignored her. "So when did she get out? She *did* get out, right?"

"She left shortly after you disappeared. One day, you were in high school, and the next, you were gone from the face of the earth. Your mother was inconsolable, so I sent a friend of a friend to talk to your foster care parents about what had happened to the little girl they were caring for."

"What did they say?"

"That you had beaten a boy up and gone to jail."

I shook my head. "Jail, huh?"

"Not true?"

"Nope. I was shipped to a psych ward of my own."

Jig smiled sadly. "No wonder I couldn't find you. I searched everywhere. Every jail, every hospital, every CPS-type system in the state. You had vanished. This time, for good. It took me nearly three months to convince your mother to come out of that horrible place. When she did, she spent the next three years looking for you. She spent every waking hour trying to locate you. In the end, she figured the Genesys group got to you and she would never see you again."

I blinked several times before asking the question I wasn't sure I was ready to ask. "Is she..." My heart leapt into my throat and I couldn't bring myself to say the word.

Jig nodded. "She is. Alive and kicking down in Santa Cruz."

Years of angry resentment disappeared. Alive. My mother was alive! She was alive and close enough for me to drive to in less than two hours. She hadn't just given me up because she didn't want me. I wasn't a throwaway. I had been loved. Loved.

"And my dad?"

She shrugged. "That's where it gets sadder and even more complicated. Your father left the country shortly after your mom was admitted."

"He left the country?"

"He did. He felt it was the best way to make everything go away, so he gathered up...his things and flew south. It was two and a half years before I heard from him."

"You're kidding. Where was he?"

"Living in a small village in Peru. He'd spent most of his time traveling around Asia and Russia. Your father is fluent in Russian and Ukrainian, and several other languages by now, I'm sure. Brilliant man, your father. Not so much in the son and father department."

"Did he ever come home?"

"Oh no. As far as I know, he's never returned to the States. He is far more afraid of Genesys than even your mother, and believed th...believed he was being pursued by them even in Russia." She paused here, not allowing herself to spill a secret I sensed was rising to the top. "Your father preferred hightailing it across continents than to come home and face the truth with your mother. I'm not proud of the way my son handled this whole thing, but second-guessing how someone handles this sort of problem isn't in my job description."

"So, you don't know if he is dead or alive?"

She shook her head, and I knew she was being honest. "He

stopped calling or writing eight years ago. For all I know, he died in a car accident, or is living *la vida loca* somewhere in Mexico."

"I'm sorry."

She waved this off. "Don't be. I know this is a lot to take in, but you have to know, deep in your heart, that both of them gave up their lives so you wouldn't have to go through whatever those other poor children had to endure. Your mother once called the Genesys Project pure, unadulterated evil. She hated them."

"What ever happened to it?"

"I have no idea. It was best not to know or care. My son may have ended up being a coward, but he started off being a hero. He loved you enough to let go of everything, including your mother."

I hadn't been abandoned because I was a burden or unwanted. I was given up so I could escape the fate of the poor little girl whose corpse stood in as my stunt double. My parents had known what I was from the very beginning, and that knowledge had sealed all our fates.

"What did you mean when you said I was too smart for my own good?"

Jig came around the counter and sat next to me, taking my hands in hers. "Charlie, I don't know if Genesys still exists. I imagine it does. You managed to piece together the fragments of a child's life enough to wind up here. Now that you've opened the doors to the truth, we have no idea who or what is going to come marching through them, and frankly, that scares the poo out of me."

I nodded in understanding. "You think they have been watching your house all these years?"

"I don't know what to think. I know my daughter gave up nine years of her life so you could live a good life. You owe it to her to make sure that happens."

"It has been, Jig. Really. I've had a wonderful life. The half of it spent in foster homes sucked, but the last fourteen have been excellent."

She leaned closer. "Then where have you been? Where did you go that no one could locate you?"

Grandmother or no, I wasn't about to share my truths with

her. "I was taken someplace far away to live with a woman who could teach me how to use my powers. She taught me how to live in the natural world as a supernatural. She gave me a sense of family, a sense of belonging. She helped mold me into the woman you see before you. From there, I went to Mills College and received my degree in English with a minor in journalism. Currently, I am a reporter for the *San Francisco Chronicle*. My name is Echo Branson."

Her eyes grew wide as her hand flew to her mouth. "Oh my. You're that Echo? *You're* Echo Branson? I read your articles all the time." She was beaming. "I can't believe it. My granddaughter is a famous reporter! My, but you *have* lived, haven't you?"

"Considering I've been living without a memory of my past and am a product of the California State Child Care System, yeah. I've done pretty well for myself."

She picked up the vehemence of my words and patted my thigh. "Your anger is understandable, hon, even if misdirected."

"Seems to me there could have been another way. They could have taken me with them. Who decided that leaving me was the best thing to do?"

She shrugged. "You'll need to speak with her about that. Am I wrong to assume that's where you'll be headed next?"

I had no idea where my next step would take me. I had arrived at this step so quickly, I hadn't had time to formulate any plan.

"We never expected to see you again, Charlie. After those nine years, it took me three months to get her out of the psych unit and another three years to get her to stop searching for you and to start living her *own* life again. She had to stop looking and get a job, find a place to live, discover a whole new life for herself. It was time for her to join the rest of the world without you." She gazed into my eyes, tears clinging to her bottom lashes. "As angry as you're going to be in the coming days, you need to remember how much they both sacrificed for you. Your hindsight can't see into the twisted world of Genesys and the horrific things they did to those children. I promised your mother a long time ago if this moment ever came, I would *not* tell her side of the story. It's not mine to tell."

"Will seeing me freak her out?" I heard a car door slam.

Jig rose and peeked out the blinds. "I would have said so five years ago, but I don't know now. It took her a long time to regroup when she finally let you go. You'll need to be very patient if she doesn't come right to the party. Just remember for every ounce of anger you carry within you is equal to a pound of heart-wrenching sadness she has carried within her. There's no heavier burden than not knowing the fate of your child. Trust me. I know."

I slowly rose. I needed air. The walls were closing in around me. "Do you mind if we go outside? I could really use some fresh air."

Jig led me to her gorgeous backyard, where the main feature was an enormous koi pond filled with huge yellow and gold koi. We sat on a wooden swing overlooking the pond. "I'm glad you found me, Charlie. I know it's a lot to absorb, but you have made this old lady very happy."

I turned to her. "Jig, would you mind not calling me Charlie? Charlie is a little girl completely detached from who I am."

"Oh. Sure. I'm sorry. It's all I know. I'll try to remember."

"Thank you. It's just...it took me a long time to figure out who I am. I am not Charlie Hayward. That little girl died inside the mouth of an elaborate lie." We rocked a little before I asked, "So, were they ever going to come get me?"

"Oh, yes. Once you turned eighteen and went off to college, she was going to introduce herself and tell you everything that happened. She wanted to make sure you were safe from them first before she initiated any sort of contact, and then she was going to see if you'd leave the country with her. She had it all planned out. Some days, when I would go visit her, it was all she would talk about." Blowing out a huge breath, she shook her head. "But then...you were gone so abruptly. Any hope of that reunion went with you."

"Is she happy?"

"You'll have to ask her."

"Are you?"

She grinned, and it was the smile of a much younger woman. "You've made an old woman's dreams come true, hon. Many a day I've sat on this swing wishing you were sitting next to me, and here you are. So, am I happy? I am ecstatic." She faced me. "What about you? How has your life gone for you?"

Watching the koi, I reached for her hand. "I'm very happy. I've had a good adult life so far. I have dear friends. I make a difference in the world, and I have a wonderful family."

"A family, huh?" She looked for a ring on my hand.

"Not that kind. I've learned that a family is what you make it, and I made a really good one. For as surely as my mother saved my life, so did they. I am loved."

Jig rocked the swing, but said nothing. We sat in the swing a long time, just rocking back and forth. She was comfortable with me, maybe remembering times when we had done this very thing. Sad for all the lost times, I felt Jig's emotional pendulum swing this way and that.

"So, you call yourself Jig from the Hemingway story."

She lit up. "Yes. And you are the first person I've ever met who knew that."

I grinned. "Too smart for my own good."

She chuckled. "Or something like that."

I rose and helped her to her feet. "Can I get my mother's address from you? I think it's time."

"Indeed."

She walked into the kitchen and jotted down an address on the back of one of her bank deposit slips. "You know where to find your old grandmother, hon. We'll have lots of catching up to do once you get your questions answered."

Taking the deposit slip, I nodded. "I'd like that." Reaching into my purse, I pulled out my silver business card holder and handed her one of my embossed business cards. "That phone rings both ways. When I come back, we can go out to dinner and get to know each other better. Let's replace my blank whiteboard with some real memories. How does that sound?"

"That sounds marvelous."

We hugged for a long, long time, and I felt so many emotions from her, I couldn't single just one out. When we pulled away, she placed her palm on my cheek. "She is going to be so proud of the woman you have grown into. I know I am."

As I started down the driveway, I stopped and turned back

to her. The sunlight was like a halo as it fell on her. "You know, I take it back."

"Take what back?"

"I'd really like it if you'd call me Charlie."

She lit up once more. "Really? Oh hon, I'd like that."

I grinned warmly. "So would I."

I called Danica as soon as I got into the car and had to listen to her screech for five minutes about how in the world could I have gone out there by myself. I knew the truth of her badgering had more to do with the fact that she hated more than anything being out of the loop. When she finished harping at me, I told her all about my visit.

"And you're heading to Santa Cruz now? Without me?"

"I'm just getting on the freeway."

"Like hell you are. Pull that stupid little car over and let me get a driver to take us down. You do *not* need to be driving those freeways with your head in the clouds. I mean it, Clark. If you don't pull that piece of shit over, I will come after you in a helicopter if I have to. You know I will too."

That was no idle threat. As much as I wanted to disagree with her, I didn't. I liked the idea of having a driver so we could sit back and talk about my plan of attack—so I could debrief and sort through the quagmire of emotions I was lost in.

Two hours later, we were doing just that.

"I appreciate this, Dani," I said after filling her in on everything that happened with Jig. We sat in the plush leather seats of the Lincoln Town Car with the windows rolled down as we cruised effortlessly down the 680 freeway.

"You okay?" She shook off her question. "Of course you're not okay. How could you be? You just found out your mother has been alive all these years. Wow." Shaking her head, she threaded her arm through mine. "We never saw this coming."

"My head is spinning, my stomach is doing backflips, and my legs are like two soggy noodles. It's a good thing I'm not behind the wheel. We might end up in San Diego."

"It's my job to help you navigate these uncharted emotional waters. Someone has to have one of those cooler heads that prevail. Today, it's mine."

I smiled. "It's a bit scary to think that that head is yours."

"Pshaw. Who do you know who is even half as cool as I am? Nobody, that's who. My cool head got us a driver so we can sit back and relax. Don't you worry, Clark. I gotcha. So, tell me, is Jig from *Hills Like White Elephants*?"

I chuckled. Our professors would be proud. "Yes."

"Cool. And you let her call you Charlie?"

I nodded.

"Can I call you Chuck?"

"Only if you want to lose an eye."

She laughed again. "I'm starting to lose count of all the names I can call you now. Charlotte, Charlie, Jane, Chuck, Clark, Echo. It's a damn good thing you are finding out who you are. You're using up all the pages in my address book."

"Don't make me hurt you." Looking over at Danica, I was so happy to have her with me, and thought briefly about Delta's explanation of our relationship. If she was my yang, I was certain I couldn't do better than Danica.

"Okay, okay, I'll stop. Tell me more about your grandmother."

"She was so incredibly sad about losing Charlie. I felt it in every cell."

"Did she explain why they chose that way out? I mean, why couldn't they have just left the country together?"

"Believe me, that's the first question I intend to ask."

"Does *she* have a name?"

I looked at the piece of paper Jig had handed me. "Her name is Patricia, but she goes by Trish. My dad's name is Harmon."

"So, Harmon Hayward hasn't been heard from for a few years, eh? You have to wonder if your mother's heard anything from old Harm. Tell me your thoughts about this Genesys crapola. Let's get some sort of bead on those fuckers." Danica pulled out her vidbook and called the boys.

"Yo, Boss. What up?"

"Bad grammar, apparently. Roger, no Cal graduate would be

caught dead sounding like a boy from the 'hood."

"Sorry, Boss. We're playing the beta of a new game called Street Cred. Gory, violent game, but damn, it's fun. I'm a gang leader who—"

"Glad my money is well spent on you guys. Listen up. I need you to find information on a company or a government group called Genesys. Spelled s-y-s."

"Genesys. Got it. What are we looking for?"

"Intel. Deep, dark intel. Look, but be sly and fleet of foot. These guys are scary shit, so you need to use your best ops. Don't let anything be traced back to us. I mean not one damn thing."

Roger's face lit up like a little kid seeing his first Christmas bike. "Nuh-uh."

"Again with the Berkeley educated language?"

He blushed. "Sorry, but come on! Intel? We haven't gathered intel since—"

"Ahem," she said, nodding her head toward me.

"Oh. Sorry. Hey there, Princess!"

"Hi Roger. I appreciate the legwork on this."

"It's for you? We're all over it."

"Well, *be* all over it with incredible discretion. Use the satellite, buy new laptops, the whole deal. Nothing traceable."

"You got anything else on this Genesys?"

I looked over to get a better view of the small, checkbook-size monitor and could see the other two boys' faces on the split screen. They ate this stuff up with a shovel-size spoon.

"Yo Princess!"

"Hi guys. Look, Dani means it when she says discretion. This company is ruthless. Go as far back as the mid-forties on this. I have a feeling they started as a result of World War II."

"We talking Secret Service kind of stuff? CIA? NSA? FBI? HSO?"

"HSO?"

"Homeland Security Organization. It's a new group Old Georgie and his cronies threw together. No one knows about it, of course. I think it's a place for his retired checkbooks to play. Beats golfing."

"Yeah. Check all of those, but be really careful with this, Roger. These people play for keeps."

"Will do. We'll buzz you when we got something."

"Do that."

"One more thing. Can we put Connie on it also? She's coming over in about an hour to run through some locked files. She's a genius, you know. Makes the three of us look like amateurs."

"Do what you have to—break through firewalls, security systems, whatever you need to do. Just don't leave a trail or get caught." Closing the book, she turned to me. "You know, sooner or later, you're going to have to come out to them, and I'm not talking about the lesbian gene, either."

I growled, "It'll have to be later, I'm afraid. I can't take any more emotional upheavals at the moment."

"Clark, you know those guys would go to the mat for you any day of the week."

"I know. It's not that I don't trust them. It's just…I don't know…seems not quite right to tell anyone before I tell Finn. Know what I mean?"

She nodded and slipped the vidbook back in her big bag. "I understand. Can't be easy always having the weight of that piece hanging over your head."

I shook my head. "It isn't." I watched her sip the ice water that was always stocked in the Town Car. "So Connie is hanging out at the Bat Cave these days?"

Danica stared out the window. "Maybe."

"Want to tell me about it?"

She turned to me. "I will if you swear you won't put your hands over your ears and say lalalalalal."

I crossed my chest. "Will you accept my apology first?"

"No need to apologize, Clark. If the roles were reversed and I had seen you with a man, I would have freaked too."

"I did not freak out." I sighed. "Okay. I freaked out a little. I have enough secrets in my life. I'd like to think that I at least know what's going on with my best friend."

"And you do. Look. You know I love you to death, and I would do anything for you, but trying to talk to you about sex is like talking to a vestal virgin. You just get all nutted up."

"Fine. I'm a prude. I can own that, but can you talk to me about it now? It will help take my mind off the fact that I am going to be seeing my biological mother for the first time since I can remember and I am scared to death."

"Playing the sympathy card, are you?"

I grinned. "Am I?"

"No. Save it for a rainy day. I'll tell you what I think you want to know so it will save us the pain of watching you formulate sentences with words that make you blush. You already know I've slept with women before. Christ, Clark, we went to an all-female college where lots of hotties roamed. You never noticed because you were so wrapped up in the Big Indian, but trust me there were some gorgeous women there to play with."

"Is this your bisexual coming out line?"

She chuckled. "No. No line. I refuse to pander to that or any other label. It's hard enough being a mixed race black kid. To heap the bisexual label on top of that is a little like adding sugar to a hot fudge sundae. Let's just say I'm a woman of loose moral fiber and leave it at that."

Shaking my head, I grinned. These were the times when I realized why I loved her so much. "So, somehow, you managed to get Connie into your bed. What are you, Black Magic?"

Danica tossed her head back and laughed. "Oh, it wasn't as hard as you think. Face it, Clark, there aren't a lot of women out there who possess the kind of computer acumen she and I do. That totally turned her on. We went out to dinner to talk about things like software and Microsoft, and the next thing I knew, we were tussling in the sheets. It was, I repeat for the record, incredible sex, the likes I haven't seen with Mr. Penis in a while. Very give and take. I've made a mental note to require Mr. Penis to visit certain places prior to entry, so I can have that kind of sex more often."

I wanted to put my hand up to signal her to stop, but I had already said I wouldn't be such a prude, so I remained silent.

"And no, she's not looking for a relationship and neither am I. It was good, consensual sex...heavy on the consensual, heavier on the good."

"And that's it? Just good, clean fun."

"Sure. What more do you want? You know, not every woman thinks there needs to be a ring on her finger in order for her to enjoy a romp in the hay. Connie has abstained for a long time...too long...and she decided this chocolate hottie was worth her time and effort." She smiled softly. "I appreciate you worrying about my love life, Clark, but the truth is, I really am phobic about commitment, and I sure as hell am not ready to be anyone's stepmom." She shivered. "Eww..ick."

I laughed. "Thanks. I guess...I guess it was a bit unnerving to think I don't know who you are just at a time when I'm pretty damn sure I have no idea who I am. I just needed something to hold onto."

Danica reached across and took my hand. "No matter who comes or who goes in our lives, you can always hold on to me." She gave my hand a quick squeeze. "Always."

We arrived in Santa Cruz a little after four p.m., which was a good thing, considering every freeway in the Bay Area becomes gridlocked right after two in the afternoon.

After the 1989 earthquake destroyed much of the downtown area of Santa Cruz, it had regrown like the limb of an octopus, only cleaner and nicer. The city had a state university whose mascot was the banana slug, and the most popular vegetation was marijuana. Santa Cruz made Berkeley look semi-normal, with all of its tie-dye clothes and hemp sandals.

"Every time I come here, I wonder why I don't come here more often," I said.

"Traffic, Clark. Traffic keeps us all apart. It is the great divide, if you ask me." She paused for half a beat. "That would be a great title for an article about how traffic has changed our lives in the twenty-first century." She stuck her head out the window like a dog and I thought that she and Bailey would be a better match than her and Connie. "I'm telling you, Clark. I think I see a series of articles in your future." Bringing her head back in, she yawned and stretched. "You're nervous, huh?"

"Totally."

"No matter what, you will always rock, sister, and don't you forget it."

As we drove through the small, narrow street along the shoreline, I realized we were headed for Capitola, a little town nestled on the edges of the beach. It was a little bedroom community sporting multimillion dollar cracker box houses that weren't worth a fraction of that, but location, location, location was everything.

When the driver pulled up to 100 North Seaside Drive, my heart rate picked up speed. It was a beach house; one of the smaller homes originally built to be a vacation getaway, but had now been converted to a million dollar mansion.

"Someone has *dinero*," Dani remarked, getting out of the car.

I couldn't respond. My knees were weak and I thought I was going to throw up.

The driver got out and opened my door. I sat there, staring at him, as if I was too dumb to figure out what he wanted. When Danica came around to my side, she helped me out and slid her arm through mine. "Remember, Clark, she gave up a helluva lot to save your life. Put your anger aside for the moment and just experience the emotions."

We walked together to the front door and Danica rang the doorbell. "You'll be fine," she whispered. "You've waited your whole life for this moment, and it's going to be great. Just don't forget to *feel*. Come out of your head for this one, okay?"

The front door opened and a tall, thin man with graying sideburns stood looking down at us. He wore a red and white Hawaiian shirt and black walking shorts. His feet wore Teva sandals. "You must be Charlie," he said, grinning. "Jig called about two hours ago to let her know you were on the way. Please, come on in."

I'm pretty sure I would have just melted into a puddle had Danica not had a firm hold on my arm. "It's going to be okay, Clark," she whispered. "I promise."

"I'm Brian," he said, reaching his hand out to me. I read nothing but kindness and genuine concern from this man, but I just couldn't seem to get my appendages moving.

"I'm Danica, and my mute friend is…well…she's Echo now."

I reached out and shook his hand. "Nice meeting you, Brian." My eyes left him and scoured the rest of the house.

"She's not here. She's down the beach a ways, waiting for you. Liked to have fainted straightaway when Jig called. She never thought…never really imagined…" He shook his head. "I offered to leave and give you guys some privacy, but Trish has always preferred to handle tough things outside."

Danica did not let go, but steered me to a sliding glass door that opened to a Trex deck and the Pacific Ocean. "Wow. What a lovely view. This is gorgeous."

"Thank you. It was my parents' summer home. When they passed, they left it to me. I can't even imagine living anywhere else."

Danica slowly slid the door open. "I'm going to send Echo off in the direction of her mother, and then I'm going in the opposite direction. Is there anything further up the beach?"

"There's a Starbucks."

"Perfect. Clark, call me on my cell when you're done, but take your time. I have plenty of work to do." She turned to Brian and thanked him before closing the sliding glass door behind us. "You gotta let go, Clark," Danica whispered. "Lower your shields, and let go. You'll know which one she is. Just let go. I'm just a phone call away, okay?"

Nodding, I grabbed her hand as she retrieved it. "This is the right thing to do, isn't it? I mean…I *should* go see her, right?"

"Of course you should. Take a deep breath and steady yourself. You've been ready for this for a long time. I promise." Taking her arm back, she stepped down the stairs going in the opposite direction from where Brian had pointed. "Call me when you're done…or if you need me. Whichever comes first. You can do this, Jane. It's the right thing you can do."

I looked down the stretch of beach and saw a jogger, someone flying a kite, two teenagers on a beach blanket and a woman sitting on large towel with her knees drawn to her chest. I turned to say something to Danica, but she was already gone. I stood there, immobile, thinking, of all things, of the Langston Hughes poem *What Happens to a Dream Deferred*? And then I wondered what happens when a dream comes true. No one can really walk you through it or tell you what to do or how to react when our dreams land at our feet. We won't ever know what to say or how to say it. The moment it arrives, we know we will be changed forever, but we don't quite know how or to what extent.

And I wasn't ready.

How could I be? I had spent my life believing she was dead. What does one say to a ghost who suddenly springs to life?

I had no words.

But someone else did.

"Hey, darlin', what in the hell is going on with you? I'm getting some whacked out vibes from you ringing like church bells. You okay?"

Tip and I had broken up for this very reason, yet now, I was glad for the intrusion. *"It's my mother. She's alive and about thirty yards from me."*

"Ah, man, that explains it. Where's Dani?"

"Here, with me, but I have to do this on my own and I am scared to death."

"That's normal, don't you think?"

"You know I've never done normal very well."

"Better than most of us. Look...don't be scared. No matter what happens, you have a family who loves you and will always be here. She can either add her name to that long list of people who care about you or she can fuck off. It's really that simple."

Was it? Was anything really that simple? I didn't think so. *"Did you know?"*

"That she was alive? No."

"I don't even know what to say. How do I start? I stopped dreaming of this moment when I was a little girl. I have no idea how to start off a conversation."

"Yes, you do. Don't get all wimpy just because your mom is alive. You're a much stronger woman than that. You came for answers. Be the reporter first and go in there to get your answers. You've waited a long time for this moment. Make it a good one."

I took the stairs slowly, one at a time. *"Thank you, Tip. You're a good friend."*

"It's what family does for each other, darlin'. Holler if you need me." And she was gone.

It was no wonder I was having a hard time letting her go. She always knew when I needed that little bit of love and support to get me through a crisis. Tip had honed in on my erratic emotions and found me when I needed her most. Poor Finn didn't even know where I was.

As I walked across the hot sand, I could see the woman was deep in thought as she stared at the ocean. Not once did she glance my way, but just looked out straight ahead. How odd this must be for her; a mother who had given up a child in order to save her, only to lose her for fourteen years. I imagined her guilt was a hundred times worse than my fear.

When I was about ten feet away, she shielded her eyes from the sun that was at my back. When she saw me, she slowly stood, her hand still shielding her eyes. She was taller than I. I figured about five eight, five nine. She wore her auburn hair short, like a boy, and the red highlights collected the sun. She looked at me through blinking eyes the shade of sapphires. This woman was my mother, and she was beautiful.

"I've played this scene in my head thousands of times, and yet, now that it's here, I don't quite know what to say or do." She stood before me. Her voice had a Lauren Bacall quality to it; refined, polished, educated, but not as deep.

I said the first thing that came to my mind. "In the movies, they always hug."

I stepped up to her and let her wrap her long arms around me.

"I would have known you anywhere," she whispered, clasping me tightly. She smelled of cloves and something else I couldn't put my finger on; something sweet.

When I could, I gently pulled away. "Jig called."

She nodded. "That was our deal, and she has always kept her promises to me. It was a good thing, too, Charlie, or else I would be standing here a babbling idiot." Taking my hands in hers, she looked me up and down. "You have grown into a beautiful young woman."

I blushed. I was not nearly as pretty as she was. "Must be the genes."

For a long time, she just looked at me. In my face, at my hands. She surveyed me as if she had just gotten her sight back. I did the same, only with my powers. She was experiencing the same mixed bag of emotions Jig had experienced.

"You are beautiful. You look so…happy."

"I am. I have a good life. A really good life."

Her eyes teared up quickly. "You must have a million questions for me."

"A million and a half, really."

"Come. Sit with me." She sat down, cross-legged and I sat across from her—a mirror image. "I can't get over how much you look like I did when I was your age." Her eyes roamed all over my face, taking in every blemish, every freckle, every wrinkle. I knew she was taking snapshots of me for her mind's eye, in the event I disappeared from sight once more.

"I got a lot of background from Jig. She said you're a scientist."

"Was. I *was* a scientist. I teach cell bio at the university now." She paused and smiled. "You have your father's mouth."

I didn't know what to say to that, so I said nothing. After my movie comment, I wasn't sure I trusted anything intelligent to come out of my mouth.

"I'm sorry," she said softly. "I can't help staring."

"It's okay. It must be weird to see what I look like after all these years."

"Oh, I've seen photos of you. Jig took some pictures of you one night when you and Danica were walking home from a football game. She got very good at stalking you."

I nodded, not sure I cared for the notion of being stalked by anybody. It was creepy. "She stalked me, huh?"

"She did everything she could to keep me in your life. Then…well…then we lost touch."

I nodded. "Jig told me all about Genesys, about the telepath. She explained why you did what you did."

"She told you about the telepath? Then you—"

I grinned faintly. "Am one? No. Nor am I telekinetic; at least, I haven't displayed that power yet. It could still come." I searched her energy for any kind of fear. I did not want her to be afraid of me. "I don't remember anything that happened in my childhood, so I can't tell you what was happening to me during those times when you saw me use a power. What I *can* tell you is that you probably did save my life."

"You mean...you're—"

I nodded. "I'm an empath."

She stared at me knowingly. I let this sink in for a moment. "My God...all these years, I questioned whether or not we'd done the right thing...and now...to know we did...it makes all these years without you worth it." Her eyes filled with tears. "I'm sorry. I promised myself I wouldn't cry."

"It's okay, really."

"Is it?" She reached out and took my hands again. "It must be so hard to understand why we did what we did, but we had to do *something*. Genesys had managed to get their hands on an incredible telepath whose job was to locate others and point them out to the committee."

"Spotter. We're called spotters."

Her mouth opened, but no words came out.

"And no, I don't work for Genesys, but I do belong to a group of paranormals who are my family." I leaned forward, locking eyes with hers. "And before we go any further, I need you to know if I feel they are in *any* danger from any conversation I have with you or Jig or Brian up there..." I paused. Licking my parched lips, I continued. "You see, I *do* have a family now; one I would die for; one I would kill for."

She tried pulling her hands away, but I held on tightly, surprised at my own strength. "One I *have* killed for. If I read anything off you that even implies you'll use what I share with you with someone who could hurt us, you'll be dead before sunset." Letting go of her hands, I leaned back, somewhat rattled by the force of my own convictions. "In our world, trust is more precious than gold, Trish, and I don't know you from Adam."

Visibly shaken, she cleared her throat and nodded slowly. "Apparently, protecting family runs in our genes. I...I understand your concern, Charlie, and, to be honest, you're wise to be suspicious."

I studied her and read no deception. I shook my head. In the thousands of times I'd played this scene over in my head, it had never included threatening my own mother. "Being suspicious isn't natural to my personality, Trish, but taking care of those I love is."

Her smile was sad. "Your father was like that once. Loyal to a fault, willing to lay his own life on the line, but Charlie...if you're as strong as you say, you'll know if I'm playing you."

"I don't know how much you know about me and my kind, but self-preservation is second to protecting the whole."

"I am aware of that, and I understand perfectly. Tell you what. Why don't you ask the questions and I'll answer and then you can be the judge."

I had so many questions, I really didn't know where to start. I started in the middle. "You really were afraid of them so much that—"

"That we'd trash our home, our careers and our entire lives? Absolutely. You would, too, if you had seen what they're capable of. We thought we were doing good work—noble work. Then suddenly, kids were accidentally dying. Things started to go sideways when the CIA and others wanted quantifiable proof. Suddenly, I began seeing more and more of our test subjects in the morgue. No one would admit it, but whatever we were doing, it was deadly. We were murdering innocent children and no one even questioned it."

I suddenly thought of Shirley's ranting and raving, horrified by the truth in what had sounded like craziness.

"How could anyone allow children to be hunted and used as human guinea pigs?"

"People were afraid. The CIA and NSA funded Genesys to find the genetic makeup of psions like yourself. It started as far back as World War One, but really kicked into high gear during the Cold War when the Reagan administration realized the viability and potential of having telepaths in any meeting with any other world leader. It snowballed from there. Scientists started believing humans can spontaneously combust." Her eyes narrowed. "Can you imagine having a supernova weapon you could walk through any airport and get through any metal detector? The kind of damage a fire starter could do..." She shook her head. "Or any of you for that matter."

"You worked with one," I said.

"Yes, I did. A little girl named Frida." Trish shook her head, tears springing to her eyes again. "Never seen anything like it. Could make a flame appear at the tip of her finger."

"What happened?"

"They pushed her too far and she snapped. We tried to warn them she was unstable, her powers were erratic at best, but they wouldn't listen. She took out three of our geneticists when she imploded. It was awful."

"Frida was the little girl you used to replace me, wasn't she?"

The sadness in Trish's eyes was answer enough. "Shortly before Frida died, I saw you move something on the desk without touching it. At first, I just figured I was overly tired and seeing things. Then, I saw you do it again. You cannot imagine the fear that coursed through my body. With that creepy telepath always lurking around, I knew we were in trouble. I was certain he was reading all of our minds and keeping tabs on everyone who came and went. One day, he was staring me down. I don't know if I was just paranoid or what, but I knew what I had to do. Quitting wasn't really an option. Our positions were highly classified and we were highly trained in the field of psionics. There wasn't anything else we could do to keep you from harm except remove you."

"So you faked my death then erased me."

She nodded and sighed. "We had to protect all of us quickly and surgically. We were desperate, Charlie. Believe me. Over the past twenty-three years I have thought about a million different ways I might have solved our problems and still kept you safe, and in the end, I always return to that one. We couldn't have gone on the run. Running was a fool's mission. None of us would have made it back alive." Her blue eyes got bluer as she took my hands again. "I've spent years covering every single angle, and if I had to do it all over again…I would do the same thing with one exception."

"And what would that be?"

"I'd find a way not to lose sight of you." She shook her head.

"That was the worst part—losing you. You just disappeared. Where have you been? Where did you go? I thought—"

"That Genesys got me?" I shook my head. "No. I ran away, found others like me, and have been living a relatively normal life ever since."

"Jig and I looked for three years. Your trail went so cold, I was sure the government had something to do with it. We watched Danica's house for months, hoping to see some sign of you, but she came and went as usual."

"You could have asked her."

Trish shook her head. "I couldn't ask her without exposing her. We needed to keep Danica from harm. As long as she knew nothing, she couldn't be used as a weapon to reach you."

"I appreciate that, Trish. Really. I don't know what my life would have been like without her. She's been my rock for over half my life."

She nodded, tucking her hair behind her ears. "I know. When it was obvious she had no contact with you, we feared the worst."

"And eventually stopped looking."

She answered sadly, "I had to. Hanging on to that hope was draining my life away. Jig convinced me that's no way to live. It was time for me to move on. Wherever you were, you were too far out of my reach, and after having you erased, we knew there would be no getting you back."

I looked out at the ocean as it lapped the shore, like the ebb and flow of my emotions. "And what about Harmon? What happened to him?"

"After he checked me into the psych ward as a babbling, bereaved mother of a dead child, he took your sister to the jungles of—"

My eyes grew wide and my heart leapt into my throat. "Whoa. Wait. Hold on." I suddenly jumped to my feet, sending sand flying everywhere. "I have *a sister*?"

Trish looked up, surprised. "I thought Jig told you."

So *that* was the secret Jig was hiding. "No. Pretty sure I would have remembered that little piece." I paced back and forth. "I have *a sister*?"

"Oh, Charlie, I'm so sorry. I guess—" She shook her head. "It wouldn't be the first time Jig and I got our wires crossed."

"She...she did start to tell me something, but said it would be better coming from you." I paced back and forth some more, my mind fractured by dozens of questions bouncing into each other.

"Charlie—"

"Wait. Please." I held my hand up again. "I need a moment to process this. This is a little much. I never...it didn't occur to me that—" Shaking my head, I gave up. Somewhere out there, I had a sister. A sister! It was exciting and scary and crazy all at the same time. Pinching the meat of my thumb, I relied on Bailey's calming technique to give me clarity. "Not once," I started, my voice barely audible above the waves. "Not once in all my years, did I ever lay in bed at night wondering if I had a sibling. It never dawned on me I might have a sister. I always thought I was alone. To find out I do—" Shaking my head, I ran my hands through my hair. "Where is she?"

Trish was blinking rapidly. "I don't even know if she is alive. I haven't heard from either of them in years."

I sat back down. "Okay. Okay. Tell me about that. I know Harmon left the country after you burned the house down. He took—"

"Kristy. Her name is Kristy."

My sister's name was Kristy. "So his part of the plan was to get Kristy to safety."

She nodded. "We were afraid she carried the gene as well. Harmon and I decided it was best if we looked like the grieving family who just couldn't hold it together after the death of our daughter."

I reached over to lay my hand on top of hers. "You lost everything in that fire, didn't you?"

Trish blinked back tears. "It wasn't supposed to be that way. I never thought when I kissed Kristy goodbye that I would never see her again. I never envisioned losing you before I could get you back. So much went wrong. So many, many regrets." Tears fell as she bowed her head.

"You haven't seen her in all these years?"

Shaking her head, she whispered, "No."

"Where did they go?"

"At first, they went to the Amazon. Harmon had done some research down there when he got out of college, so he knew where to go and how to disappear. They stayed down there for about two years, and then started crisscrossing their way through Asia and Russia. Harmon thought they were being followed, so he spent two more years on the run trying to shake any possible tails Genesys might have sent."

I nodded. "So by that time, I was nine or ten. Why didn't they come home? Was it that dangerous?" I knew by the shift in her energy what the answer was before it came out of her mouth.

Trish glanced away. "Harmon...he...was gone for so long... he eventually fell in love with a Russian scientist he met in Peru. She convinced him to leave South America and go with her to Asia, where he continued working for the next couple of years."

"He *left* you?"

She looked at me with utter devastation in her eyes. "Your father left me long before he met her."

"And where was Kristy?"

"With him. They went everywhere together. By the time she was twelve, she was fluent in Spanish, Portuguese, Chinese and Russian." She said it with such pride it made me smile. "She was a bright little thing, to be sure, and to Harmon's credit, he always put her in the best school no matter where they went."

"But she never came home?"

She shook her head again. "It wasn't until your...until Harmon left the country that we realized the extent of the government's paranormal research. Every major industrialized nation was also involved in tracking down the gene responsible for these special powers. I'm pretty sure he continued on with his research in Russia with Svetlana." She brushed a tear away. "By that time, they had already started a new life somewhere in Russia. I never expected Kristy to come home even though Harmon told me when she turned eighteen she was free to choose her own life. He was happy in Russia and sent the divorce papers explaining that he just didn't want to come back."

I stared at her, thinking of the many sacrifices this woman had made in order to keep her daughters safe. It all seemed cruelly unfair. "I'm so sorry."

Again wiping her eyes, she shrugged. "Oh, it wasn't so bad for the first nine years, when you were nearby and I could hold onto the hope that someday you would know me and be my daughter again, but once you disappeared, I did everything I could to try to convince Harmon to send Kristy home. He felt it was still too dangerous. The last time...the last time we spoke was on her seventeenth birthday." Sighing, she continued. "Harmon went with Svetlana, but Kristy didn't want to go. She was in her senior year at a boarding school in China and begged to stay until the year was over. I couldn't take anything more away from her, so we agreed to let her stay in China for one more year. That decision cost me my daughter. I haven't heard from her since."

"Did you try to find her? Did you contact the school?"

Trish contemplated lying, then changed her mind. "I called every boarding school in China and none had ever heard of Kristy. I was pretty sure, then, that much of what Harmon had told me over the years was nothing but lies. Kristy never attended a boarding school. I doubt she had even been to China."

"But you spoke with her. Didn't she ever say?"

She shook her head sadly. "And it was foolish of me to think that she would have done or said anything that hadn't been of her father's design. The truth is...something happened to Harmon when he left the country, and he was able to carry on the charade for a very long time. More than likely, that web of lies was wrapped around my daughter."

I blinked several times, no words strong enough to make it out of my mouth.

"It took me eighteen months to backtrack in order to find out where the truth ended and the lies began. The trail of the truth went cold in Peru. Once he met Svetlana...everything changed. The phone calls became less frequent, the conversations less meaningful. I suppose I should have seen it coming. I don't know what happened to my husband. Maybe he snapped. Maybe being on the run finally got to him. I don't know. I just know that somewhere along the way, he started lying about where they were and what they were doing."

"And she never called you again?"

"I can't even say if the little girl I spoke to over the phone was even her. She was only a baby when they left. She could have been anyone."

"Did you ever find out if she was...like me?"

Trish shook her head. "We never spoke about it, and Harmon refused to have that conversation over the phone. He became increasingly paranoid...or at least...he acted like he was. I had to move on. I had already given up nine years of my life. I could either spend the rest searching, or I could try living it to its fullest. I chose the latter."

We sat there in silence with only the sound of the surf filling the void between us.

"Your turn," I said reaching for her hand.

She looked at me with the saddest eyes. "For?"

"What would you like to know? I'm willing to tell you anything I can about myself as long as it won't put anyone I love in danger."

"The truth is, Charlie, I've spent so much of my life in the past, I'd rather know about who you are today. If you don't mind."

I smiled softly. "I'd like that. Would you mind if Danica joined us? She'll add another dimension to my story that could prove entertaining."

A smile lit up her face. "I'd love to. She's been your friend for so long."

I nodded. "Can't live without her."

"Are you lovers?"

"Hell no!" I laughed. "I didn't mean it like that. I just meant...she and I would kill each other if we were. She *is* the most important person in my life. My anchor most of the time, but we've never been together like that. Ever."

"Then by all means, bring her."

After I called Danica and she came over, she inspected Trish with open and avid curiosity before we chatted about our current lives until it was almost too dark to see each other anymore. Danica was her usual brilliant story-telling self, regaling Trish with stories about what a geek I was and what it was like having an empath for a best friend. Trish hung on her every word, soaking up my life then and now like someone who had never heard a story before. She laughed at some points and nearly cried at others, as Danica and I filled her in about our lives growing up in Oakland, and life in and after college. We never mentioned the bayou or the time I spent there.

We spent another hour sitting in the house with Brian, and finished up to where our lives were now. She promised she would get a subscription to the *Chronicle* so she could read my stories. She seemed so proud of what I did and who I had become.

When it was time to leave, I felt the heaviness of her heart. She didn't want to let me go and yet, she had already done that a long time ago.

"Thank you so much for tracking me down; for caring enough to find me even though—"

"You did the right thing, Trish. I know you probably didn't know it then, but if you had a telepath working for you, he would have found out sooner or later. You saved my life...and probably Kristy's as well. Rest in the peace of that."

Tears came down her face—absolution twenty-three years later. "Thank you so much." Tentatively wrapping her arms around me, she pulled me to her, hugging me tightly. "My God, I never thought I would get to do this again."

"Thank you for the lengths you went and the sacrifices you made for me, Trish. I've had a wonderful life thanks to all you did for me."

As Danica and I turned to get into the waiting car, I stopped for one final question. "Trish, I know it's been a long time, but do you remember the telepath's name?"

"Remember? I'll never forget that bastard's name. Not now. Now ever." As she stepped up to me, I felt pure enmity coming from those icy blue eyes. It felt like a Chicago chill blowing through my bones when she whispered, "His name was Malecon."

"That's just fucking crazy," Danica said as we settled into the car for the nearly three-hour commute through traffic ride home.

"Which part?" Shaking my head, I stared out the window.

"Malecon! Can you even *believe* the asshole responsible for taking your family from you is Melika's fucking psycho twin brother?"

I couldn't believe it. We had just dealt with Malecon in the bayou, where he'd attempted to kill Melika and the rest of us. The fact that *he* was responsible for me losing my whole family was too much for me to digest. That news just sat in the pit of my stomach like bad potato salad. It was just too much. "I can't go there right now, Dani. I can't give that asshole one second of my energy when all I can think about is that out there somewhere, I have a sister." I looked at her. "A sister, Dani. I have a *sister*."

Danica reached over and squeezed my hand. "Pretty damn cool, Clark. That's pretty awesome in a freakish sort of way. Pretty fucking cool."

We drove along in silence, both with our own thoughts to keep us occupied. I wondered what Kristy was like. If she was happy. Where she might have ended up. I wondered if she was still alive and then quickly dismissed any thoughts to the contrary. If she was alive, I had the means to find her...and I would.

"Guess this means we'll be keeping Delta and Connie on the payroll a little longer, eh?" Danica asked, as if reading my mind. "You are planning on looking for her, right?"

I looked back out the window at the half moon hanging lazily in the sky. "Yeah. I am."

"Well, if anyone can find her, it's those two and our three. They could find a piece of dandruff on the North Pole."

I smiled, then it quickly dropped from my face. "She could be dead."

"And if she is, then you can put Trish's mind to rest so she can move on. That poor woman's been through a lot."

I turned back to Danica. "She had that haunted look, you know? Too much sorrow and not enough joy. I can't even imagine what it must be like to walk away from your children the way she did."

"No kidding. If I had any doubts she was being honest, they evaporated the moment she spoke *his* name." Danica rolled the window down and stuck her hand out. "You *know* he was reading everyone's mind in Genesys because he's so egomaniacal. Can you even imagine the power trip he must have been on back then? They gave him the power of life and death over other supernaturals. He must have eaten that shit up with a spoon."

That was when it hit me full force. Slowly, I turned back to her. "Shit."

"What?"

"They knew."

"Who?"

"Tip and Melika," I said through gritted teeth "They *had* to know the Genesys Project existed, but they have never mentioned it. They never, not once, said a word about its existence. Why wouldn't they have warned us?"

"That was a long time ago, Clark. We don't even know if it still exists."

I faced her, glad for the fresh air entering the car. "Dani, those experiments were going as early as the fifties. What makes you think they're not still going on?"

"Don't borrow trouble yet, Clark."

"I'm a reporter. Borrowing trouble is what I *do*."

"And being a supernatural is what you *are*. You would be crazy to mess with this thing, especially if the government is still involved. Besides, there's no fucking way Tip would allow it."

"She doesn't need to know."

She shook her head. "Now you're talking crazy talk. *Of course* she would know...and if she didn't *I* would tell her. You are so not taking on some government group in order to find a sister who may not even want to be found. No way. Ain't happenin'. Not on my watch. Tip would kill me."

"Can we make that decision once we see what the boys find out?"

"No." She crossed her arms over her chest. "This is serious shit, Clark. If you're gonna do anything, you do it with Tip's blessing. Otherwise—"

"You'll tell on me?"

She did not smile. "Or something."

I was quiet for a minute. I knew she was right, but I also knew I had a sister out there who might need me. "You know I won't let this rest."

She didn't look at me. "I know. Dog on a bone is what you are, but that's one bone that can and *will* bite back. Let it go for now, Clark. If you want help finding your sister, I'm all for it. I'll call out the National Guard myself. But going after Genesys without Tip or Mel knowing? No way."

"I never said I was going after *them*. Just Kristy. I just want to find my sister. To hell with some jacked up secret government agency."

Danica shook her head. "Do I look stupid? You can never let sleeping dogs lie. Even if you found your sister, you'd be compelled to go after anyone you think threatens your people. It's only a matter of time."

I opened my mouth to protest but then closed it. She was probably right. Getting in over my head because of my emotions had never really ended well for me. Still, there were now more questions than ever and I wanted answers—answers I knew I could only get from Harmon Hayward. "Then let's go after Harmon."

Danica slowly turned. "Go. After? *He* would be that piece of dandruff I was referring to."

I shrugged. "It's worth a try."

She nodded. "We have something poor Trish doesn't have."

"Supernaturals to help?"

She shook her head. "My bank account."

I grinned warmly at her and turned on the overhead light. Trish had given me a bunch of photos of me and Kristy when we were kids, but it was like looking at photos of someone else's children. None of them rang any bells for me. "Dani, when Trish was talking about what happened right after the fire, did she say it was Harmon who took me to an eraser?"

"Yeah. She was too busy getting introduced to the nuthouse. Why?"

"Erasing is nearly impossible to do to a super. You would

have to be incredibly adept and actually *know* you were dealing with one. My...Trish...said she had seen me do things, but they had no idea what kind of powers I had."

"Your point?"

"I should still be able to remember *something*, especially after looking at these photos. Erasing may be permanent, but it's not complete."

"You still can't remember one thing?"

"Nope. It's just as dark as it was before I saw them. I think Harmon Hayward is the key to finding my sister and maybe even recovering my memory."

Danica stared at me. "It's that important to you?"

"To get my memory back? God, yes."

She nodded. "Then that's where we'll start. What are you thinking?"

Tapping my chin, I blew out a breath. "Well, all those years, Trish thinks he lied to her about where he was and what he was doing. So what else did he lie about? Did he lie about being followed? Did he lie about there even *being* a Svetlana? I think it's best to believe everything he told Trish was a lie and start from there."

She nodded. "I'll bring you everything the boys come up with on Genesys if you *swear* you won't go after them until we have all the facts and Melika and Tip on our side. You are *not* doing this without them."

"Fine." I leaned my head back to rest.

I don't know how long I was asleep, but when I woke, I turned and saw Danica's eyes were closed and she was breathing deeply. "Dani?" I whispered.

"Yeah?"

"I'm really sorry for being such an ass about Connie. I was way out of line."

"Yes you were, but you're my best friend. It's your job to rattle my cage if you think I'm losing my marbles."

"But you haven't, right?"

She chuckled under her breath, her eyes still closed. "It's debatable. I'll forgive you on one condition."

"Name it."

"You let me call you Charlie."

"Not a chance."

"Chuck?"

I shook my head. "You're incorrigible."

"And you're..."

I swore under my breath. "Chuck."

She laughed. "I forgive you."

"Thanks."

"Chuck."

When I got home after dropping Danica off at her office, I was surprised to find Cooper, our escapee TK, still bound and gagged on the couch with a large white pit bull with an enormous head and Down Syndrome eyes staring at him.

"Uh...Bailey? What happened? I thought—"

"That kid's a *total* asshole," she said, standing and stretching. She had been watching a *20/20* segment on ghost hunters. "Ass. Hole."

"Okay. What's with the dog?" I asked, glancing around for my cat.

"Buster and Tripod are cool, don't worry. I made sure I got one who gets crushes on cats. She digs the milk stool." Milk stools are three-legged, like my cat, and Danica, true to her own bizarre nature, nicknames everything. Milk Stool was what she called Tripod.

Cat crushes? I was too tired to ask. "And he's sitting there because..."

Bailey walked up to me and showed me the shiner growing just under her cheek. "The little rat bastard head-butted me when I was trying to let him go."

I stepped closer. "Ouch. Did you put something on it?"

"Yeah. Luigi gave me some ice. That's one sweet little Italian man. He gave me some ibuprofen as well."

"So, what's his problem?" I looked over at Cooper and realized he hadn't moved a muscle since I walked in.

"Oh, I force-fed him some of my special nighty-night potion.

I got real tired of trying to explain what was really going on and that we are on his side. He didn't want to listen. Just kept coming at me with that big boy head of his. So, I got me a sentry so I could close my eyes and rest without worrying about him lunging at me." She stretched again. "How did it go?"

I shrugged, not sure where to begin. "I have a grandmother and a mother, and a sister who seems to have vanished. I'll tell you all about it, but I have to talk to Tip first. You mind?"

She appeared nonplussed at my news. "Not at all. I need to get some fresh air and get a bite to eat. I'm not used to being cooped up all day. Pardon the pun."

"Take your time. Is the dog...uh..."

"Buster rocks the Kasbah, E. He won't let Cooper move an eyeball without giving him a good old pit bull growl. You'll be fine."

I studied the dog's large head. "And you say Tripod likes him?"

"Tripod *loves* him. You'll see. If Cooper so much as looks at you sideways, Buster's teeth will be embedded in his flesh." She glared at him. "Asshole."

"Good to know."

Bailey nodded and started for the door. "You look beat, E. You need some rest."

"I'm wiped." Every ounce of energy I had was gone.

"Well, I'm glad things went well. Tell Tip she owes me for bagging this neophyte."

I looked at her and laughed. "Don't sprain your tongue."

She laughed. "Did that the other day. Wanna hear about it?" She laughed and left before I could reply.

After Bailey was gone, I checked on Tripod, made sure the dog statue guarding Cooper had a pulse, and then sat in my favorite recliner and phoned Tip. I phone her when I need to keep my thoughts to myself. As soon as she answered, I dove right in. "Why didn't you tell me about Genesys?"

There was a long pause followed by a protracted sigh. "For what purpose? We steer clear of those people. They're bad news. Unless they threaten any of us, we give them a wide berth." Her use of the present tense didn't go unnoticed, and pieces of our earlier conversations began falling into place. "We do what we can to get to the young ones before they do. Some days, it feels like a footrace. We win some, we lose a few. "

"So...all these years, when you would disappear for days at a time...you weren't really seeing Shamans and learning more about your own powers, were you?"

"Sometimes, but not always, no. Mel does send me for training a couple of times a year, but yeah, most of the time I am trying to get to them before Genesys does. It's what I do. Hell, it's what I've been doing more than half of my life. It's what Mel trained me to do all those years ago when I first came to the bayou. I'm a hunter, darlin', it's all I know. I hunt supers and try to get to them before Genesys does. Genesys is pure evil, and because they are an extension of the government, they're virtually untouchable."

"How is it we can be okay to let something like that even exist?" I turned when Cooper stirred slightly. The dog merely blinked but never turned away.

"They've been involved in the paranormal trade for over half a century in various guises. We're the next super weapon, the next super spy, the next super soldiers. We know exactly what they want and why. We don't *let* them exist, Echo. We let them locate supers *for* us. They are the net that catches those who fly under our radar. It's a chess game our kind have been playing for decades. Why do you think time is of the essence for us?"

I ignored the question and repeated my question. "Why didn't you tell us?"

"Because of the very conversation we are having now. *You* want to stop them. *You* want to create an army and go after them, and that would be the greatest mistake we could make. This isn't a battle we can win, Echo, so Mel keeps it on the down low."

"Tip—"

"Where it needs to stay. Mel knows what she's doing where they're concerned. It is not up to us to second-guess her."

"What about The Others? What do they say?"

"The same. Look, Echo, I know you want to jump in there and save the world, but that's not how it works. You're going to have to cool your jets on this one."

"I don't see that happening, Tip. This is personal."

"No, it isn't, and the fastest way to find your way back in the bayou is to step over that line."

"What line? What do they want with us?"

"Genesys believes if they can isolate the gene responsible for our powers, they can find a way to replicate that code."

"You're talking about cloning."

"I'm talking about more than that. Cloning is just the beginning. Designer babies have nothing over the direction Genesys is heading."

I watched as Cooper struggled to roll over. "That's a frightening thought."

"Yes, it is. If you think cloning is in the far future, you're wrong. Every country with a test tube is trying to be the first to figure us out. We're not only in the future, we *are* the future. For every Genesys in the U.S., there are a dozen more in other countries."

My mind was reeling at the possibilities.

"It would be worse than a nightmare. It's what they've been trying to do for decades. The problem is not many of us live through the Genesys experimentation. We're not sure what it is that causes our minds and bodies to crash and burn, but we do know many do not make it out alive—or sane. The fact that we got to you before they did was the luck of the draw. Had you gone to any other psych ward, we may not have gotten to you in time."

"So, they have spotters too."

"Oh yeah. Only *theirs* make a living gathering up those who wouldn't be missed. Like us, they have people who scour newspapers all across the country looking for anomalies that might point them in the direction of another super. Like you for example. The way you apparently went nuts and clobbered Todd over the head with your math book for no apparent reason would be one such anomaly. They read the clipping, do some digging, and find out if the target is an orphan or has a familial situation ripe for the picking. This red flags them because taking a kid who won't be missed is much easier. They do their homework and then send a collector."

"Is this…" I couldn't bring myself to even say it.

"Why some of the kids in the U.S. disappear? I'd be lying if I said no. Genesys has no ethical code. If they suspect you have powers, they go for it. They don't care who you are or where you came from."

"And they're too powerful to shut down?"

"Absolutely."

"What's The Others' stance on this?"

"They want to save as many as we can, but not at the cost of the rest. Long ago, even before Melika, it was decided our stance would be one of peaceful resistance. We do what we can, but we stay out of their way. Let me repeat that: *we stay out of their way.* That means no digging, no stories, no dirt, nothing. You got me?"

I ignored her question. "Why didn't Melika tell me this all those years ago? Why is it such a big secret? Shouldn't we *know*?"

"Back in the day, she used to, but that knowledge made her students paranoid and suspicious. Some started living in a fearful state and it wasn't healthy. She decided nothing good came of knowing. The younger boys all want to pull a Rambo and go postal, and that would be a grave mistake. Now Mel only talks about the Project if it becomes an issue for us."

"So you've had run-ins with them before."

"Yeah, and it wasn't pretty. I hate that group with every fiber in my being, and the last guy who crossed paths with me…well… he's pretty much a vegetable now, but The Others had to do some real cleanup to make that go away."

"If they know you exist, why don't they come get you?"

"Because they can't control me. Don't you get it? That's why they use children. They need weaklings they can promise the world to, not a six-foot Indian who can fry their brains. That's our advantage: they have no idea how to stop us from using our powers. They are only interested in learning how to *create* our powers, not how to control them."

I nodded, thinking back to my lessons with Melika. "That's why Mel taught us layers and layers of firewalls, isn't it? It wasn't just to keep us from reading each other; it was to keep *us* from being read by *them*."

"Bingo. We don't want them gaining access to the rest of us, but I'm telling you, they're not interested in us. We are too hard to handle. Unless they design cells capable of holding us, we're too much of a risk. No, these assholes prefer to prey on the little ones—the ones with no training."

I started pacing and decided on a change of tactic. "Did you know about my parents?"

"No." Her answer was swift in coming. "I know nothing other than what you've shared with me, which wasn't much. How you holding up?"

"I found my mother today."

The pause told me she already knew, so I continued. "She told me Malecon worked for Genesys."

Another pause. "He did. He was their very first super who had the strength they had been searching for. They had had two others before him, but they weren't like us."

"What happened?"

"No one knows for sure. One day, he was their ace in the hole. The next, he vanished. Mel hadn't seen him in nearly ten years, and when he finally resurfaced, she managed to lock him down before he could hurt anybody."

"Until Katrina."

"Right."

"And no one knows what he was doing all that time?"

"Honestly, I don't think anyone cared. He was no longer a pawn for the group so fewer and fewer kids were being taken in by Genesys. Who knows what happened? Maybe he got tired of being a human pin cushion. Maybe he got bored. Whatever the case, he got out and in a few days, vanished. Melika heard from him a few times via postcards from Europe, but that was it. Once she saw him, she realized whatever they had done to him had made him crazy, so she locked him up."

"She thinks Genesys is the reason he's insane?"

"Yeah. She won't talk about it, but I get the feeling she has always blamed them for his lapse into the world of nutcases."

Cooper was struggling to sit up, and the pit bull emitted a low, threatening growl.

"Do you think he went mad?"

"I do. His power was too off-balance. It isn't just the power he had when he was born. It was augmented somehow. Now, I hate to bring you back into the real world, but is Bailey bringing in that kid in this century or what?"

"Yeah. Yeah she is. It might have helped if we knew what he was running from. He is definitely on the run. Bailey will be bringing him in shortly. We've got him pretty wrapped up. He's not going anywhere."

"Good. What about you? You okay? I know this must be a shock to you about your family. You want me to come to you? I can be there in a—"

"No. No, I'm okay. Dani's with me. It's going to take a while to sink in, but right now, I'm just a bundle of emotions I need to sort out. Thanks for being there for me, Tip...you know...with my family and all. I...I needed you more than you may have realized."

"Oh, I realize it, love. It's what we do. I'm here if you need me. Always."

Quickly hanging up, I knelt in front of Cooper. He was more docile than when I knocked him out—a testimony to Bailey's concoction. "Hey there," I said, offering him my best grin. He glared at me through groggy eyes. "You're running from Genesys, aren't you?"

His anger toward me diminished slightly. My phone rang, I ignored it. I knew it was Tip calling me back. "Genesys had you, didn't they?" Again, I felt his anger lessen and there was less hostility in his eyes. "I don't blame you for not trusting anyone, but everything Bailey has told you is the truth. We're the good guys. We're on your side. If you let us, we can get you to a safe place away from them, where they will never find you. You can learn how to control your powers. Learn more about what's happening to you." I reached over to remove the gag. "Please don't yell, Cooper. It will only make the dog mad, and we don't want him to get mad, do we?" He shook his head. I knew by his energy he believed me so I removed the gag.

"I don't want to go anywhere safe, Miss..."

"Call me Echo." I felt his true emotions for the first time, and I smiled in understanding. "Oh. I see. This is about a *girl*."

He looked away. "Fuck no."

"You can't lie to an empath, Cooper. That's what I am. I know it's about a girl. They have her, don't they? That's why you don't want to go to where it's safe. You want to go to where *she* is."

He nodded reluctantly, still not looking at me. I could tell he was trying not to cry.

"And that's why you went back to San Jose, isn't it? You went back for her, didn't you? What's there, Cooper? A Genesys Project?"

He turned back to me, eyes flashing anger once more. "And I would have gotten to her too, if you assholes didn't—"

The dog growled.

I held up my finger. "Careful. The dog doesn't like cussing. You think you can find your way back there?"

Anger gone once more. "Yeah." Cooper sat erect, proud. Challenging.

I nodded, feeling the tingle at the back of my neck. I did not respond to Tip's knock. "Turn around and let me get those off you."

His eyes grew wide. "What about Bailey? That bi—"

I glared a warning, stopping him in mid-word. "She's a good one. She's someone you always want on your side, and believe it or not, she is. *We* are. I'll prove it to you by cutting the cable ties, but if you use your powers in any way, either Buster or I will bring you down, and that's gonna hurt one way or the other. Are we clear?"

He nodded, his eyes shifting from me to Buster as he tried to decided which would hurt more.

Just as I cut his cable ties, in walked Bailey with a pizza box in her hands. "What are you doing, E?"

"I'm letting him go."

"Why?" She set the box on the table and bent over to pet the dog. "Not a good idea."

"Because he's going to take us back."

"Back? Back where?"

"To Genesys."

The three of us, plus Buster the dog, were up at dawn and finished with coffee and breakfast by seven. Danica had brought coffee and doughnuts and had roused the boys from their office bunk beds at six thirty. They'd worked all night gathering information on the Genesys Project. Their first report wasn't great—they came up with very little we could use. They had stock information, base of operations, the CEOs for the last two decades and where the money went, but nothing indicating anything about paranormal activity. As far as the public knew, Genesys was a company searching for cures for cancer and other terminal illnesses.

My comment was, "Shit."

"They're deep underground, Princess," Roger said, "but that just means we dig deeper."

Once I filled Danica in on all I knew, we agreed to meet Delta and Connie at For Yours Eyes Only, Delta's detective agency.

In the meantime, I outlined everything Cooper had told us. He had spent all of breakfast telling us what he remembered of the warehouse complex being used as a temporary lab for the Genesys Project. There were rows of warehouses out in the unincorporated part of San Jose and Genesys had renovated them into makeshift labs. It was there they had taken Cooper after one of their spotters located him.

A runaway from Los Angeles, he was the perfect candidate for a lab rat. His father was in jail and his mother was a crack whore, and he ran away from a foster home the moment his powers kicked in. Genesys snagged him outside Bakersfield and took him to a place everyone referred to as The Farm. It was at The Farm where he met his girlfriend, Eve, a clairvoyant who had been caught in Vegas. Eve's father knew she had some kind of special gift and he used her to help make him money on the Strip, but her father owed the wrong people lots of money, and he got a one-way ticket to the desert for his troubles. Eve managed to get away, but not before a collector grabbed her. Eve was sixteen and Cooper was only fourteen, but they managed to find each other at The Farm. She helped him escape when she *saw* an unlocked door on the side in one of her visions. She did not see herself making the same getaway as Cooper did, so she begged him to leave and return with help.

Cooper had tried shaking any tails by coming to the city. He had even gone to all three airports in the Bay Area hoping to throw off the scent. His plan was to backtrack to The Farm and free Eve himself. He didn't know how he'd go about it, but he was determined to free her.

And I was determined to help him.

As we all filed out of the house, Buster emitted a low growl stopping us all in our tracks. At the bottom of the stairs stood a scruffy-looking woman in an oversized army jacket, a beanie and dark glasses. Raising my arms, I was about to throw out a blast of energy when Buster charged ahead. Bailey stopped her halfway down the stairs. The woman, who I had already discovered posed no threat to us, threw her hands up in surrender.

"Hey! Whoa! It's me! Echo, it's me!"

Me turned out to be Finn. Undercover Finn.

"Crap," I muttered to Bailey. "Not now."

"Talk to her, E. I'll get Cooper and Buster situated in the car. Take your time." She said hi to Finn on her way past her, and Finn gave Buster a wide berth. I went down the stairs and hugged Finn, who smelled of stale cigarette smoke and old beer.

"Ugh. You need a bath," I said, backing away.

"Good to see you too."

Her eyes had dark circles underneath and her energy was sagging and tired. "What are you doing here?"

She took off her beanie. Her hair was unkempt and dirty. I'd never seen her look so bad. "Not quite the welcome I was expecting."

"I'm sorry, Finn. It's just—"

She nodded, eyes softening. "You're busy. I can see that."

We stood in awkward silence.

"If it isn't one thing, it's another," she said softly. "Maybe this was a bad idea. I should have called."

I had to turn away, she smelled so bad. "No. Really. It's fine."

I stepped closer, ignoring the stale smoke smell. "So. This is what undercover looks like?"

"Yeah. Not pretty, but neither are the people I'm hanging out with. I can't really talk about it. Where are you off to so early in the morning? And who was that kid?"

I decided to answer only the first question. "Delta and Connie's office. We hired them to help find my parents."

"Oh." I read her hurt and disappointment. We had both been so busy, I hadn't had time to tell her what was going on with my life—as if I could. I'm sure she felt out of the loop. If there even was a loop, I'm not sure either of us were on it.

"Well, if I know Delta Stevens, she'll find them."

I nodded, Finn's hurt and angst tapping aggressively on my mental shields. "She did. Yesterday." As if that somehow explained why it was I hadn't called *her* with the most important news of my life.

"Good for you." Her disappointment was palpable through my shields.

"How's the undercover going?"

She shrugged, clearly wishing she hadn't come. "Inches of progress. These things take time to set up."

In other words, she couldn't tell me. So, here we were, once again, two people shrouded in secrecy, talking around the truth, sharing just enough to get by, and not enough to get through to each other. It was ridiculous, but I didn't have the time or the energy to really deal with it right now; not a good sign in any relationship.

"Who's the boy?" Typical cop perseverance and inquisitiveness in place of genuine concern.

"Bailey's nephew," I said, lying as easily as telling the truth. "I'm really sorry, Finn, but now is just not a good time. I have to get going."

She studied my eyes. "When can we hook up?" Slight irritation in her voice, her sadness transforming into something closer to anger now.

I looked up at her. "Hook. Up?"

She sighed, running her hand through her greasy hair. Undercover certainly did not mean under the showerhead. "Sorry.

Too much street lingo, if you know what I mean. Call me with some times that'll work for you for dinner and I'll do my best to get the night off. I'd really like to get cleaned up for a real date."

I forced a grin I didn't feel. "I'd like that." Stepping up to her, I kissed her cheek. "I'll leave a message on your cell." Hurrying past her, I jumped into Ladybug, who had never been this full since I owned her.

"That was fast," Bailey said.

"Too much to say, not enough time to say it."

"Two ships passing?"

Before I could answer, Cooper piped up. "If that's your girlfriend, you can do better."

I didn't say anything.

"She's not really her girlfriend," Bailey answered for me. "They're just hanging out."

"Cool. Well, don't get too involved, 'cause that chick reeked. Big time."

It took me a moment to respond. "She just smells like smoke."

Cooper shook his head. "You oughtta dump the greaseball. Besides, aren't you and this one over here tapping it?"

When Cooper slumped in his seat, Bailey stared at me. "Did you just knock that kid out?"

Gripping the steering wheel harder, I nodded. "Tap tap."

She and Danica laughed all the way to San Jose.

"How did it go?" Delta asked, opening the door to a small office filled with three desks and lots of electronic equipment. It looked like controlled chaos. Maps covered every wall, a large Xerox machine hunkered in the corner, and a worn speed boxing bag hung in the opposite corner.

"Well, the big news is I have a sister who needs to be tracked down. Do whatever you need to do, use whatever resources you have, but please help me find my little sister."

They scattered to their computers, fingers poised on the keyboards awaiting my directions. "Give us everything you have," Connie said. "Names, numbers, addresses, anything. We'll be all over it."

"As soon as we patch into the Bat Cave," Danica said, hooking up her vidbook to the largest monitor in the room. Instantly, all three boys' faces appeared on the screen.

I gave them everything I had so far, which wasn't much.

"I think that's good for now," Delta said. Connie's fingers had been skimming across the keyboards the entire time I spoke; she never paused or asked me to slow down. It was amazing.

"What do you think?" Danica asked, stepping behind Connie. I had to hand it to her; I would never have known they had slept together. They spoke in a businesslike manner with no lingering looks or outward signs of attraction.

Connie took her fingers off the keyboards and turned to me. "It won't be easy. I won't kid you. Even with your boys, there are just too many unknowns. What name did she travel under? Did they ever get new passports? Where did they really go? How long did they stay in each location? Was there really even a Svetlana? Even if we could go to Russia or China or Peru, which we wouldn't, but even if we did, we don't even have a photo to show. We've got a whole lotta nothing."

My hopes sank. "I understand."

"But." Connie looked at me, eyes afire. I could practically feel her intensity seeping through my walls. "This sort of thing is right up our alley, Echo. Storm and I love a good challenge, and this one will test our limits. We won't give you false hope or promise something we can't deliver, but we *will* give it everything we have."

Danica came over to me and put her hand on my shoulder: her signal for me to read the room, including her. Long ago, when I first came out to her, I promised I wouldn't read her without her consent. It was an enormous violation to use one's powers for personal gain, and though she never made me keep that promise, it was something I had to do for me and our friendship. And after being in a relationship with Tip, who came and went as she pleased in the corners of my mind, I was resolved to maintain that distance between me and Danica.

But now, she wanted me to read both these women whom we had come to trust and respect. Lowering my shields, I wondered what it was I was looking for.

When my shields are lowered, emotions hit me in the form of heat and color, like the heat rising off pavement. The stronger the emotions, the brighter and hotter the wave washes over me. There were some big emotions coming through loud and clear. From Connie I read an excitement of the challenge, and the sort of frenetic energy athletes get prior to a competition. She was eager to see if she could pull this off.

Delta's emotions were a bit more subdued and dubious. She was unsure—hesitant. She didn't want to disappoint me because...because she really liked us. No...wait...not so much *us*, as it was Danica. There was a feeling of gratitude toward Danica.

Gratitude?

I wondered what that was about. Was it because Danica had helped Connie move beyond the pain of her loss? Whatever the reason, Delta held Danica in higher regard than I knew and was willing to move mountains to assist her in any way she could.

How many loops was I out of?

Trying to find that answer, I read Danica. She believed in these two women with a faith she usually reserved for machines. I knew now why she wanted me to read the room. She wanted me to see just how strongly *she* believed in *them*. She wanted me to go for it, regardless of the cost. She wanted... Looking up, I realized there was more to her feelings about Connie than she would admit. The wave hitting me was soft white and warm. Her feelings for Connie wrapped me like a down comforter. This was more than a night's romp in the hay. Danica knew I would see this, but she cared more about me finding my family than trying to hide her true feelings. She wanted me to put my faith in them, too, even at the risk of seeing how she truly felt. It wasn't love; I would have pinpointed that in a nanosecond. This was something else—something between love and lust.

Then there was Bailey, who wanted nothing more than to help me find myself.

And there was something else: a loyalty to me etched deep within her.

"Let's do it."

The room let out a collective sigh.

"Okay," Connie said, looking over at Cooper as if seeing him for the first time. "Who's the kid?"

That proved to be a stickier wicket. "He escaped from Genesys. Cooper got out and went back to get his girlfriend. We're taking care of him until we can get his girl back."

Connie eyed me with a suspicion only an empath could feel. "Escaped. Interesting choice of words. Apparently, there's more to this than what you've let on. So let's make sure we're all on the same page here. We're trying to locate two females, one you're related to. And what else? What aren't you telling us?"

I swallowed hard. "A lot. I wish I could, but I can't."

Delta and Connie looked at each other. "We're okay with that. If you want our help with that as well, you've come to the right place. We're a full-service PI agency."

Delta motioned for Cooper to sit with Connie. "At the very least, let us get you wherever you need to go safely."

"What do you mean?"

"Well, you're planning on returning to this Genesys place, right? Give us an hour with Cooper and we can get a lay of the land; see where you're going, what you need to look out for; entrances, exits, danger zones, those sort of things. Con can create a blueprint out of his words. At least you'll know exactly where you're going."

"The sort of thing we're really good at," Connie added. "We'd feel a lot better sending you into some fanatical compound knowing you were armed with good intel."

I nodded. "Good intel. Okay. Good start." I looked at Cooper, who was now sitting next to Connie. "Coop? You okay with this?"

He nodded. "I just want to get Eve out of there before they do something bad to her."

Delta and Connie kicked into high gear, dividing jobs up between themselves and the boys. "We'll pull up everything we can on this Genesys. Dig deep. See who funds them, who backs them. We'll come up with blueprints, topo maps, the whole nine yards."

"Mind if I stay with Cooper?" Danica asked. "The dog and I might be the best way to make sure he doesn't act up or do something stupid."

She was right. It was wise for one of us to stay in case Cooper got carried away and told them more than we wanted them to know, so I gave her the green light.

When Bailey and I got in Ladybug, we were without Cooper, Buster and Danica. "Where to?" Bailey asked, buckling up.

"Golden Gate Park."

"No kidding? For a minute there, I was beginning to think you never take a moment to relax."

I grinned and shook my head. "Actually, I don't. We're going to see Shirley."

"Why?"

"You'll see."

When we got to the park, Cotton and Midnight ran up to Bailey, and Shirley waved one of her multicolored fingerless gloves at us. "If it isn't our vet! Hidee-ho ladies!"

"It's a good day," I whispered to Bailey.

She knelt down and reached into her pocket to pull out doggie treats. "Hey there, kids. How is everyone today?"

"They love you," Shirley announced, grinning. It was a really good day. "How are my kids? Do they feel healthy today, Bailey?"

Bailey rose. "Yes, ma'am, they're good as gold. You take good care of them, Shirley."

"I try." She patted the bench and had me sit down. It was a beautiful, fog-free day in the city by the Bay. "What's on your mind, Echo? It may be an up moment, but it's just that: a moment."

I nodded. "When you're having a bad day, you tend to rant and rave about the CIA and the government coming after you. I used to think you were just delusional and maybe a bit paranoid, but I'm beginning to think there's more to it than that. What can you tell me about the Genesys Project?"

Shirley's mouth dropped open. "Those bastards still exist?" She got that faraway look of someone remembering. "I should have known. Dirt like that never goes away, just creeps under the carpet."

"What happened, Shirley?"

It took her a moment to come back to us. "They came for me like some force, but they were just scumbags mugging an old homeless person. They were foolish in thinking I was defenseless or that I would willingly go like a lamb to the slaughter. Oh no. Not me." Shirley rose and faced us. "There were three of them. Ha! Send three of your henchmen for a bag of used bones? Made me sick, they did, all high and mighty."

"What did they say to you? Do you remember?"

"Of course I remember. They woke me up and asked me if I wanted to live in a nice, clean place and have three squares a day and all the medical attention I needed. I told them I ate just fine and didn't need medical help."

"I'm guessing they didn't take no for an answer."

"Not a chance. They didn't understand that being out here is a *choice*. I told them as much, and then realized that going with them wasn't a choice. They started to hem me in. I don't do so well when I'm cornered."

"What did you do?" Bailey rose and sat on the bench.

"I'd been on the street for half a dozen years when they came the first time. Better men than they have tried to mug me before and barely lived to talk about it. I did what I always do; I took out an eye."

Bailey covered her mouth. "No."

"Oh yes. Took it out with a fountain pen, I did. Kid screamed like a wild banshee. Blood was everywhere, but people came running when he started howling."

"He was howling?"

"Like a wounded animal, and when they started scrambling, I drove that same pen into the neck of another and then took off running. The one who wasn't bleeding made a grab at me, but old Midnight leapt on his back and sank her fangs into his neck. I escaped unscathed."

Bailey clapped.

"Did they ever come back?"

"Oh yes. Only this time, they sent a young, cocky woman to talk with me. Nice young thing. Pretty. Slightly better mannered than the three thugs who limped out of here holding an eyeball in their hand." Shirley shook her head. "That's when I got Cotton; to keep assholes like them away from me."

"What did the girl want?"

"Same thing. Said I was a great fortune teller and that they would take good care of me."

"In exchange for what? What did they want?"

"What else? My cooperation. They knew I had the sight. They wanted to use it, to use me. I wasn't playing."

"What else did she say?"

"She wanted to know if I knew others like myself. I told her it was rude to ask a question she knew I wouldn't answer."

"Was she one of us?"

"Nope. They actually sent a natural." She chuckled. "Can you believe that? A natural! I explained in plain English that the next folks they sent to me would be sent back in body bags. I told them I might be old, but I wasn't feeble. She got my meaning and they haven't been back since."

"You're certain they never came back?"

"Oh, they watched me for a few months, but after that, they didn't send any more after me."

"How do you know they were from Genesys?"

"How else? I saw it. The young woman, silly thing that she was, gave me a bland business card and I used it for scrying. I saw their nest, their sign, their business. I saw more than they would ever have wanted me to see; more than I cared to see, truthfully. I decided then and there that I'd rather die than let those fuckers get to me."

I inched closer. "When you saw things, is there anything you saw that might keep me safe if I were to…engage with them?"

Shirley slowly turned to me, one of her scarves falling off her shoulder. "Engage with them? Honey, these are not people you want to do *anything* with. That would be a needlessly foolish thing to do. No, no, you need to forget whatever you're thinking about doing, Echo. Those people are dangerous. What's the matter with you? Didn't you get enough fight in New Orleans?"

"It's not that."

"No? It's a fool's mission, my dear. Whatever you're thinking about doing, let it go. This time, let it go. They have the backing of powerful folks."

Bailey rose and I rose with her. "You don't think we have enough power?"

Shirley shook her head. "I don't know if anyone does, Shaman." She turned to me. "I like you, Echo. You're one of the good ones on God's green earth. This world needs you. There will always be groups like them. They're like crack houses. One goes down, three more pop up. We're a hot commodity, and someone is paying big bucks to get us. Live your life, and let this alone."

Bailey said goodbye to the animals and I hugged Shirley and thanked her.

"Whatever you're chasing, Echo...isn't worth it. You must believe me when I tell you that it isn't worth it."

I nodded. "Maybe not, but I guess this is something I need to find out on my own."

Shirley shook her head. "Youth is so impetuous." She smiled and shook her head. "I can tell you plan on going anyway. If you go, take help...lots of it. You got good help?"

I nodded. "I've got really good help."

"Thank God, because you are going to need it."

We got back to Delta and Connie's office almost two hours later. Danica and Cooper had slipped out to get a bite to eat. Like all teenage boys, he was a bottomless pit, and was eating us out of house and home.

"Quite an interesting little project you plan on attempting, Echo," Delta said, pulling out a chair for me. "Danica's boys came up with some enlightening pieces about the company. I have to say I am impressed...impressed and a...well...a little scared for you."

Connie had multiple windows opened on three different

laptops. All three laptops had information regarding Genesys. "Company's been in business since nineteen fifty-two, when it was originally looking for ways to genetically modify beef cows."

"Ah...that explains why they're based in Texas."

Connie nodded. "They were well ahead of their time, that's for sure, and we have multiple reports indicating successful cloning long before Dolly the sheep was cloned."

"And they hid it?"

"Hell yeah they hid it. These people aren't connected to the science community. These folks are scientists working to further government projects for warfare. The boys had to go places reserved for hackers to get that intel. They're very good."

Danica nodded. "Yes they are. The best money can buy."

Delta came up behind me. "Which means, in shorthand, that you are attempting to go somewhere and do something not even Connie and I would attempt; at least, not without a really solid game plan." She grinned. "And some of our best friends."

Connie nodded as she tied her hair behind her in a ponytail. "If you were to get caught..." She shook her head. "This is a really bad idea, Echo. People like them make people like you disappear all the time."

I whirled around. "What do you mean, *people like me*?"

Connie cocked her head. "Reporters. What did you *think* I meant?"

"Oh. Yeah. Reporters."

"People like Karen Silkwood, Don Ramon, Cass Sherwood. Whistle-blowers. People who would embarrass the government or big business too much have a way of vanishing."

"But Cooper's girlfriend..."

Delta held up her hand. "If you want our help, which I strongly suggest you do, you'll need to be straight up with us because you are so far out of your league, this will only end badly for you if you try this without taking proper backup."

Connie nodded. "So...you want to come clean? We can't help you unless we know exactly what it is we're up against. Are you comfortable telling us as much as you can?"

I looked at them, wishing like hell I could just blurt out the truth, but I couldn't. "If only I could tell you the whole truth, but I can't. I'm really sorry." I started to get up, but Delta's hand on my shoulder stopped me.

"That doesn't mean we won't help you. It's just...we'll need to bring in more help. There are certain people we know who can do certain things better than either Con or myself. Will that work?"

I nodded. "That would be great. Thank you for not pressing the matter. I'd like to explain it all, but sometimes they're just not our stories to tell."

"And we understand that," Delta whispered. "More than you know. If we're gonna put our asses on the line, you need to be as straight up with us as you can. Tell us as much as you are comfortable telling us. We'll piece it together as best we can. Sound good?"

I nodded. I couldn't tell them the truth, yet I needed their help. "You'll be with us from here on out. Trust me on this, you'll be observing everything you need to know."

Connie scooted closer. "Okay. Here's what we know. We have the general location of The Farm. Based on Cooper's marvelous recollections, we've been able to pinpoint a block of warehouses they're using."

"A block?"

"Oh yes. This is a big operation. Huge. The boys are working on getting the data for electricity usage in a fifty-mile radius from where the warehouses are located. One look at that usage grid and we'll know whether or not those are the warehouses we're looking for. We're pretty sure they are, but the usage grid will let us know for sure."

I nodded.

"Once we have the physical location, we'll go satellite and get topography of the area; hills, gulleys, trees, et cetera. After that, it's just a matter of zooming in on their security system, the mainframe, and what we need to do in order to get closer without being detected."

"How will we do that?"

"As you've seen with The Echo, your namesake," Delta interjected, "Con can get around just about any security system ever made. With us and the boys, we should be able to get this party started from the inside out."

"You're going to break in first?"

"Oh no. Not us. *We* don't do breaking and entering anymore. To get in and out of a facility like this will take an expert—a professional thief as it were—someone who can get in and out undetected."

"And I suppose you know one of those."

"No, we don't know *one* of those. We know the *best* one of those, and she'll be arriving tomorrow."

When we were finally all ensconced back in Danica's estate, it was almost eight o'clock. We had spent the day doing various errands for Connie and Delta, getting them supplies needed for the job. I had to stop by the office and produce a story, and Danica had to check up on the boys and throw food at them so they wouldn't starve. Once we got there, Danica spent an hour showing Cooper around her palatial home, gave him a soda and an Almond Joy, and let him go wander around her place while she made the rest of us coffee and waited for her files to print.

"I'd like him to go over everything with us one last time," Danica said, pulling out a notepad. "He needs to be precise. We can't send our people out in uncertainty."

I took a cup of coffee and inhaled the aroma. "People? Or are you concerned with one person in particular?"

When Cooper re-entered the enormous family room, his soda was gone and he was finishing his candy bar. "I suppose you want to go over it all one more time," he said, flouncing down on the couch. "We need to get a move on. Eve needs help."

I leaned forward. "Good people are willing to put themselves in danger to help you. We want those good people to have all the facts so they can come home in one piece, so pay attention."

Cooper reached out and played with Buster's ears. "Okay. Sorry."

I leaned back and let Danica take over. She consulted her

notes before kicking one of his dirty sneakers. "Sit up."

Cooper shot up and mumbled a half-hearted apology.

"So, you were approached by three guys…"

"Who wanted to know more about my special talents. Said I could be on TV."

"Is that what he called your abilities? Special *talents*?"

"Yeah. They wanted to know if I could teach them how I do it. It was a dumb thing to do, but I needed the money and they seemed cool at the time."

Delta looked at each one of us, her eyes boring into us. She was trying to figure out what we were talking about, but said nothing.

"And they took you straight to The Farm."

He nodded. "They said they needed to do things on the down low so their new TV show didn't get scooped by another station. I bought the whole stupid line. So did Eve."

"Keep going. We'll stop if we have any questions."

"So they take me to this warehouse, which looks like old rundown barns on the outside, but the inside is like something from a sci-fi flick. Floors are all white and there are labs everywhere. They took me down this long hallway to a dorm room, only without windows. They show me how to use the clicker for the TV. The room is nice, the bed was more comfortable than anything I'd slept in, in a long time. I fell asleep and didn't wake up till morning. They came in, took blood and showed me to this small cafeteria. They explained to me what they wanted to do."

"Dog and pony show?"

He nodded. "They wanted me to show them what I could do, so they started me through my paces in this other lab. I did shit for them all day, and by the end, I was beat. I kept asking what this had to do with a TV show and they said they needed to make sure I was the real deal." He shrugged. "It sounded real until I met Eve in the cafeteria. She told me this wasn't anything like I thought it was and I needed to get out if I ever had the chance. We didn't have much time to spend together, only a few hours here and there over a couple of days, and then she told me I had to get out. She told me what door would be unlocked and then I promised her I'd come back for her. We met a few times when we thought it was just the two of us, but that was before we realized they were watching everything we did."

"Cameras?"

He nodded. "Like I told Connie, there are cameras everywhere except in dorm rooms."

"Are you sure?"

"Yeah. It's not like the cameras are hidden. They're not. The dorm rooms are dead simple, all white with nothing but a bed, a nightstand and a TV. No cameras. I'm sure of it."

Danica consulted her notes. "And you said the hallways are camera-free as well?"

He nodded. "Cameras are mostly in the labs."

My shields were lowered for any signs of dishonesty. He was telling the truth. The more I watched him, the more I liked him. With shoulder-length curly brown hair and blue eyes, he would normally be the boy that teenage girls swooned over in high school. He had the Peter Brady kind of looks that made you think of wholesome and clean.

"They came in once when I was sleeping, and I was so scared, I blasted both guys against the wall. Broke one guy's collarbone."

"You think it was a test?"

"Unless they were looking for the tooth fairy, yeah."

Danica grinned slightly. She liked him too. "Anything else?"

"Weird things like...once someone chucked a fork at me in the dining hall. I..." He stopped and looked at Delta before continuing. "I sent it back. Lucky it missed him 'cause I have zero control over this shit, but they were always doing crap like that."

"You said earlier they tested you?"

He nodded. "Yeah, they brought in Eve to see if we could read each other's minds. We couldn't. They were really bummed about that. One day, this super prick named Reynolds got all uptight and yelled we weren't trying hard enough. That guy treated us the worst. A real wanker, that dude was."

"And this is how you and Eve got to know each other?"

"Yeah. They had us wired up to electrodes and shit all day. She really hated that. It...I think it hurt her, but she never complained. I just kept talking to her so she wouldn't feel it as bad."

"When did you realize you weren't really going on television?"

"About ten days in. I mentioned to Reynolds that my brother might be missing me and I wanted to see him. Reynolds told me I didn't have a brother and I could walk away any time, but they would have to cancel my contract, which, he added, would be about half a million a year."

"So why didn't you go?"

"They started amping up on Eve. The last time I saw her, she was so doped up she barely knew her own name. That's when I knew I had to get us the hell out of there and do something before they killed her."

"Why did they drug her?" Delta asked.

He shrugged. "No idea. All I know is she made her way to me one evening to tell me about the unlocked door and that she would create a diversion so I could get out."

"And she did."

Cooper nodded, looking back at the memory. "At first, I didn't think the diversion was her, because she didn't have those kind of...skills."

Danica and I looked at each other. "What kind?"

"Electrical kind. I'd never seen that before."

I nodded. "That was when you realized there was more than just the two of you in there."

"Yeah. The lights started flickering and shit, and this kid..." Cooper shook his head in amazement. "He seemed to be...like... controlling all of the electricity in the place. I mean, he wasn't afraid at all, but he should have been. That was a lot of power."

"How come you never saw him before that?"

"I don't really know, but I saw him that night. Said his name was Pedro, but that was all he had time to say."

"And you think he used his powers to shut down the entire electrical system?"

"Every light in the place flickered and then went dead. If I hadn't been near the door, I would never have found it because every single light went off. Pedro managed to shut it all down."

Danica shifted in her seat. "Tell us about the door again."

"It led down a hallway that opened to the side of the building. It was unlocked, just like Eve said. So I opened it and hightailed it out of there. I knew they'd start looking for me along the gravel road that leads to the warehouses, so I took to the hills. I got about halfway up the hill when I heard the dogs. I couldn't fucking...oh...sorry...I couldn't believe they were coming after me with dogs! That was when I knew whatever this was, it wasn't about Hollywood."

"And how did you get away?"

"I got to a ranch or a farm of some sort and hotwired a motorcycle. I rode that thing across the hills until I came to a road. And I was off. I finally ditched it to be safe."

Danica turned the questions over to me. "When did you see them again?" I asked.

"In a mall. I saw them coming up the escalators. No way they could have tailed me, so I figured I musta been wearing some sorta tracking device."

I smiled. Smart boy.

"I got out of the mall and headed toward a bunch of homeless kids my age. I told a girl I'd give her five bucks if she could find something on me that looked like it didn't belong. At first, she thought I was some kinda perv, but when I told her she could have a friend stand there while she looked me over, she said fine, but it would cost me twenty. That nearly wiped me out, but I knew I had to get that thing outta me."

"Where was it?"

"In the middle of my back, in a perfect location that kept me from reaching it."

"How did they get it out?"

"They didn't. I decided to use it to make them think I was moving away from The Farm."

"Risky."

He ran his hands through his hair. "I owed it to Eve to be smart, to throw them off track. I couldn't go to the cops because I already have a record and with a wild story like this, they'd toss my ass in a padded cell. I couldn't find my way back yet because the way I left was very different than the way I got in."

"Yet, you still planned on going back."

"I had planned on going to the airport and seeing if I could get someone to get it out of me, then I was going back to San Jose."

"That's when you saw us."

"Yeah. You guys came too close a bunch of times, so I went into a tattoo parlor to see if they could get it out."

"And they did."

"Yep. Pulled that mother out with needle-nose pliers. The dude was so stoked, he let me get a small tattoo for free."

"What did you get?" Bailey asked.

Cooper stood up and lifted his shirt. He showed us a small Chinese character. "It means freedom."

Bailey got up and lightly ran her fingers over it. "Hurts there on the bone, huh?"

"Like hell, but I didn't care, as long as that thing was gone."

"What did you do with it?"

He grinned. "The tattoo guys dropped it in the bag of a girl they knew was traveling to Canada. We all had a good laugh over that one."

Cooper yawned and I realized he was probably exhausted. "Okay, kiddo," I said. "That's good enough for today. You've done really well."

Danica rose. "Come on. You'll sleep like a baby in my guest quarters."

"Can Buster come?"

Danica deferred to Bailey, who nodded.

"Just remember our deal. Failure or success, you're going where someone can help you learn how to control your...skills."

Once Danica got him all situated, the three of us made ourselves comfortable and she poured us all a Baileys on the rocks.

"Well?" Danica said, folding her long legs beneath her.

"Suicide mission," Bailey said. "Odds are totally against us." She paused, rubbing her hands together. "Sounds like fun to me."

"Don't you guys need to get Mel to sign off on this or

something?" Danica inquired. "She's gonna be pissed when she finds out."

"Like that would ever happen," Bailey replied. "Look, for all we know, E's sister could be basking in San Tropez, but she'll never rest until she knows for sure those bastards don't have her."

I nodded. "As it is, Mel will flip to know we've taken it this far, but I'm not backing down from this. Those people destroyed my family. If they have or if they had my sister, maybe they'll know what happened to her. If not, at least I'll know where she isn't."

Just then, Danica's vidbook beeped and she opened it. "Don't you guys ever sleep?"

"You don't pay us to sleep, Boss." It was Roger. "You pay us to do illegal things and we come through without getting arrested. Is this a bad time?"

She chuckled. "No."

Danica rose and plugged the vidbook into the 72-inch screen HDTV hanging on the wall. Then we saw Roger's big head on the screen. He grinned and pushed his glasses back up the bridge of his nose.

"Hi there, Princess," he addressed me.

"Hi Rog."

"Another adventure, I see." Roger had a slight crush on me.

Bailey made a throat clearing noise, and so I made the introductions. "Roger, this is Bailey."

"Hey," he said, trying to sound cool. He turned back to Danica. "It took a lot of breeching and slithering, but we finally came up with a few undisclosed tidbits about Genesys."

Danica flipped on a recording device and stood in front of the screen. "Fire away."

"Their headquarters may be listed in Houston, but we found out where they *really* started. Are you ready for this? Area 51." He paused while we made the appropriate noises. "You may not know this, but the number refers to a six-by-ten mile block of land where an air base sits in Nevada. It was the site where the U-2 spy planes were first tested in the mid-fifties. The government won't talk about it anymore, and it's all super-secret spy stuff out there, but that's where Kip Reynolds got his start."

We all exchanged glances.

"Dr. Reynolds is the Dr. Frankenstein of our time. Before they cloned Dolly the sheep, Kip Reynolds was suspected of attempting to clone humans. Some reporter found out about it and then disappeared after the first article of what was to be a series. Reynolds was never a suspect, but according to a couple of conspiracy sites, he's currently doing experiments with so-called mutant genetics. You know how dumb those sites are. Sift through them and you'll find one tiny grain of truth. Anyway, a couple other sites have him listed as a scientist working for the Lawrence Lab in Livermore. We pulled up an employee roster and sure enough, there he was." Roger consulted his notes and when he looked up, pushed his black-rimmed glasses back up the bridge of his nose. "Doesn't prove anything, though. It's just a name on a list. Craig and Franklin went poking around at the mutant angle, just for kicks and giggles, but nothing much came of it. You know how they are with all that sci-fi crap. A few bloggers wrote about being abducted by Genesys, but those people are whack jobs, you know?"

"No doubt."

"Genesys made it big in the seventies with artificial skin for temporary healing of burn victims, and they print a lot of scholarly articles on genes and genetic mutations, but there's little other than that Area 51 piece to link them to any government agency."

"Isn't the lab a government facility?"

"Technically, it's part of UC Berkeley."

"So, we don't know if they're still in Nevada?"

"Nothing comes out of Nevada, Boss. We gave it a try. So did Connie, but we got zilch." Roger consulted his notes again. "Genesys has some patents pending, but that's about all we have on them."

"What about their firewalls?"

Roger's face went slack. "Sorry, Boss. We tried that too. We've been working nonstop, but it's heavily encrypted and secure. It would take months. The only way to get to that is from the inside. We've done about all we can from here." He paused. "That's the thing bothering Connie and us the most. It's too secure, know what I mean? We can get into the FBI data banks, but Genesys?" He shook his head.

I spoke up. "Can you send us the information from the bloggers who said they were abducted?"

"Seriously?"

I nodded. "We need to try out every angle."

"Will do, Princess. I'll send it over right now. I wish I had more. We all agree they're too heavily fortressed not to be government. We *did* find some interesting pieces on some legislation regarding what was termed *genetic rearrangement*. It passed during the Reagan administration. No one paid attention to it, of course, but a few million dollars goes into that fund annually until twenty-thirteen."

Bailey and I looked at each other. Genetic rearrangement sounded like a very scary something we needed to know more about.

"Send me a list of everyone who voted for it."

He nodded. "Already on your desk along with the bill authorizing genetic rearrangement. It reads like something out of *Star Wars*. In case you don't know, it's manipulating the DNA in creatures in order to create a superior species. Have you heard of a liger? A liger is the offspring of a male lion and female tiger."

"Wait." Danica turned and looked at Bailey, who was nodding. "Those species don't mate or interrelate sexually at all."

Bailey was now on her feet as Roger clicked on a slide of a striped lion.

"Tell that to the tigons—tiger males that mate with lion females. Or zorses or wolphins," Roger answered, changing slides as he spoke.

Bailey stepped right up to the TV and stared at the designer animals. Danica had to pull her back. "The camera is on the vidbook, Bailey, not the TV. He can't see you if you're that close."

Stepping back, Bailey said softly, "I've heard of those things, but I didn't think they really existed. I mean…what's the point?"

Nodding, Roger answered, "Hybrids occur when two species

are closely related enough for there to be a viable embryo. Hybrid cells have a mix of chromosomes from the parent species, hence, the ligons and others. There is no point…yet. Creating better farm animals was their excuse."

Bailey shuddered. "That makes my skin crawl. Men playing God."

Looking at Danica, Roger nodded for him to continue. "Hybrids may have a mix of chromosomes, but that's not the case with chimeras. That's when we go totally sci-fi." Roger changed the slide to show something I'd never seen before.

Bailey's hand went to her mouth. "Oh my God."

Roger continued. "The geep, a mix of goat and sheep embryos is more like two jigsaw pieces formed using identical cutters, but from two different puzzles. The completed puzzles will show both parts from both pictures."

I now realized what Genesys was really attempting to do, and my blood ran cold.

"Roger, is there anything about Genesys working with humans?"

"We looked for that, and other than the whacked websites, we came up empty. Not much has been heard except for their hybridization of the cow and bison called the beefalo. They've also created the turken, which is, of course, a chicken and turkey. There are a couple of weird things, but other than that, they've been off the radar since the late eighties."

Bailey sat back down, holding her head in her hands. "This is awful."

"If they're messing with human genomes or chromosomes, they're in deep cover, Boss."

"And rightly so. Good work, guys."

"Doesn't feel like it. We *did* get the topo information about that area you wanted us to check out. The buildings may appear old, but they were built just eight years ago. Aged chemically."

Danica turned to me. "Didn't Cooper say they were decrepit?"

I nodded.

Roger shook his head and pulled up Google Earth. Zeroing

in on the buildings, he gave us a street view of them. "They've been built to look that way, but trust us, they're pretty new." He circled a rain gutter with a green pen. "Connie went hunting and found these gutters have only been sold on the coast for eight years. If we zoom out," which he did, "you can see these little black boxes in the trees. Pretty sure those are security cameras."

"Who owns the land?"

Roger flipped through info on his laptop. "That trail was a dead end too. We expected it to be Genesys, but they're nowhere in sight. The land ownership is buried deep, Boss. We had to follow a paper trail that even the IRS couldn't have found. We finally found a dummy corporation called Summer's End who owns the land. They lease the buildings to someone named Don Syler." Roger paused as if he was waiting for us to get it. "Yeah, it's okay. I didn't catch it, at first, either, but Connie did. It took her two seconds to realize that Don Syler is an anagram…for… who else? The man listed as having been in charge of Genesys in the eighties…Kip Reynolds." Roger was beaming as he shuffled through his notes. "Which is interesting because Kip Reynolds hasn't filed taxes in over ten years. For all intents and purposes, Kip Reynolds has been dead for a decade."

I could feel the tension in the room as we all realized the extent of this covert government operation. "So, outside the warehouses, he is Don Syler, but inside, he's Dr. Reynolds."

"We doubt that's who he goes by in the real world. If he is still working for Genesys, it's well out of the limelight. Younger scientists are doing all the hybridization he once got panned for. His name is on none of the hybrid successes. We can't find anything on him in the last decade."

"How old is the guy?"

"In his early sixties maybe." Roger looked at his notes. "I'm out. That's all I got, Boss."

"Connie?" Delta asked.

Connie stood behind Roger and stared into the webcam. "It's bad, Storm. The place is a garrison. How that kid got out and away is beyond me."

"What if there were an electrical disturbance that shut the cameras down for a few minutes?"

Connie nodded reflectively. "That might do it."

"Oh wait, Franklin's sending me an IM that says he wants me to tell you one more thing about this Don Syler."

We all waited.

"We're running all possible anagrams of Reynolds and matching them against properties owned by companies with those letters in the name. We have a feeling this is what this guy does." Roger looked into the camera. "Not sure what it is you guys are after, but these people are dangerous. Genes and scientists, land and anagrams. Is there something you need to tell us?"

Danica shook her head. "Not really. We're just helping a young boy."

Roger nodded. "Sure you are. We're still working on a few other angles for you, but I have to say, Boss, that these people value their privacy. Be careful."

"Absolutely, Roger. Thank you for all your hard work. Go home and get some rest. That's an order."

"But—"

Danica shook her head. "But nothing. You guys look beat and I'm sure you smell bad. I want you to clear out in ten. Come back in the morning no earlier than nine. That intel can wait."

Roger nodded like a scolded little boy. "Okay. We're outta here, but we'll be back at nine oh one."

"See you then. Connie? I'll send the car around for you. Roger'll lock up." Flicking the TV off, Danica unhooked the vidbook and returned to her seat. "They are worth every penny I pay them. Indispensable they are."

"Up shit creek is what *we* are," Bailey offered. She had finally stopped holding her head. "He's messing with the very fabric of nature. Ligers? Give me a fucking break."

"If he were that untouchable, don't you think Mel would have taken care of him? Or, The Others? Don't they do that sort of thing?" Danica heaved a sigh I think we all felt.

"There's one way to find out." Reaching over to the phone, I put it on speaker before dialing Melika's cell phone.

"It took you longer than I thought," were her first words.

"We had a lot to work out."

"I see. Tip warned me you were up to something. I take it you haven't pulled the trigger on any grand scheme yet."

I couldn't tell by her tone if she was angry or annoyed. Maybe neither. "You know me too well."

"Is Bailey with you?"

"I am," Bailey admitted.

Melika chuckled. "I should have known that the two of you becoming friends would cause waves in the world. Add Danica to the mix, and the three of you start believing you're unstoppable or something."

"Did Tip tell you about my sister?"

I could hear her intake of breath. "Yes. And no, I did not know you had one or I would have told you. I've not kept secrets from you about your life, Echo. There is nothing in your past, nothing I could see, nothing Bishop could ever see."

"We have a few things we need to know."

"I'm listening, but that doesn't guarantee I'll answer your questions. Some things are better left in the darkness, Echo, and Genesys is one of them."

"We've done our homework, Mel."

"On Kip Reynolds?"

"Yes." I looked at Bailey with a can-you-believe-she-knew-that look.

Bailey shrugged.

"My dears, you couldn't dig deep enough to get the kind of dirt that man has in his soul. He is a very dangerous person who is exceedingly well-connected. We give him a wide berth because he is a Hydra. If you cut off his head, two more grow back."

"I understand that. Why didn't you tell us about Malecon's involvement?"

"For this very reason. All of you youngsters come out of the bayou with your powers blazing like John Wayne's six-shooter. You actually believe you have what it takes to take on a Kip Reynolds and live to tell about it. Well, let me be the first to tell you, you don't. He has too much backing from too high a position on Capitol Hill. He—"

"Is he trying to create a hybrid between naturals and supernaturals." I let that hang in the air a moment.

"With our government's blessing, Echo. Look, we do what we can. Sometimes we succeed, sometimes we don't, but we won't be any use to anyone in jail or dead or in a lab somewhere. It's not worth it. I want you all to have lives: normal, happy, healthy lives. The last thing I want is for any of you to go after a man who will only be replaced by another man who might even be worse than he is. That isn't a life; it's a mission, and I didn't raise any of you to go on some dangerous mission. So far, Dr. Reynolds has managed to wrest only a half dozen or so away from us, so, by and large, we've been far more successful than he has been. The Others decided long ago it didn't serve our best interest to take on our government head-on. It was not wise to engage in a war with the likes of Genesys. We do what we can and cross off the few we can't help or get to as collateral damage. We cannot hope to save everyone, my dear."

"*Collateral damage*? I can't believe I'm hearing this. That's just not acceptable, Mel."

"Maybe not, but it's not our call. It's not *your* call. People older and wiser than us decided long ago what our calling was to be, and it isn't to ride in like some superhero and save the day. That is short-sighted and foolish. I've trained you better than that. There are those who make these decisions, and we are not them."

The Others.

They were a mysterious group of geriatric supers we met when we were about to get our heads blown off in New Orleans. They had powers far beyond my own capabilities and I was impressed and in awe of the things they could do. They cleaned up our messes, stepped in when we needed help, and made laws and rules we were to follow. To second-guess them would be madness.

But then, I always was a little crazy.

"I just need information, Mel. We don't intend on calling an all-out war against Genesys. We just want to get in, get out and call it a day."

"Would that it were that easy. Did you not hear what I just said? We don't mess with them, Echo."

"We just need information."

"Is this about your sister?"

I knew Tip must have told her. "Partly."

"And you think you're going to try to get Cooper's girlfriend away from Genesys?"

"If we can. He won't leave without her. If you want him there, we need to get his girl out."

"We don't make deals, Echo."

"He's powerful, Mel."

"Power without control is dangerous. Look at Cinder."

"I'm going to help this kid get his girl. If Genesys wants to get in my way, then I'll deal with them. After that, I am going to find my sister. These are just things I have to do. Surely you understand that."

"I most certainly do. I only wish you'd wait for Tip."

"We can't wait. With Cooper's exodus, we don't know how long Genesys will be around. By the looks of it, they are very mobile. We can't afford to wait. We have a really good team in place."

"Naturals?"

I hesitated. "Yes, but—"

"You haven't told them, I hope."

"Of course not. They're just very good at what they do. They're the ones who helped track down my folks."

"I see. Well, if they knew of Kip Reynolds' reputation, they might think twice. He has contacts all over the world. He is a ruthless human being who would crush you under his heel if he thought it would bring him glory. He is a megalomaniac of the highest degree who sees us merely as pawns in his own game of genetic chess. Everyone is disposable to that man. Everyone. Chances are Cooper's girlfriend is already dead."

I glanced over at Bailey, who shrugged. "And my sister?"

"Probably the same if, and that's a big if, she even came in contact with the man. Girls, let me tell you about one poor child who managed to get to us after eight months with Dr. Reynolds, then you decide whether or not it's worth it to get in harm's way. She was a young telekinetic who escaped when a new nurse saw what was happening to her and helped her get out. Genesys had to bring in a nurse and several doctors because the poor girl's mind had been so damaged by the many experiments they had performed on her, she lost the ability to push energy out, and instead, pulled everything she reached toward her. Everything."

"Oh no..."

"Oh yes. She stabbed herself with knives, knocked herself unconscious several times reaching for books, and finally, the thing that required medical attention was when a row of metal shelves fell on her, breaking her collarbone, two ribs and both arms. She got so bad, all she could do was lay in a bed with her hands restrained by leather cuffs. It was a horrific existence for her. When a new nurse was assigned to care for her, she started working on getting her out of there, which she did."

Our collective horror seeped through my shields. "What happened?"

"They shot the nurse. At least, that's what Kyoto thought happened. There was a shot, the nurse went down, and Kyoto kept running. Her fear was so intense, she saw a car and started to flag it down. She actually pulled it toward her. The car hit her and broke both her legs and put her in a coma for weeks. The Others were dispatched when she screamed for help deep within her mind. A psychiatrist, not a spotter mind you, just one of us, heard the scream, and because the doctor was a telepath, was able to calm the poor thing down. The doctor contacted us and once she was out of the coma, we were able to take her from the hospital."

"What eventually happened to her?"

I could hear her heavy sigh. "She still needed special care once she reached us, so we put her in a hospital here. She was recovering nicely when...when they got to her. They made it look like she killed herself, but we knew better. They had slipped something in the guard's coffee, got in, killed her and then got out undetected. They tracked her across the country, Echo. That's how serious they are. That's how dangerous they can be. And do you know why they killed her?"

"They didn't want her to talk?"

"No. They did it to send a message to the rest of us. That was when The Others sent an edict out to the mentors that we were to stay far away from them, and though it never set well with the younger generation, it is for self-preservation that we leave them alone. There are thousands of reasons why you weren't told; all of which are meant to spare you grief and suffering. You can't stop progress, Echo."

"Progress? Creating mutant genes isn't progress, Mel."

"Perhaps not to us, but there are many who would disagree with you. It is an uneasy truce we have with them. They seem only interested in children and those new to their powers. They have stopped going after people like the homeless or older folks who have lived their lives. Can you imagine them trying to wrestle a Zach or a Tip?"

"Would The Others take issue if we were to send a natural in so we can gain access to their computers and their data? We can't hack into their computers from the outside, but if we got someone in the inside, we might be able to get information we need."

"As long as any trail leads back to us, it is not advisable. I have no doubt they would come after all of us if they ever felt backed into a corner."

"Then we won't back them into one. We'll just...hover inside their CPU."

"And this is something you believe you can do without notice?"

"Yes, ma'am. I've employed the very best computer folks money can buy. They'll leave no trace."

More hesitation. "Echo...I cannot condone any interference with these people, I hope you understand that. I know you three girls well enough to know you'll go regardless of what I say, so I'll ask one thing."

I expected her to ask me to wait for Tip.

She didn't.

"No stories on Genesys or Kip Reynolds, or anything connected to them. If you do this, no matter how enraged you may get when you uncover what they do, you will refrain from dragging them to our doorstep."

"No stories about Genesys or anything connected with it. You have my word."

"Good. Be sure to keep in touch, and let me know what outcome, if any, occurs. I know finding your sister is important to you, but it cannot ever be more important than the safety of the rest of us."

"Agreed."

"Then I'll leave you to your mission. When can I expect Bailey and Cooper?"

"A couple of days," Bailey answered.

"Excellent. See to it Cooper is well-briefed."

"Yes, ma'am.

"Oh, and Danica?"

"Yes, ma'am?"

"Watch over my girls. They are going to need it."

We allowed ourselves the luxury of sleeping in. We would need to preserve our energy for the coming days, once we figured out the best way to get in. It was nearly nine o'clock by the time we stumbled into Danica's kitchen.

"I don't think anything Mel told us changes anything," Bailey said, accepting a cup of coffee from me. "We're either going to help Cooper get Eve out of there, or we need to cut him loose and wave bye-bye because he won't come with us without her. I, for one, vote for the former."

Danica nodded. "If he tried to get her out by himself, Clark, we might as well send him in with two pine boxes on his back."

Sipping my coffee, I nodded. "I know, but Mel's right. We can't put everyone at risk because of the foolhardiness of a boy."

Bailey shook her head. "There could be worse reasons than young love."

"You can bet they've doubled up on their security since Cooper got out."

"Maybe they've pulled up stakes."

I shook my head. "I'm sure they're waiting for him to return." I looked toward the hallway. "Shouldn't we get him up and ready? We've got a lot to do this morning."

"Teens need lots of sleep," Danica said. "I'll go get him."

"Stop worrying so about her." Bailey told me when she left. "Don't fret. It will all be over before it even begins."

"It's just not like her to get so close to someone so quickly, and why wouldn't Connie want her? Danica is quite a catch."

"She's a catch, all right...from another pond. I'm telling you—"

"The little dickhead is gone!" Danica shouted, running back into the kitchen. "God damn it!"

Bailey and I were on our feet. "What?"

"Gone! And he took that damn dog with him!"

"He took Buster?" Bailey said, dumbfounded.

"Apparently you forgot to tell the dog that he was still on watch."

Bailey sighed. "I took the guard command off so the poor thing could sleep. Damn it!"

Running to the guest room, I lowered my shields to pick up any residual energy. I did, and it was just as I had feared.

"Did someone get him?" Bailey asked, coming up behind me.

"Of course no one got him," Danica spat. "I have one of the best security systems in the state. The jerkoff left on his own."

"He's gone after her," I said softly.

"Why?"

"After all of this, my guess is he didn't think we would go through with it."

"At least if he's still traveling with the dog, they'll be easier to find. Buster and I are connected. We'll have no problem tracking them down."

The three of us swept into the kitchen grabbing our things, swigging our coffee, and gathering our notes before heading for the garage.

"We'll take the Beamer," Danica said, tossing me the keys. "You drive, Clark."

I drove to Delta and Connie's office while Danica called and told them Cooper had taken off. When we arrived at the office, Megan let us in. She was dressed in all black. "Everything is good to go."

"But we—"

"Come in, come in."

When we walked in, Delta and Connie were standing on either side of a small woman dressed in a black leather jumpsuit much like I'd seen Halle Berry wearing in *Catwoman*. There was an intense energy surrounding her that vibrated the air like static electricity.

"Echo, Dani, Bailey, this is Taylor."

Her hair was short, cut in a boyish pixie cut, and her eyes blazed with a love of life. I liked all eighty pounds of her right away.

"We've heard great things about you," I said, shaking her hand. It was very warm in mine.

"You can't believe anything those two yokels say. Here I thought I was retired, and then I get the call." She glanced over at Delta. "And they pulled me out kicking and screaming." She chuckled, her eyes twinkling mischievously. "Okay, that was a lie. I was getting bored to tears with all that peace and quiet. How do normal people keep from slitting their wrists?"

Danica and Bailey looked at each other, but said nothing.

"So…you're really a…a thief?" I asked, releasing her hand.

"Thief? Is *that* what Cheech and Chong told you? I am no mere thief, ladies. I am the best professional thief on the goddamn planet." She shot Delta a look. "Thief? That's the best you could do? I thought we were friends!"

Delta chuckled. "Sorry. I didn't have time to print up your résumé." To us, Delta said, "Taylor has stolen things no one in their right mind would have attempted. Made quite a fortune from booty she plundered from the rich."

"Booty? Plunder?" Taylor stared at Delta.

Delta actually blushed. "Sorry. We watched *Pirates of the Caribbean* last night. Anyway, Taylor's the best in the business. If she can't break in, no one can."

"When do we get started?" She rubbed her hands together as if we were going shopping.

Then she looked at her watch. I couldn't help but notice it was a silver Rolex.

"In a few hours," Delta replied.

"I'll need to be there a few hours before dusk to get a lay of the land. I'll need to study the topo map on Connie's computer and get a feel for where everything is." She studied me for a moment. "I get the feeling I'm not moving fast enough for you."

I shook my head and apologized. "I'm sorry. It's just...with Cooper out there, he's a loose cannon we can't afford to leave alone for too long."

Taylor grinned. "Delta knows all about loose cannons, don'tcha, Storm?"

"Don't make me hurt you," Delta said, mussing Taylor's hair. "She really is the best in the business, Echo, but nobody gains by going off half-cocked. We'll get her to an area near The Farm and let her do her magic."

I nodded. "Then what's our plan?"

"Come on in to the conference room and let's discuss it."

We all followed Delta and Connie into a large room, where we sat around an oval cherry wood conference table. In the corner sat a large television monitor with a Google Earth close-up of the buildings with blue and green arrows pointing in different directions. On the right was a list of what needed to happen. I suddenly felt sick to my stomach at the thought of sending this cocky little woman into such a dangerous environment without telling her the truth about where she was going and what she was going to face. The moral dilemma of who I was and the truth behind Genesys hung heavily around my neck.

"Okay," Delta said, sitting down and folding her hands on the table. "Taylor will be equipped with a small tracking device and a microphone so we can be in constant communication."

Connie nodded. "Don't forget the camera." She smiled at Danica. "It's so small and so new, it's not even on the market yet."

Delta nodded. "We have the best equipment for this, Echo. Once we get Taylor in—"

"Forget it," I said, causing all heads to turn toward me. "I'm sorry. I...I can't let you guys do this."

"Whoa. Wait," Bailey said. "Did we miss something?"

"I can't let you guys risk your lives when you don't...you don't really know—"

"That's okay, E," Bailey said, catching my eye and sending

out vibes loud enough for the dead to hear. She was afraid I was going to tell them the truth. I wasn't, but I wasn't going to let Taylor risk her life under false pretenses. "Let's hear what the plan is first before you squash it, E."

Connie reached over and lightly touched my leg. "We can play this any way you want to, Echo, but this isn't about your sister or your parents. It's about doing the right thing by those kids. We know something almost otherworldly is happening in there. If kids' lives are at stake, it's incumbent upon us to help them regardless of the risk."

"And the right thing to do is to save that kid and his girlfriend," Delta continued. "Regardless of what you think appears to be a personal agenda. Cooper's a good kid. Whatever he's facing, he shouldn't have to face alone."

I shook my head. "I know...I just—"

Danica held her hand up. "Clark, I know why you want to back out, but you can't. These ladies have faced a helluva lot worse than the likes of Kip Reynolds. They know what they're doing. They don't need to know the full truth."

Connie nodded. "Echo, Delta and I have been doing this a long time together. We...know things about people, and we know this much: you ladies have something you're not telling us. We're aware of that. Always have been. That doesn't change the fact that kids need our help. We're not about to turn our backs. We don't need the whole truth. We just need to know what it is you need from us."

Delta nodded. "Look, we don't need to know whatever it is you're hiding, Echo. We just need to know we're on the right side of things. Are we?"

I looked over at Bailey and Danica. All three of us nodded.

Megan leaned across the table, her blue eyes shimmering with what I felt was pride. "I've seen what these three can do. They can make the impossible possible. If they thought for one second that sending Taylor into The Farm was as dangerous as you believe it to be, they would never do it. Taylor is family, and we never hang our family out on a limb. It took me a long time to learn to trust them even when everything around me screamed not to. So, take my advice on this; let them run with it. Don't take them out of the lineup before the game even starts. Every one of us is here because we want to help. Let us."

I looked over at Danica, who nodded. "Whatever your decision, Clark, it's your call and Bailey and I will back you one hundred percent, but I think these ladies have a leg up on us when it comes to facing impossible odds."

I turned to the women at the table. What had started out as a simple collection had taken a lot of detours, but in the end, this was still about collecting a young man who needed us. If they were willing to still help even when they didn't have all the facts, I would not stop them.

"Let's go get him," I said softly.

Before I could utter another syllable, Megan, Connie and Delta were whisking duffel bags into their Dodge Durango and speaking so quickly to each other, I could barely understand what they were saying.

Tossing a radio to Danica, Connie moved us all back to the conference room.

"We'll set out in an hour, get something to eat and then take Taylor to The Farm via this back route." Delta pointed to the green line on the map.

"Umm…that doesn't even look like a road," Danica said.

"It isn't. They'll be looking for cars coming up the road. We're going to do a little four-wheeling through this area here." She traced the map with her finger. "And set up base camp here."

"Why there?" Bailey asked.

"See these little hills? If they have any surveillance equipment or cameras, they won't go through those. We'll be safer from prying eyes. It's easier to go around cameras than through them."

I nodded. "What about the road?"

"We're putting Megan and Sal, a friend of ours, on the road so we know who is coming in and out. We'll have a better idea of what's happening if we have someone watching the front door."

"Front door?" Bailey asked.

"Figure of speech. It means we'll be watching to see any vehicular activity."

"Oh. Gotcha."

Delta continued. "We'll set up all our equipment at base camp; computers, cameras, weapons, et cetera. While we set up, Taylor will roam the grounds, see what's what, and then find her way in. Remember, she's *allegedly* gotten in and out of the Louvre undetected. Warehouses will be child's play for her. While she surveys the grounds, we'll be watching the whole thing from there. If anything goes hinky, we'll move to plan B."

"And that would be?"

"Blast our way in and blast our way out."

Before I could say anything, Taylor cut in. "She's messin' with you guys. There won't be any need for plan B. When I was thieving, I never had any backup. Didn't need it then, won't need it now. We just take precautions in our old age, that's all. If I get in a bind, Delta and Con will get me out one way or the other. I'm not worried about that."

I looked at her. "I don't get one thing. I know why we're doing this, but why would you do this for a kid you don't even know?"

Taylor grinned impishly. "I'm an adrenaline junkie. I've risked my life for far less. I live for the thrill of the game, not for the profit. Some gains I kept, most of it I gave away. Some papers called me Robin Hood, but trust me, I never gave anything to the poor." She rolled her head as if to release tension. At that moment, I realized who she really was.

"Oh, my God. You...you were the thief who stole the Narcissus Emerald."

She grinned and I picked up pride. "You read about that, did you?"

"Who didn't? That was you? Wow."

"Yeah, but I'll deny it if anyone asks. You see my point? I live for the excitement of it all. I'd never keep anything truly priceless or precious, but taking it is always big fun and I really *am* the best there is. You'll see. Connie can get in and out of people's computer panties, Delta can bend the law and sometimes even time, but I can get in and out of Fort Knox." She tucked something in one of her zippered pockets and then rose. "It's not an empty boast. Delta will fill you in on the rest. I need to go double-check my equipment."

I nodded and watched her leave. There was something genuine about her that made me really glad she was on our side. She looked right in my eyes as she spoke—unwavering, unapologetic. I liked that. "What do you need us to do?"

"We'll have several laptops up and running that will need eyes on them. It's imperative we know everything Taylor is seeing and hearing and her location at all times."

I nodded. "We can do that."

"Good. Then once we get there, we'll set up base camp, keep an eye on Taylor, and wait to see if she can get into one of their computers. If she can access those we'll be able to shut everything down from the inside. It will make it easier to get in."

Delta tapped her ultra-thin laptop. "Taylor is rigged up so as she moves, we get a layout of the building on the computer."

"Like a blueprint?"

She nodded. "Yeah. Just like that. Connie developed it a couple of years ago. She calls it Breadcrumbs."

Danica winked at Connie. "Good one. I might have to see if that is something we can market."

Whatever passed between them made both Delta and me turn away.

"Yeah," Delta said, looking at the monitor. "We'll follow her and just wait until she tells us it's time to move in. Any questions?"

We looked at each other. "None that I can think of," I said.

"Excellent. Then if we're all ready to go—"

We rose and filed out to the Escalade and the Durango, ear transmitters in our hands along with maps, GPS systems and water bottles. "Keep it on that frequency and turned way down. We'll meet for a short debriefing before we send Taylor in."

I looked at the group of women and wondered if it was fair or realistic of me to expect so much from them, but they seemed so competent, so self-aware. I needed women like them in my life, and suddenly, any doubts I had about the danger of this rescue vanished.

"Don't look so worried, Echo," Delta said, laying her arm across my shoulders. "We've done this kind of surveillance a hundred times. It'll go smoothly if no one panics or freaks out.

Trust us. This may be unfamiliar terrain to you, but it's old hat to us. We'll get the kids out of there one way or the other."

I nodded, wishing I had her confidence. "See you there." Hopping into the SUV, I bit my lower lip and made sure my shields were at their strongest.

"I'd like to kick that boy's ass," Danica said when we started rolling. "We should have shipped him to Melika when we had the chance."

"What's done is done," I said, feeling the same way about it. We blew it by not getting him on the fastest jet out of California. "Spilled milk, Dani. Besides, he's in love. He would have just found another way to get back here."

We drove for a while, each of us thinking our own thoughts, when Bailey said. "They're certainly fired up. I'm pretty sure I've never met anyone like them and we're the ones who are supposed to be super. Know what I'm saying? Am I the only one who's picking that up?"

I nodded. "They're something else, that's for sure."

It felt like we were going off to war with an enemy we had never seen. I wondered how Taylor was going to be able to get into someplace that appeared impenetrable. How would she get around security cameras, infrared sensors and dogs? Cooper said they had dogs. I wondered how she planned on getting the kids out. They were a lot bigger than any emerald necklace or diamond brooch she had ever swiped. I guess I was wondering about a lot right now. Maybe we should have waited for Tip. Maybe I should have put Bailey and Cooper on a plane the moment we got him. Maybe, maybe, maybe.

And I was supposed to be Melika's replacement?

The fact was...I had blown this collection right out of the gate, and now we were trying to play catch up. I'd lost Cooper, was trying to find a sister who probably didn't want to be found, and was letting my new friends fight a battle they didn't even know what it was about.

"Connie's hot, Dani," Bailey said from the backseat. "You seriously scored on that one."

Danica cut her eyes over to me before turning to Bailey. "Yes she is, but she goes to your church Bailey. She's not interested in playing house and neither am I. Knock your socks off if you're interested."

"Oh, I think someone's socks have already been knocked off, and they aren't mine."

Danica looked straight ahead. "I don't know what you're talking about."

Bailey leaned back. "You don't have to be a super to feel the energy between the two of you. It's a little like a supernova... melting the soles of my Nikes."

Danica didn't say a word, but I knew she wanted to.

"You don't have to own it, but I know what I see and—"

"What *do* you see, Bailey?" Danica looked in the rearview mirror. "What is it you think is going on here?"

Bailey leaned forward once more. "I'm a lesbian, D. I know when a woman finds another woman hot, and Connie Rivera wants you bad. Those smoldering eyes follow your every move like a tractor beam. Boop. Boop. Boop."

"We've got enough on our plate not to be worrying about Danica's sex life," I said. "Can you focus in here? Danica is not interested in anything more than a roll in the hay."

"Hello? I'm right here!" Danica said, putting the handheld radio up to her mouth. "Maybe I ought to talk to someone in the other car."

"Personally, I think Megan is a hottie." Bailey rubbed her hands together. "Of course, Delta isn't anybody's sloppy seconds, either. I tell you what, E, hanging with you has really broadened my lesbian horizons. All the lipstick lesbians are in the house." She pumped the ceiling.

"Don't make me hurt you," Danica said, depressing the receiver and speaking into it. "It looks like we're going for an area about two miles from the warehouse proper. Does that sound right?"

The radio clicked and Connie's voice came through clearly. "Yeah. Megan's going to swing off and pick up Sal, then they'll be right behind us. You guys okay back there?"

"We're good. Thanks." Setting the radio between us, Danica reached into her purse.

"I have a new gun," she said, pulling out the Glock she'd bought when we got back from New Orleans. She'd spent a few days at the shooting range getting used to it. For my part, I hated guns and hated knowing she was carrying one. Guns scared the crap out of me.

"We won't be needing that, Dani. We're just going to collect our kids and get the hell out of Dodge. No shooting. No dead people. *Nada.*"

Danica put her hand on my shoulder. "I have a funny feeling about this, Clark. You're kidding yourself if you think this is going to be simple."

Bailey set her hand on Danica's. "Call it what it is, D. This isn't a collection...it's the beginning of a war, and Echo is our Commander-in-Chief."

By the time we braved the traffic and made it to the rendezvous point, it was almost one o'clock. Once we left the freeway, Delta had us four-wheeling up and over the rocky terrain, well off the beaten path. Branches were beating the side of the SUV, and there were times when I thought we were airborne. It was all pretty scary until we got to base camp, where we set up a long table and connected the laptops to the jacks in the back of the Durango, which was no mere Durango, but a mini-computer lab on wheels. It had every techno-gadget ever made.

"Impressive," Danica said, helping Connie set up shop.

I had to agree. It was amazing. Along with the laptops was a radio transmitter, a couple of gizmos the size of an iPhone and the radios. There were several file folders filled with maps and diagrams that I couldn't make heads or tails out of.

"Everyone with a cell phone, leave it in the cars."

We did as we were told. Taylor was busy fiddling with an earplug in her left ear. "Ready for launch."

"Launch?"

Delta nodded. "Launching is when we go see the viability of a project first. The satellite photos we have tell a good tale. Taylor knows where she can run and where she can hide. It's..."

"Satellite photos? How on earth..."

Connie grinned. "Ancient Chinese secret." She pulled several firearms from the stuffed duffel bags.

"Wait a minute. What are those for?"

Delta froze and looked up. She had been putting a scope on one of the rifles. "Echo, these people play for keeps. They're the kind who shoot now and ask questions never. They have everything to lose and nothing to gain, so pulling the trigger is as easy as breathing. Trust me. When it comes down to them or us...he who has the best guns wins."

"Do we have the best guns?" Bailey asked.

Connie turned. "I don't know about that, but we have the best shooters. We're not worried."

While I admired their calm, it did little to ease my own trepidation. I had never done anything like this and it was unnerving.

"We don't want it to get violent. We won't be striking first. What we will do is take care of our own."

I nodded. Now *that* was something I understood.

Bailey shielded her eyes and looked up at the sky. "If you guys don't need me, I need some space before the fireworks get going."

"Not a problem," Connie said. "Just don't go too far. We'll need you back here in about an hour. Don't go over the hill line, okay?"

Bailey nodded. "Got it. Thanks."

When Bailey headed for the trees, Danica stood next to me. "She's an odd one, huh, Clark?"

I nodded. "I think she's grown fond of Buster, and is more than a little pissed off that Cooper took him."

"That's not why she's going over there and you know it," Danica whispered.

I shrugged and stepped away from the base camp. "I don't know what you're talking about."

"She's not an empath, but she knows about me and Connie, doesn't she?"

"Yeah, but I didn't tell her. You know I'd never say anything. She's empathic by nature, so I wouldn't be surprised if she didn't feel it. Carnal lust is a pretty powerful energy and you two are slinging it like hash."

"Shut up!" she hissed. "There's nothing going on beyond that one night. Nothing. It was what it was. End of the story."

"Why do you sound so bummed out?"

"I don't. I'm not."

I waited a few beats. Danica knew I wasn't reading her, but she also knew that I knew her well enough to see the obvious. And it was really obvious.

"I don't understand what's happening to me, Clark." We walked out to the shade of a large oak tree and sat beneath it. "I've never liked anyone like her."

"You've fallen for her, you goof. Welcome to the real world of love, my friend."

Danica flopped down next to me. "I just don't see how this could happen to me. I'm usually more careful than that."

"Some things can't be avoided. Besides…maybe it's time for you to fall in love with a woman."

"Whoa. Wait. Who said anything about *love*?"

I looked at her. "Dani, in all the years we've known each other, you have always been the coolest cucumber on the block. Other than me, you've never really let anyone in to see the real you. Doesn't that get lonely?"

"No."

I smiled softly at her like I used to when we were kids. "I'm thinking maybe it does. The only other person I've seen you truly care about is Cinder, and she's just a kid."

"What's your point?"

"My point is maybe it's time you took a chance on loving someone."

"Someone, yeah, but another woman? Come on, Clark, you know I can't be with someone better looking than me." She grinned. "Think of sharing a bathroom with another woman, and—"

"I'm not saying it has to be Connie. I'm saying that what's really got you freaked out isn't the fact that you might have fallen for a woman, but what you're feeling. I think your heart is trying to tell that thick head of yours that maybe…just maybe…you're ready for something more significant than a few rolls in the hay."

Danica shook her head sadly. "Roll in the hay? Are you nine

years old? You know, you're old enough to say the F word now, you know? You won't teleport to hell."

"I don't need to say it. You and Bailey say it enough for all of us."

We sat in silence for a few moments, watching from a distance as the Three Amigas finished setting up camp.

"They're really into all this shit, aren't they?"

I nodded. "I guess that's how it's all done. I mean, without the boys—"

"Yeah, they're pretty good, aren't they?"

"You ever think about telling them...you know...about me?"

"Honestly? No. I like being one of the few naturals who knows you guys exist." Danica shielded her eyes as she watched Bailey coming toward us. "You thinking about telling Finn?"

"No. Hell, I'm not even sure we're dating anymore. Our careers have really disjointed hours. It's crazy how little we get to see each other these days."

"Maybe that's for the best. Her coming to NOLA was a really bad plan. What would she do if she knew we were getting ready to infiltrate a secret government facility?"

I nodded as Bailey walked up.

"Good news and bad news," she said.

"Bad first."

"Cooper left Buster outside The Farm, which means he is either inside of his own free will or he got caught again."

"Jesus. And the good news?"

"Buster's okay and is lying near the door where Cooper went in. If I can get Buster to take Taylor there, it might be easier for her to get in." Bailey sat cross-legged in front of us.

"Bailey," Danica began. "Of all the supers I've ever met, your powers are the most mysterious. How in the hell do you communicate with a *dog*?"

"Dogs think largely in pictures. So do we. We like to think we're all verbal, but we're not. I can read what an animal is picturing and then respond in kind. That's oversimplifying it, of course, but you get the general idea. I don't read their minds, if that's what you think."

"And the Shaman part? What's all that creature of the earth shit?"

Bailey grinned patiently. "Echo senses emotional energies, right? Well, I sense energy from the natural world, and because I can do that, I know what flora and fauna have particular medicinal or therapeutic qualities. All of our skills revolve around energy. Mine just comes from more places than Echo's."

"Show me."

Bailey rose and placed her hand on the oak. The sunlight bounced off her blond hair as it pierced through the oak leaves. "This old guy is over a hundred years old. I know this because the energy is fuzzy around the edges, not sharp, like it is when there's youth. There might be a bug infestation of some kind, but other than that, he's healthy. I feel energy from the tree, but no pictures, of course. Still, it has plenty of life. If I needed mistletoe for an unguent, I would know if the oak had it just by touching the tree because mistletoe is a parasite, and that energy sucker would also give off an energy." Bailey sat back down.

"Pretty amazing."

"Yeah. It's cool. I love it." She studied Danica with piercing blue eyes. "You ever wish you were one of us?"

"Honestly? Sometimes. Like when I have idiots for clients. I just wish flames would come shooting out of my fingertips. That's a pretty awesome little skill Cinder has. Phoom! And you're toast. I like that."

Bailey grinned. "Then I guess it's a good thing you don't have any powers."

"Looks like they're getting ready to send Taylor off to launch...or whatever." I rose and helped both Danica and Bailey to their feet. "Let's see if there's anything we can do to help."

"Help? Have you seen all that crap they brought with them? I think the best way we can help is to stay out of their way." Danica leaned against the oak. "So, Bailey. No one special in your life?"

Bailey slowly shook her head. "I did. Before Katrina."

"What happened?"

"She didn't want me to go. She said she was tired of me jumping every time Mel called." Bailey tucked her hair behind her ears. "I can't really blame her. I did sort of come and go, but I really wanted to give back...because Mel and the bayou saved my life. When I left, I told her it was because I wanted to help...I wanted to be a collector...to help some other little girl who needed a break. When Mel called us to help out after Katrina, I knew it was my chance to prove to her I could do it, that I could be a viable member of a team." She looked off into the hills. "I wasn't much of a team member when I was growing up there. I guess I was too enamored with my powers and being out in the bayou. I pretty much stayed to myself the whole time I was there."

"So your girlfriend left you."

Bailey nodded. "She was gone when I got home."

"I'm sorry."

"It's not so easy being this different, D. We are always questioning *Do we tell? Do we not?* When is a good time to come clean? Who can be trusted? Who can't be? What if she finds out?"

"So, she didn't know?"

"Hell no. She just thought Melika was an old aunt of mine. A particularly needy one."

I held my hand up to stop her. "You said she was tired of you jumping every time Mel called?"

Bailey nodded. "Women are really high maintenance creatures, D. They don't like it when we come and go all the time. My partners don't like me to be gone and I can't really stay. In the end, I just decided it's best if I stay alone for a while...at least until I can get my collector's wings."

I smiled at Bailey. She had a great heart I was sure was easy enough for women to fall in love with, but there was so much more to loving us than merely loving us.

"Taylor's waving us in," Bailey said. "We're ready for this, right?"

Danica laughed. "Ummm...no. I'd love to swagger on over there and say that I was born ready, but the truth is, this is way outta this ghetto girl's league. Did you see the rifle Delta attached that scope to? That could bring down an elephant from a mile away. Looked like something out of *Star Wars*."

"Does that mean we're *not* ready?" I asked.

They both shook their heads. "But we weren't ready for Malecon, either, and we managed."

"That we did."

"So we're not going to back away from mere normals when we kicked his ass all over the bayou. Come on."

"If she is as good as they say she is, getting into one of those warehouses shouldn't be a problem," Bailey said.

"Getting in—" Taylor said when we walked up, "will be a piece of cake. But getting out with other people? I've never done that before."

"Nervous?"

"Nah. It's all part of the gig."

"The gig?"

Taylor grinned but I felt her trepidation. She wasn't worried as much as she was excited. "Yeah, you know...the game. I always get jacked before going in, but once I'm in there, my heart rate slows, my breathing slows, and I see with a clarity that's almost... supernatural."

I made sure I did not make eye contact with either Danica or Bailey.

"This is no game."

"Sure it is. Just about everything we do in life can be reduced to a game. Like a game, we have two sides. They're our opponents trying to keep us from getting our goal. There's a beginning a middle and an end. It ends when someone has what the other one doesn't want them to have. That means the game is over and someone, that would be us, is the winner while someone else, that would be them, is the loser. There are rules, that we, of course, are going to ignore, and penalties we'll suffer if we get caught. It's all a game, and those with a good game plan who play the right people in the right positions win."

"And that would be us again, right?" Bailey asked.

"Of course."

Connie motioned for us to come over to the equipment table. "The boys have gotten into the PG and E grid and found out their power is directed mostly into this one area." She drew a circle on the map showing the buildings. "Once Taylor gets in, we'll shut off the power for ten seconds to give her a chance to get out of camera range. From their side, it will only look like a glitch in the electrical system. The lights will flicker, fade and then go off. She'll get someplace safer and then the power will come back on."

"How will she see in the dark?"

Taylor pulled out what looked like a pair of swim goggles. "Infrared. There's a tiny camera right here, so you all can see what I see."

Connie zipped up a Kevlar vest and continued. "Once she's in, she's on her own. She'll go for the computers first, see what data she can upload. Then, she'll find Cooper and the kids, all the while giving us a layout of the warehouse." Bending over, she tucked her pants into her combat boots.

"What if they're locked up?" This came from Bailey.

"Honey, there isn't a lock or a safe around I haven't picked." Taylor double-checked all of the zippers on her leather jumpsuit. She looked all of size negative one in that skintight suit. "Locks don't concern me. I'm more worried about getting the kids out safely. It would be a snap if it was just me, but like I said, I'll be carrying a big load behind me."

"We do have a contingency plan in the event she gets caught, but we won't muddy the waters with any of that right now."

"Is that what the heavy weapons are for? Are those your contingency plans?" Bailey asked, eying Connie as she pulled on fingerless leather gloves.

Delta grinned. "Maybe. Look, if those people are really who you say they are, they can't really afford a shootout at the O.K. Corral, can they?"

"So, if we have to go in there with guns blazing to get our girl out, that's what we'll do. Remember, Cooper and Eve were *abducted*. It's not like Genesys wants to have to answer to federal charges."

It was brilliant, really. "Not likely."

Connie turned to me. "Look, we know there's a lot you're not telling us, so our guess is that the government would renounce any and all knowledge of whoever they are, so it's not likely anyone is going to risk getting caught."

Danica and Bailey looked at each other and nodded.

"Whatever it is," Delta continued, "you can trust us with it. Believe me...we have our fair share of secrets between us."

"We do trust you, Delta. It's just—"

"It's okay. No need to know. Just know that you can."

Connie joined Delta and they stood side-by-side. "You have our word that whatever you all are about will never leave our lips. Secret, we're good at, and you can rest easy knowing we'll never divulge anything we know about any of you."

"Just what is it you think you know, Delta?"

She smiled and her one dimple showed. "That you've got a helluva lot more secrets up your sleeve than the average person. Keep your secrets safe, Echo. We will. I promise."

We all nodded.

"Okay, Danica, I need one pair of eyes on that laptop monitor. That's the video feed from Taylor's camera." Delta walked to the next laptop. "This is my feed. I'll be up on that incline over there with the scope aimed on the door. I'll keep an eye on anyone else coming and going."

"My dog, Buster, is waiting by that door there," Bailey said, pointing to the monitor. "He's a big, scary beast, but if you pat him on the head, he'll know I sent you, and that will release him from the spot." Bailey took Taylor's hand in hers. She held it between hers for a moment before laying it on her chest. Taylor did not move. "He'll smell me and sense me. Trust me."

Taylor nodded. "I do."

Danica cleared her throat. "Ahem."

Taylor retrieved her hand slowly, smiling up at Bailey. "I'll head out over the incline at dusk. Is Meg in place?"

Delta nodded. "They're all over it."

My heart hammered against my chest. How did they stand this? How could they remain so calm?

"What if they move out before we can get in?"

"Megan and Justin will pretend to be broken down in the middle of the road."

"I'm glad she's not alone."

"Alone? Hardly. Justin can pull your eyeballs out of your head before you can say eyeballs. She's in good hands."

"You guys ride with a pretty interesting group of people," Bailey said.

Bailey nodded. "I'm glad the eyeball puller is on our side."

I felt the soft tap, tap, tapping of Tip. "I need to sit down and close my eyes for a bit, if you don't mind. When Taylor gets ready to roll, let me know."

Walking back to the tree, I leaned against it and closed my eyes. Centering myself with my breathing, I was glad she was there. I needed some support right now; I needed something that a phone call to Finn wouldn't get me. It was at this critical juncture I knew what I had to do.

I had to stop seeing Finn.

I had been fooling myself that we could keep our secrets and still manage to make it work. She had hers and I had mine, and though we both did not share our secrets as a means of protecting the other, the truth was, secrets erode the foundation of every relationship, one piece at a time. I remembered Melika quoting to us once when we were out on the river, saying, "If you reveal your secrets to the wind, you should not blame the wind for revealing them to the trees." It was an apt quote to a fourteen- year-old girl who was trying to decide whether or not Danica was my wind. At fourteen, you don't realize that the people you go to school with will seldom be in your life once you grow up. Melika wanted me to understand the gravity of revealing my secret.

"Mel also told you that, 'To him you tell your secret to, you resign your liberty'."

"Oh, there you are. Where are you in real life?"

"With The Others. I've been trying to explain to them what you're up to before they send someone to pull the plug on your little scheme. They're not pleased."

"What did you tell them?"

"They have cleaners on standby, kiddo. If this thing goes south on you...they're ready to bail you out."

I'd met some cleaners when I was in New Orleans. Cleaners were older psis who had retired into the service of The Others— the watchdog group of supernaturals who keep the youngsters in check. Cleaners do just what their title implies; they clean up our messes. They make sure naturals don't inadvertently discover something they shouldn't. I had seen what they could do, and, quite frankly, it was frightening. We had quite a few powerful weapons in our arsenal I hadn't been aware of until our battle with Malecon.

"*Hopefully, there will be no need for them.*" I sighed loudly. "*I'm sorry, Tip, really I am. I know I've royally screwed this collection up and this isn't what you thought, but…*"

"*Whoa. Back up. Don't apologize to me, kiddo. Believe it or not… and I'll deny saying this…but I admire your chutzpah. I'm proud of you for stepping up to the plate. It might be a big plate, but at least you're finally in the supernatural game.*"

Game. There it was again. Could Taylor's simplistic view of the world really be reduced to that? "*I thought you said they weren't happy with me.*"

"*That's what I was supposed to say, but the truth is you're doing something I've always wanted to do. Melika would kill me if I did something like this.*"

"*She knows.*"

"*Of course she knows. She always knows. She's not happy, either, which is why I'm here with The Others. We want Cooper alive. She's not sure we'll get him back that way if we don't hurry.*"

"*You're with The Others?*"

"*I had to leave New Mexico to make sure they don't overstep and ruin whatever it is you've got planned.*"

"*It's happening tonight.*"

"*What?*"

"*Yeah. He got away from us again. Went straight back to get his girl. We're here to get them both.*"

"*Damn it, Echo, you're not making this easy on me.*"

"*I'm sorry.*"

"*You got a good plan? Backup? You know what you're doing? Do you—*"

"*I have it all covered, Tip, really. I couldn't ask for a better group of people to be working with on this.*"

"*I'm trusting that you do, darlin'. Reynolds isn't someone you want to piss off.*"

"*Oh, he's going to be pissed off, Tip, when we snag two of his precious lab* rats away from him. But I don't care. When this is all over, we're going to sit down with Melika and talk about what we can do to stop this."

"Stop this? You want to stop this? We don't—"

"Maybe it's time we do. Times have changed, Tip. Maybe we need to as well."

"We'll talk about it when you get back."

"I'd like that."

"There's something I need you to know about that time I dealt with Reynolds's men."

"I don't need to kn—"

"Yes, you do. When I had a run-in with his guys, it didn't end well. I...I killed one of them."

"Oh."

"Yeah. The cleaners were barely able to make a clean sweep of it. My actions put us all in danger that day and Mel made me swear I would never get involved with them again. As hard as it's been, I've kept that promise to her all these years. I've stood back when all I really wanted to do was kick some ass."

"I see."

"No, no you don't. I should have told you all of this, but I couldn't because—"

"Because you knew I'd go here anyway, and you secretly wanted me to."

"I wish I could lie and tell you that's not true, but it is. I'm tired of sitting on my hands while these assholes do what they do. If I had to do it all over again—"

"You'd never have promised Mel."

"Right."

"I understand, Tip, really I do."

"Just tell me that you really do have a plan...that you've got this covered."

"I really do. We're sending in a professional thief first. She's going to—"

"Please tell me you haven't told them."

"I haven't. They don't press, either. They just know that Cooper is in trouble and we're paying them good money to help get him out; though I suspect they would do it for free...that's the kind of women they are."

"*Women? Natural women? You're going against Kip Reynolds with* natural *women?*"

"*I am.*"

"*Echo—*"

"*I royally screwed up Bailey's collection of Cooper, in part because I was too focused on finding out about my family and...and—*"

"*And because you thought they might have taken your sister.*"

And there it was; the understanding and support I could never expect to get from Finn. That was what my secret prevented me from experiencing with her; this was what I had been needing the last couple of days. "*Yeah, I did, and because I wasn't tuned in, I screwed up and now Cooper's in trouble. I have to fix this, Tip.*"

"*And you think tossing a bunch of normal women into the mix is going to help?*" Tip wasn't being accusatory, just inquisitive.

"*They're not really normal. They're not supers and they're not really normal, either. I don't know and I can't explain it, but there's something about them that defies definition. I can't put my finger on it. I just know that from what I've seen, they're really good at what they do.*"

"*Then I guess I have no choice but to trust your instincts on this.*"

"*That's a first.*"

"*Hey, people can change, you know.*"

"*People can, but can you?*"

"*Why don't you come home with Bailey and find out?*"

"*Tempting, but I just found my mother and grandmother. I think I'm going to spend some time getting to know them.*"

"*All right. You guys be careful. We're rounding up a team of cleaners as we speak, so hang in there, okay? If you succeed without casualties, I'll be impressed. Just remember that Cooper can be crossed off the list as collateral damage.*"

"*Don't say that!*"

"*It's true. We need you. We don't need him. Remember that.*"

"*I better go.*"

"*I have faith in you, darlin'. Have some in yourself. For as long as I've known you, you've always done the right thing. I'm sure now is no exception.*"

A branch snapped and I opened my eyes to find Delta

standing there. I should have felt her energy long before I heard her. "How did you do that?"

She smiled. It was the first time I noticed she had a lopsided grin. "I've spent a lot of time skulking around in the dark after people who would rather my head not be attached to my shoulders. You get sorta good at it after a while. Mind if I join you?"

"Please." I let my connection with Tip go, knowing she was there if I needed her, that she would be on her way in a matter of minutes. It was comforting to know she always had my back.

Delta sat next to me, her long legs outstretched. So many of her mannerisms were masculine, but there was still an edge of softness to her she managed to keep hidden from view. I imagined only Connie and Megan ever got to see that side of her. "Anything I can do to ease your worries?"

I cleared my throat. "Actually, there is. While I can't tell you the whole truth about what is really going on, I *can* tell you this much: Cooper isn't a normal kid. He needs special care. That's why they grabbed him. They want what they think he has, only he probably won't give it to them."

"Is he worth dying for?"

I shook my head. "He isn't, but keeping their secret is. The… tests they perform in there, the things they do to human subjects would be difficult to explain to the public."

"I see. You know, I've faced my fair share of baddies myself. Government projects funded in secrecy may not be on that list, but criminals are criminals, Echo, and it doesn't matter if the collars they wear are blue or white. I spent a lot of time on the force trying to reconcile right from wrong. In the end, I can't say I didn't cross that fine line more times than a person should, but I did. I'd do it all the same way, though, if I had to do it all over again."

"Is that why you guys are no longer cops?"

She stared off for some moments before nodding. "We've lost some really good friends over the course of our law enforcement careers. Sometimes we lost them to the crooks, and sometimes we lost them to the good guys. Truth is, it doesn't much matter which side gets them, they're gone all the same. We finally faced an issue that just couldn't resolve itself, and knew it was time to lay our badges down. Sometimes, Echo, doing what's right isn't necessarily what's best."

I nodded and wondered how this woman could be so perceptive, so intuitive, and not be a supernatural herself. "I think this may be one of those times."

She turned to me, her green eyes dark and intense. "Trying to save two kids from something that scares the shit out of all three of you sounds to me like it's both the best *and* the right thing to do, Echo. Whatever is happening in that warehouse needs to stop. *Right now.* Today. We get that. We're not second-guessing any of that, and neither should you."

I nodded, wishing I possessed a fraction of the self-confidence of this woman. I was in awe of her; not only her, but Connie and Taylor as well. "She really stole the Narcissus?"

Delta chuckled. "Yeah, and a helluva lot more. We were able to convince her to retire only by offering her gigs like this one. Believe me, she doesn't need the money. Taylor has more money stashed away than Trump. She's been thieving for over a decade, and has amassed a fortune. I can't even begin to tell you about the paintings, sculptures and jewels she's snagged from private collectors. And if it's a piece she knows was stolen, like so many of those pieces taken during WWII, she'll send it to whatever museum she thinks should have it. Taylor has a heart of gold, that one."

"But she's like an addict where stealing is concerned, isn't she?"

She grinned. "Oh yes. She is addicted to the game. I have no idea what we're going to do with her when she gets too old to leap tall buildings in a single bound. My guess is she'll turn into one of those little old ladies who steals a pair of socks just to see if she still can."

"Scary."

"Retiring is scary. Taylor is damned good at what she does, but it's best to go out while you're still on top."

"So, what does she do for you now?"

"Little jobs."

"You call breaking in there a little job?"

"Hey, did you see any armed guards? No. Any perimeter

with watchdogs? No. What's in there are scientists, and if we can't beat a bunch of propeller-heads, we don't deserve to take people's money."

"Then why all the heavy weaponry?"

Delta rose and helped me to my feet. "It's been my experience that people do what you tell them to do when you point really big weapons at them. If this doesn't go as planned, Connie and I will do what's called a simple John Wayne and Sly Stallone, and go in there with guns blazing, taking out everyone we can. They'll never know what hit them."

"Aren't you…you know…afraid of getting caught?"

"Guns blazing doesn't mean we *plan* on shooting everyone. It just means we point them at people and get what we want."

"That makes me feel a little better."

Delta grinned. "Really?"

I looked at her and sighed. "Honestly? Shit no."

She chuckled. "I didn't think so."

As dusk approached, Taylor double-checked her equipment against the computer. The infrared, the camera, the audio all flashed green. She checked her headset and the dozen or so pockets on her as well as the two sets of throwing knives in the pockets along the sides of her thighs. I didn't want to know if she had ever had to use those. I was pretty sure she had.

"Knives?" Danica said, folding her arms across her chest. "You're kidding, right?"

Taylor stopped and cocked her head. Then, in a move so fast I barely caught it all, she whipped one out and threw it at a tree about thirty feet away. It stuck solidly. "They incapacitate more quietly than guns."

"Oh." Danica left it at that.

"Okay, gals, looks like I'm ready. You yahoos ready to watch a pro in action?"

I nodded. My heart was racing a million miles an hour and my palms were sweaty. She seemed so cool and confident. Was it in the water or what? These women felt no fear.

"Good. Now, unless I give you the high sign that I am in trouble, you are to stay put. Stay put."

I looked over at Delta. "What's the high sign?"

"A flare."

"She's got a flare in that tight little Emma Peel outfit of hers?" Danica asked.

Delta nodded. "Of sorts."

Walking up to Taylor, Delta hugged her. Something passed between them that felt like love; no...not just love...the camaraderie soldiers must feel toward each other prior to going to battle. Whatever these two had shared at one time ran deep—really deep. "Don't mess around in there, Taylor. In and out, just like we planned."

"Gotcha. Don't leave me hanging, Storm."

"Never."

With that, Taylor set out over the incline and Delta grabbed her duffel bag and said something to Connie before walking up to us. "This is it. If this thing goes south, you do exactly what Connie tells you to—to the letter. Don't ask any questions, don't doubt, wonder or stop to think. Just. Do. It."

Danica and I both nodded.

When Delta was gone, Danica turned to Connie. "What's the deal with the two of them, anyway?"

Connie looked up. "Them? What do you mean?"

"You know what I mean."

Connie turned back to the monitor. "Those two women are almost as connected as Delta and I are."

"How is that possible?"

"Living through some pretty hairy life-and-death situations brings people closer together, don't you think?" Connie looked at me when she asked this.

"They weren't lovers then?"

"Hell no. Delta would never cheat on Megan. Ever. It's not in her character. No, this is something very different. They actually started out on opposite sides and came together when Megan needed help. She's been part of our family ever since."

"Family, huh?"

"Hell yeah. We've been through a lot together. They trust

each other with their lives. You don't feel that from someone unless you've been in the trenches together. Believe me. They have."

Danica and I both nodded. "So, what all is in that duffel bag of hers?"

"The usual: smoke canisters, rifle, handguns, infrared binoculars and an assortment of other goodies to help us out if things slide sideways." Connie held a finger up as she spoke into the Bluetooth perched on her ear and told Megan everyone was in position. With military precision, they moved like soldiers on the battlefield. It was pretty amazing.

Connie motioned for Danica to take the folding chair next to her. Bailey hadn't left the table the entire time.

Standing at Bailey's right shoulder, I looked at the monitors as they started to life. Taylor was swiftly moving through the fields toward the back of the warehouses.

"Won't they have security cameras on the exterior?"

"We've taken care of those. Don't worry."

I marveled at how swiftly Taylor moved in that leather outfit of hers—a throwback to some comic book character, I was sure. The suit was so tight, it looked spray-painted on.

"She found the dog," Connie said. "She'll wait a bit now, before going in. See if they send someone out after her."

I looked at Danica, but said nothing. "Taylor knows how fast or how slow to take this. She's a pro. It's good the dog is outside. If Taylor comes out the same way she goes in, the dog can act as her shield, maybe nab anyone thinking they're going to follow her."

"Is that what you want him to do?" Bailey asked.

Connie turned and studied Bailey a moment. In that moment, something transpired between the two of them that I felt, but could not quite grasp. "Actually, yes. That would be good."

Bailey nodded and returned her attention to the monitor. If she was communing with Buster, I did not feel it.

We watched Taylor not move for almost twenty full minutes. How they could all remain so calm was beyond me. They seemed to actually be enjoying this. I would be gray-haired if I had to do this more than once.

"She's moving," Connie whispered into the Bluetooth. I thought she meant Taylor, but she was talking about Delta.

"I thought she was—"

"She'll get in the best position to protect Taylor and the kids. Hang on. I'm getting something from Megan. Yeah? You sure? Okay. Taylor, did you get that? Good. Good to know. It's all a go, Taylor. Your call." Connie turned to me. "Megan's just saying the roads are clear, but they found an odd roadblock on the other side of the road. Could be nothing." Connie returned her attention the monitor and I watched as Danica tucked her Glock into the back of her pants.

"What in the hell are you doing?"

"Precautions, Clark. Always be prepared, right?"

"Taylor's going in."

I watched her kneel down and pick the lock as easily as it would have taken me to open it with a key. I thought I was going to heave, I was so nervous. "What if it's a trap?"

"We don't play monkey mind, Echo. Taylor will show us exactly what's going down."

The four of us watched the monitor as we saw Taylor crack the door open in order to get inside. The door barely moved; it was like her whole body was double-jointed or something. It had to have been open less than six inches.

"Okay. Get ready to jack their power. On my count. Five, four, three, two, one, go."

Suddenly, Taylor's camera went dark and then I realized it was on infrared and we could still see everything she was seeing even with the lights off.

"She's in."

None of us moved. We just stood there, eyes glued to the monitor, no one breathing.

"My God…" Bailey uttered. "They've turned those warehouses into…hospital corridors?"

She was right. You would never know by the outside façade that the interior looked like the inside of a hospital or laboratory. The floors were slick-looking, and it was as if Taylor were standing in a hallway of a hospital.

As she moved from room to room like some black cat in the night, she managed to get by the first of three cameras before the lights went back on. When they did, her camera flickered as it made the adjustment back to white light. She moved so quickly now, it was as if she knew her way around.

At first, it appeared as if no one was there and maybe we were too late. She passed a couple of the rooms Cooper had described as being like dorm rooms, but there wasn't any sign someone lived there. She made her way across the hallways more carefully, sure to look around to locate any security camera before moving.

"Temp ceiling," she whispered, looking up. In the background I could hear footsteps approaching. It took everything I had not to wet my pants.

Before I knew it, before I could even blink, she had pulled herself up and was now moving along the horizontal beams holding up the ceiling panels. She went from black cat to spider monkey in two point two seconds. I was riveted as she used some sort of wire gadget and attached herself to the beam above her head. This kept her suspended above the ceiling tiles and she was able to move more swiftly across the beam.

She was almost in complete darkness now, making her way toward the sounds I couldn't distinguish from the Bluetooth.

"She's inhuman," Danica muttered. "How can she move so quickly in the dark?"

"She sees the world differently than the rest of us," Connie explained. "Some people are naturally born with better night vision. Taylor's one of them. It's just one of her many skills. Told you. She was born to this."

We watched in silence as she made her way over the beams, nearing an area where light beamed up through the cracks, and voices could be heard. She was finally nearing human activity, and the closer she got, the closer we all moved to the monitor. When she was right above the voices, she stopped moving. For almost ten minutes, she remained motionless and I'm pretty sure I stopped breathing.

"What's she doing?" Bailey asked.

"Gauging. Something might be going down."

"How long can she just stand there?"

Connie sighed. "Hours if she has to."

I was dying here. The stress was killing me. I was sweating, my heart was racing, and my stomach was up in my throat. I wasn't cut out for this.

Suddenly, the lights went out, and I heard Taylor mutter, "Shit."

"Uh-oh," Connie said. "Storm? Did you get that?"

"Ten-four. She been made?"

"I don't think so, but something's happening. Hold tight."

We waited for what felt like forever, until Taylor whispered. "They're jamming."

"Shit!" Connie spat. "Meg, did you get that?"

"Affirmative."

"They're on the move. There may be too many to stop, so wait for a count and an advisory."

"Got it. Where we are, we can run a nail trip and taken them all out. They won't make it to the freeway."

"Hang on." Connie turned to us. "They either know she's in there, or are moving because they have him. I don't want to scare you, but Cooper and the girl could already be dead." Connie fiddled with the contrast on the monitor. "However, the fact that they're cutting and running means they're afraid of someone or something. I'd like to think that someone is us." Connie pressed the Bluetooth closer to her ear. "Are they leaving *en masse*?"

The camera moved up and down.

"Chief?" It was Delta. "I'm moving closer. If I go in—"

"I'm right behind you." She turned to Danica. "And that means *just* me. I'm sure you know how to use that thing, but this is serious and we can't be worrying about you guys. Unless you have superpowers, I'd rather not put any of you in harm's way."

The three of us looked at each other, but no one said a word.

Connie adjusted the volume on the Bluetooth so we could hear better.

"They're taking two girls," Taylor whispered. She was on the move again, only this time, she had her face down near the ceiling. "Drugged. Loading in plain white vans."

"Got it. How many?"

"Vans? Garage full. Can't tell for sure from here. Ten maybe? All white."

Connie pulled up the layout of the land on the screen as well as the blueprint made by Taylor's movements. "Looks like she's at the northern end, Del."

"We can't stop a mass exodus of ten vans, Con, but we *could* be taking on more than we bargained for. If we assume they have weapons in those vans, we're way outnumbered."

Connie nodded. "Agreed. Hold your position. Meg, unless we get a positive ID on the right van, we're going to have to let them go."

"Let them go?" Danica said. "Are you kidding me?"

Connie did not take her eyes from the screen. "Even if there was only one person in each van, we're still outnumbered. We're not suffering any casualties here, Danica. The animal with the worst bite is that which is cornered. Since they appear to be on the run, they must feel cornered."

I thought my heart was going to leap from my chest. How could things move so slowly one minute and then race by me the next? I was barely able to keep up, and there was a strange sound in the air I couldn't place. It felt like I had vertigo or something.

"Only one thing to do," Taylor whispered.

"What?" All four of us said in unison.

We watched in silence again as she quickly maneuvered to the crawl space. Her camera was all over the place now as she got closer to the ceiling and then, in one swift motion, almost supernaturally fast, slid under one of the ceiling tiles and landed on the floor of what looked like a large garage. There were several identical vans facing her. Their lights were off and it didn't appear they were running, but there was a loud sound, like a generator running in the background.

"What's she doing?" Bailey asked.

"Wish I knew," Connie replied. "Taylor?"

We waited for her to answer. Nothing. We could see what she saw, but she obviously didn't feel it was safe enough to talk or explain.

"What's that sound in the background?" Danica asked.

"Van doors sliding open." Connie whispered. "Shit. Del, Taylor is trying to see which of the vans they're loading the kids into."

"You can't stop them from the inside, Taylor. They'll kill you." Delta's voice was sharp.

We could hear voices now; voices of people barking orders and feet flooding into the garage area. I couldn't tell where Taylor was by the camera. In the blink of an eye, she was under the carriage of one of the vans and staring up at the chassis.

"She's not going to—"

"Shh." Connie turned the volume up. We could only hear bits and pieces, but it was enough to scare the crap out of me.

"...charges set?"

"Less than ten..."

"...handcuffed and gagged...don't..."

"Fuck!"

The last one was Taylor's voice. We couldn't hear much over the van doors opening and closing and people yelling and moving about. She lowered herself slightly so she could see the legs of all the people scrambling to get in and move supplies and equipment in as well.

"She's looking for the kids," Connie explained. Now I saw beads of sweat on Connie's upper lip. The tension she felt was palpable even for a non-empath.

"From down there?"

"When Taylor first looked through the ceiling, she saw a pair of Converse tennis shoes," Delta said softly.

Danica looked at me. "I never saw that."

"I've been doing this a long time, Dani. I knew what Taylor was looking at. It's what she's looking *for* now."

More talk and chattering ensued as people loaded the vans with equipment from the warehouse.

"...the girls..."

"...time in less than three..."

"Con?" Taylor's voice was barely above a whisper.

"Right here, Taylor. What you need?"

"Tracking device," she whispered. Taylor moved to one side of the van, dropped onto her back, rolled across the floor, and then lifted herself up to the undercarriage of the next van. She repeated this maneuver until she was under the third van. Then, she showed a small, circular disk and placed it on the van.

"She's located which van they're on. Megan, we've got a tracer on the van with the Converse."

"Copy that, Con. We have it here as well. We need to separate it from the group."

"Can you do it without alerting the other vans?"

"We'll go with the nail strip, see if we can't slow it down some. Sal will block off the path of the other vans. I think we got this one covered from our end."

"Good. We move on Taylor's go."

"Copy. Be careful."

We watched as the garage doors opened, but could see little of that from Taylor's ground-level position.

"How's she—"

"Is she going to ride out like that?"

Connie shook her head. "I don't know. Taylor? You need to roll when that van leaves."

"No can do, Chief. I didn't get what I came here for." Then the vans' engines started and light flooded the area.

It made sense to me now how easy it had been for Taylor to get in. They didn't care who was coming in; they were more concerned with getting out.

"They're leaving," Delta said. "Taylor's not with them."

I could feel the energy in Connie's demeanor change. Something was wrong.

"The vans are all pulling out. The tracer is on the move as well."

"The boy..." Taylor was still whispering, but it was hard to hear her above all the noise. "He is still here." Taylor suddenly dropped to the ground and rolled to the side of the garage just as the last of the vans pulled out. We watched as the garage doors closed, cutting off any light she may have had.

"What do you mean he's still in there?" Connie asked. I felt a slight panic rise in her.

"Get the kids," Taylor said, standing up now. "They're in the fourth van."

"Megan?"

"We're all over it, Con. Taylor going after the kid?"

"Looks that way. Taylor, they gone?"

"Don't know yet. They're blowing this thing in less than two minutes. This place is huge. Keep my time, Con."

"At two. One fifty-nine." Connie nodded and wiped the sweat from her top lip. "Del? Get closer, but hold your ground. Do not, and I repeat, do *not* go near that warehouse until I give the okay."

"Gotcha, oh bossy one. Moving forward."

We watched Taylor's webcam as she moved swiftly through all the rooms. "Something's not right. They wouldn't have left the kid alive unless—"

We all huddled together as Taylor came to a locked door. She rattled the doorknob and then stopped to listen. "Might be in here."

"Dead?"

"Won't know till I get in here. Time?"

"One forty-three."

Taylor stepped up to the door, examining it. Her camera took in every bit of it. "See anything I ought to be nervous about?"

Connie looked closer at the monitor. "Can't see anything you need to worry about," Connie said. "One thirty-three. Do not let this wind down, Taylor. You get out with thirty seconds on the dial."

A familiar sound reverberated in the air in the distance, but I was too worried about Taylor to pay it any mind. Taylor reached into one of her zippered pockets and pulled out her lock picking tools. In a matter of seconds, which was about all she had now, she had that lock picked and the door thrown open.

Before she could take a step inside, an invisible force smashed into her, sending her crashing hard against the wall. We could hear the breath leave her body as she hit it, and then slide to the floor.

"What the hell?" Connie was on her feet now as the webcam crunched against the cement floor. "Taylor?"

Danica and Bailey were also on their feet.

"Taylor? Taylor, come in! Are you all right? Shit! Both her camera and her audio are offline. Taylor!"

"Goin' after her, Chief."

"Of course you are. Get the lead out then, old lady. Time's tickin'. Meg?"

"We've got it covered from our end. Get in your car and get the hell out of there!"

Yeah. Like that was going to happen. The sound I couldn't place was getting closer.

"What are you…why are you…" I couldn't make out the rest of Taylor's words. She must have gotten to her headset.

"She has less than a minute."

I looked down at the monitor and saw Delta was about twenty yards from the door. We were too far to be of any help to Taylor, but Delta wasn't. The sound got louder, Connie felt more anxious than ever, and all four of us held our collective breath waiting to see what Delta was going to do.

When Delta did finally make her move, what I saw wasn't anything I expected.

I don't know what I thought would happen. Did I expect her to just go running in there like a crazy woman in order to get Taylor out? I had counted on a lot of things happening; what I hadn't counted on was Buster.

When Delta got close enough to the door, Buster bared his teeth and barred the door.

"Bailey?" I said, but she was already nodding.

Out of nowhere, Bailey hit a running speed humanly impossible, and when I turned to look at Connie, I realized she was thinking the same thing.

"Holy shit….How…"

"Not important," I replied. "What's going on with Taylor?"

"Cooper won't let her near him. Says he'd rather burn up than let Taylor get him."

"He knows Delta," I said.

"And Buster," Danica added.

Connie took a deep breath and nodded. "Go for it, Storm," she said into the headset, but Delta could not get around Buster.

"Release her," I muttered, wondering why Bailey wasn't letting Buster loose so they could go inside. "Release Buster God damn it!"

Things slowed down at that point, and it felt like time had

slipped a cog. Delta, ignoring the growling and raised hackles of Buster, reached for the doorknob. Buster leapt at her and knocked her out of the way; but not before Delta had turned the handle.

It was too late to see why Buster had been guarding the door until seven enormous rottweilers emerged from it, snapping and growling in a vicious parade of black fur. One huge dog hurled itself at Delta, teeth flashing, snarling like some rabid creature bent on tasting Delta's blood.

It would have too, only Buster met the rottweiler in midair, knocking it away from Delta, who had fallen back when the door swung open. The two dogs landed in a heap of fur, tumbling end over end.

"Run, Storm!" Connie yelled, going down on one knee to shoot the second dog emerging from the warehouse.

Delta got up and started running, but there was no way she was going to out run all of those dogs and no way Connie was going to be able to shoot them all before one of them was able to sink their teeth into Delta's flesh.

Luckily for Delta, she didn't have to outrun them, because Bailey blew by Delta, and stopped on a dime near the entrance of the warehouse as several more dogs exited the building.

"No!" Delta cried, pulling her handgun out and taking aim.

I couldn't let Delta take a shot at creatures I knew Bailey was capable of stopping, so I pushed out an energy shield and knocked Delta to the ground. When I looked up, my eyes met Connie's and for a brief second, I wondered if we were still on the same side. She may not have seen me attack Delta with my shield, but she knew something weird had just happened.

When we turned back around, Delta was picking herself up off the ground, and Bailey had all of the dogs plus Buster sitting at attention.

When Delta got up she looked for her weapon before looking at Bailey and the dogs. "What the hell?"

Before anyone could answer, that strange sound came at us from over the side of a larger hill.

"Chopper!" Delta cried as a black helicopter like one of the

Blackhawk helicopters whooshed over the hill coming directly for us.

"Run for it, Clark! Get in the SUV!" Danica pushed me toward the incline, but I knew it was too late. The helicopter was on us before we could get around it.

Danica pulled her Glock and fired at the now grounded helicopter, but all four shots missed. After the fourth shot missed, she looked at her Glock as if there were something wrong with it. "I shoulda kept my old piece."

Kneeling, Connie and Delta both fired off rounds that seemed to miss the big machine as well. Their reaction was much like Danica's had been. The bullets seemed to pass right through it. There should have at least been some pinging noises, but the only sound came as the rotors slowed down, spewing dust and leaves into the air around us. The dogs all scattered as dirt and debris flew into their snouts.

And then, it happened.

The warehouse behind us blew like something you'd see in a movie. Big, fiery balls shot up straight in the air. Several more explosions went off after the initial one, lighting up the night sky and rattling the ground beneath us.

"No!" Delta cried, turning back to the now destroyed building. "Taylor!"

But Connie had her arms around her preventing her from charging back into the burning building. "It's too late, Del. It's too late!"

"No no no no!" Delta threw her arms around Connie and gripped her hard. They stood there like this for only a moment before Delta pushed away, picked up her gun, and started walking right toward the helicopter—a woman with a score to even.

I didn't have the faintest idea what she thought she was going to do. Taylor and Cooper were dead, our weapons had proven useless, and the people in that chopper were probably going to kill us all anyway.

The way I saw it…things could only get better.

The sliding door on the side of the helicopter opened and five people in black jumpsuits jumped out. I knew I could throw a protective shield around us all, but I couldn't stop bullets. If they drew down on us, we were toast.

That's when I realized they weren't even carrying weapons. They didn't have to; they were supers.

As Delta aimed her weapon at the tall blonde leading the way, one of the psis waved his hand, kicking Delta's gun about thirty feet away. Delta looked down at her empty hand and then over to Connie, who looked at the gun in her own hand before tossing it on the ground. The only two people moving now were me and Bailey.

"Don't move, Delta," I ordered. "This is *our* fight now."

"I can take her."

I shook my head. "Uh-uh." I turned to her and we locked eyes. I needed her to do as I said and not to fight me on this. I needed her to understand that this thing had just taken a turn for the worse and I needed her alive. I needed her to be as perceptive as she had shown me she was these last couple of days. I needed her to let me take charge now. "Trust me. Please. Let me handle this."

She looked from me to Connie and back to me. Ever so subtly, she acquiesced and nodded slowly, motioning for Connie to do the same. "You're on. Get us out of this."

I turned back around to face the young blonde who stood in the center of her pack. I kept my shields up and reinforced them. I didn't need to read her to know she was not on our side. Everything about her said she was a worthy adversary. I needed to be at the top of my game.

Bailey leaned her head toward me. "They're—"

"I know. Let loose the Kraken." Bailey nodded and stepped back. I felt Danica next to me. It would have been futile to ask her to stand back. We were in this together. Win, lose or draw, Danica Johnson would never leave my side.

From behind me I heard Delta say to Connie, "Chief, I don't think we're in Kansas anymore."

The blonde approaching us with a smug look on her face mistakenly thought this battle over.

She was tall; close to six feet, with an Uma Thurman look about her that made me dislike her immediately. It must have been those *Kill Bill* movies or maybe it was just the arrogant way she approached us—as if we could do her no harm.

"Where's the kid?"

"What?" I was buying Bailey as much time as I could to get the dogs ready. So far, I recognized the energy from two very strong TKs, a telepath, a seer, and the one I was most afraid of: a fire starter. They had quite the arsenal in their lineup, but the one I couldn't read at all was the bitch standing before me, arms akimbo.

"Cooper. All we want is him and we'll leave you alone."

I glanced over her shoulder and into the chopper. We were screwed. They had two girls bound together. Too late, I turned to see Delta flying toward her.

With a wave of her hand, the redhead behind the blonde knocked Delta out. As Delta fell to the ground, Connie made her move and was treated to the same courtesy. Side by side, they lay unconscious.

I knew they could kill Delta and Connie before I could stop them, so I raised my hands in surrender. "Cooper's dead. He never made it out of the warehouse. Those two don't know anything."

She turned to the telepath, who shook her head. *Yeah*, I thought. *Try to read this, bitch.* She couldn't read me and wasn't at all sure why not.

"My girl says you're full of shit."

"Your *girl* needs to get her powers readjusted...or maybe she ought not to assume that because we haven't blown her brains out the back of her head that we're just average, everyday folks." I stepped closer and the other TK raised his hand to me. I projected a field preventing him from touching me with his. The look on his face was priceless. "Cooper's dead. Take your two prizes and be off. We don't have an ax to grind with you, but we will if we have to."

The blonde cocked her head. "Well, well, well. An amateur

member, eh? I didn't recognize it with all the riffraff you've surrounded yourself with." Then she laughed and jerked her thumb over her shoulder. "Those two are hardly prize worthy. They're zombies. Brains are fried to hell and gone. We came for the boy. Get in our way and you're history." She turned to the fire starter, a kid barely out of her teens who grinned at me.

Suddenly, I picked up an energy I hadn't expected to feel. Ever so slowly, the tide shifted, and my hopes rose that we might just get out of this alive. "What did you do to the two people at the end of the road?"

"Dismantled their engine, that's all. We're not into the mass killing of naturals, Peanut. We merely disrupted all of their electrical energy so they couldn't communicate."

Ah, so that was the power of the one I couldn't quite put my finger on. Electricus was a being who could manipulate electricity and currents.

"We're not sociopaths. We just came for the boy and will leave as soon as you tell us where he is."

I took one more step. "I told you. He's dead. He never got out of the warehouse."

"I know what you *said*. Maybe you even believe it, but he's alive and we're not leaving here without him." She cocked her head toward me and leaned in slightly, as if to get a closer look at me. It was weird. Pulling away, she turned to the telepath once more, who shook her head.

Yeah, she'd been trying to read me, but I ate telepaths like her for breakfast.

"Who *are* you, anyway?" She asked me.

I stared at her. It was *Cooper's* energy I had been feeling all this time. He *was* alive and they knew it.

We were about six feet apart now. I was almost close enough to blast her with my most powerful shield, but the timing had to be perfect. What in the hell was Bailey waiting for?

I answered her. "I'm just someone who cares that Cooper is safely away from those people."

She cocked her head once more. "*Those* people? Aren't you funny? Look, we know you belong with them. Supers like you

make me sick; turning our kind over to the likes of these scum."
She fairly spat as she spoke.

"Look, you got the girls, and that's all you're getting, so scoot
along now, before someone gets hurt." I was getting anxious
about Bailey. Where *was* she?

The fire starter telegraphed her move, enabling me to deflect
the warning shot she threw at me.

"Honey," the blonde growled, "if anyone gets hurt, it won't
be us. Look at you. You're totally outnumbered."

"Oh, really? If you're so good, how come you don't have
Cooper?" I took another half step. I felt Cooper strongly now.
He was nearby. So was...no...yes! So was *Taylor*. I didn't know
how they got out of that warehouse alive, but they were and they
were coming to help.

"Take the girls and go." I said this with as much calm and
cool as I could muster. I heard nothing except the beating of my
heart and...and hers. She was bothered by my noncompliance;
bothered that I wasn't afraid when I should have been. But there
was something else bothering her. She couldn't place my powers
and her telepath couldn't read me, so she wasn't sure how to
handle me. That hesitation would cost her.

"We're not leaving without Cooper." She growled at her
telepath. "Why can't you reach him? He's not experienced
enough to know anything about blo—" then she turned back
and stared at me. "*You* taught him how to shield? That's a new
one for Genesys. Fuckers."

"You want to fight for him? Bring it."

She stepped up to me, her energy changing back and forth
like a decision she couldn't make. Something was really bothering
her, distracting her. "*Bring it*? Look around you, Peanut. Your
guns are useless, and you—" She was right up on me, but instead
of towering over me, she recoiled as if I had slapped her and
took a half a step back. "What...what the fuck happened to your
ear?"

My hand instinctively went to my ear, where my scar was.
"What?"

"That scar. How...how did you get it?"

"Are you A.D.D or something?" I turned to Bailey, who

barely nodded. Suddenly, out of nowhere, came the remaining six dogs, including Buster. Walking slowly, they encircled us and stood rigidly awaiting Bailey's instructions.

"If you think you can get to us before these dogs tear your fucking throats out, then go for it, *Peanut*."

She looked at me and then wheeled around and glared at Bailey. "A fucking creature."

I could hear sirens in the distance.

I stepped up and closed the gap between me and the blonde. She couldn't take her eyes off my scar. "Beat it."

She worked hard to keep her glare going, but she was truly distracted. "Do you...do you have *any* idea what I could do to you?"

My lip curled. "Go for it, honey."

Then everything about her energy changed, and it changed so fast, I didn't have time to read it. "Oh my God. Charlie?"

My breath caught in my throat. "What?"

She blinked several times and then moved in closer. "Son of a bitch. It *is* you."

I stared at her. "You're not—"

She swallowed hard and nodded. "I am. I'm Kristy. Your sister."

The entire group gasped their surprise at this turn of events.

"Kristy? My sister? You're my *sister*?"

She nodded and motioned for the TK holding Connie and Delta down to release his hold on them. Then she cocked her head. She heard the sirens as well. "Yeah, and those marks are mine."

"Uh-uh. A dog bit me."

"Who told you that? Look carefully at those marks. Those aren't dog teeth prints. They're human, and they're mine. Ask the creature. She'll tell you." She shook her head. "Holy shit. I always wondered if we might meet, but I never let myself believe you just might be alive."

"Well...I am, but I don't remember you biting me. I don't even remember *you*."

"You have to believe I'm your sister. Our parents are Harmon and—"

I held up my hand for her to stop. This was too much. "Kristy."

"Kristy died a long time ago, probably about the same time Charlie died. Who are you now?"

"Echo."

"I'm Scion. Do you know what a scion is? It is a detached shoot or twig containing the buds from a plant. They use the shoot when grafting a foreign branch to another tree. Grafting, Charlie. They do that in farming to make a tree or a crop better...more viable...more disease and resistant to pests. It's how we got the tangelo and the limon. It's how you get this." Stepping away from me, she put her hands out at her sides as one would who was hanging from a cross. She closed her eyes and turned into a giant lightning rod. I had to jump back to avoid whatever it was that came from the heavens and struck her. After they struck her, lightning bolts hurled from her hands, her head, her hips, her knees, everywhere. She glowed like a red-hot poker, only so hot she was white. Turning her head, she opened her eyes and blew up a boulder. Then she closed her eyes and powered down.

That display of power was *very* scary, but I wasn't going to let her know it.

"There's no time to go into it. I'm a hybrid: a genetically altered being with powers artificially constructed in a lab."

I blinked rapidly. "I don't understand."

"Of course you don't. The fact that you and your motley crew are here speaks volumes about just how much you *don't* understand. I am a half-finished project of those fuckers at Genesys. Like you, I was born with powers. I was a mere telekinetic before those bastards got their hands on me. Somewhere along the way, they stopped wanting to poke and prod us or understand what we were. They decided they wanted to play God...to actually *create* a new species. They thought it might be fun to have a TK who could shoot lightning out of her ass. Well, you're looking at what a half-finished project looks like. I'm one of the few to get out with my life intact." She shook her head. "I got away and not only lived to tell about it, but made sure *I* became the biggest pain in the ass they'd ever met."

"You were—"

"One of their guinea pigs? Test subjects? Experiments? Try all of the above, Charlie. They had me for three of the longest years of my life, poking, sticking needles in me, drugging me, and then giving me a nice little genetic modification that royally screwed my life up. When my body started rejecting the genome, they sedated me. I spent a year of my life under sedation. It was worse than any nightmare you can ever imagine."

She brushed something off her face. I thought it might have been a tear, but I doubted it. This woman wasn't telling this story with sadness. She was angrier than hell. "And what did I find out about my little powers? If my body has absorbed enough lightning energy, the next time I put my arms around someone, I'll fry them in a matter of seconds. Yeah, you shoulda seen the look on my first boyfriend's face when I cooked him like I was some kinda fuckin' microwave. He was dead before he hit the ground."

The sirens were getting louder. "But I thought you were with Harmon. Did he know?"

"Know? Know?" She chuckled bitterly. "Charlie, he's the one who set it all up. Daddy dearest handed me over to Genesys the moment my powers kicked in."

My hand went to my mouth. "No."

"Oh yes. And he would have come back to the States to get *you*, but you vanished, didn't you? He sold us out, sis. He knew he had something he could use to bargain for a new life. He dealt when the time came."

"For what?"

"His freedom, I suppose. Lots and lots of money. Who knows? Who cares? If I ever run into him again, I will kill him on the spot, but it won't be a quick or painless death. Oh no. That would be too good for that asshole."

I felt like a computer receiving too much information. "I had no idea."

"Ten years ago he picked me up at the boarding school when I called and told him something weird was happening to me. He dropped me off at the Russians' doorstep and left me there. Left me like he left me the first time he dropped me off at a boarding school in China. Do you have any idea how frightening it is for a four-year-old to be in school where she doesn't understand the language? I waited every night for six months for him to come get me. When he did, I was nine years older and moving shit with a wave of my hand."

"Kristy, I—"

"I told you. It's Scion now. Kristy died a long time ago. Scion rose from the many ashes of the lab techs she fried both accidentally and on purpose. I was a killer before I turned ten. Do you know what that does to a little girl's soul?"

I shook my head and tried not to think of Cinder. The sirens grew louder. They were almost to us.

"Kristy and Charlie died the day we became something more than human."

"I don't know how you can say that."

"You don't know. Honestly, the sad truth is, you don't know jack. Saving other paranormals from Genesys is what I do, Charlie, and after I save them, they can choose to return and try to live a normal life, or they can become one of us." She touched the patch on her jumpsuit. It bore the acronym S.T.O.P.

"Stop?"

"Save the Other Paranormals. This crew joined me after I rescued them. We're an elite squad who comes in and handles the tougher assignments. We travel all over the world helping those like Cooper." She closed the gap and looked down at me. "Join us, Charlie. Make a difference."

I shook my head sadly. "I have a life. A good life."

She made a sound of disgust. "There will be no *life* for us as long as there are people in the world like Harmon who see us as a commodity. The writing is on the wall. There will come a time when the world will acknowledge that we exist. If we don't establish that we will *not* tolerate deviant or aggressive behavior toward us right away...we'll be like Jews during World War Two."

"I'm already a part of something; something that's more family than any foster family I ever had."

"Look, Echo, Melika served a purpose in her day, but times are different now. *Life* is different. Her methods are passé."

I had never mentioned Mel's name to her.

"It's time for us to unite and stop pretending we blend in. We *don't* blend. We are different. We have capabilities naturals can only dream about. That's why *we* need Cooper more than you do. We need offensive power. We need those who can hit back or strike first. So, where is he?"

"I'm right here."

We all turned to see Cooper coming over the incline. Taylor was not with him, but she wasn't far.

"How in bloody hell—" Bailey stammered.

Cooper marched up to where Delta and Connie were. "Taylor's okay. She took some flying debris to her shoulder, but we made it out alive, thanks to her." Cooper turned to the TK who had held them down. "Don't touch them again."

"Cooper," Kristy said. "These women would gladly put a bullet—"

"I said, Leave. Them. Alone." Cooper squeezed his fists near his cheeks and sent a shockwave so hard, it knocked all five of them to the ground. The dogs tightened their circle and I stepped back.

When Delta, barely conscious, tried reaching for her weapon, Bailey stopped her. "Don't. This isn't your fight."

I stepped back to my sister. "You underestimate me, little sister." I whirled to the TK and shook my head as he started to raise his hands. "Use your powers again against my crew and we'll let those dogs tear you apart. Think you can stop all of them in time?"

"You're making a big mistake, Charlie."

"The world isn't so black and white. We're both helping young supers the best way we know how. There's room enough in this world for both methods."

She shook her head. "No, Charlie, there isn't. You give them a false sense of security that they can actually live normal lives among the naturals. I'm offering them a chance to actually *make* the rules. I'm offering them a freedom you haven't even experienced yet. Just give us the boy and we'll call it even."

"Even?"

"Yeah. Somehow, you managed to get your paws on our little fire starter. We could have used another tank."

Tank was a familiar gaming term in discussing characters who went on the offensive. They were killers pure and simple.

"She's young yet. We might still—" Kristy stopped speaking when a loud, ominous clicking sound came over my right shoulder. I didn't need to see to know who it was.

Danica moved with such deliberate precision, she had the muzzle pressed against Kristy's cheek before anyone could move.

"You or your crew go anywhere near Cinder, *ever*, and there won't be a rock on this planet big enough for you to hide under. Not your power, not your sister, not even God himself will stop me from blowing your fucking brains out."

"Dani—"

"No, Clark. I want to hear her *say* it. I want her word she'll forget she ever heard about Cinder." Danica pressed the muzzle deeper into Kristy's cheek. "Go ahead and bring your lightning bolt, Thor. By the time you charge up enough, that bitch behind you will be wearing your brains like an apron." Danica's finger pressed slightly on the trigger. "You see, there's not much I care more about than Cinder, so you best give your word that she's no longer on your radar or I will drop you right here and take my chances that those dogs will tear your precious crew apart before they can hurt me."

My sister nodded slowly. "Vicious little pet you have here."

Danica leaned in and whispered. "This dog is all bite, Uncle Fester. Swear to whatever creature you pray to that Cinder will forever be safe from you."

Scion nodded again. "Fine. You have my word we'll leave Cinder alone. However, don't blame me if she ever comes to us willingly. Fire starters are killers by nature. Your kumbaya bullshit will wear thin on her one day."

Danica held the Glock steady, "Now shove off. The cops are coming and you can't have Cooper. End of story. Beat it."

Kristy looked at me, never taking her eyes from mine. "You understand, don't you, that all I needed to do was look at your bodyguard and she would have become hotter than a french fry."

"And she would have been the last thing you ever saw."

Kristy smirked. "Why don't we let Cooper decide where he wants to go. It's your call."

"No it isn't," I said.

Bailey put her hand on my shoulder. "Yes, E, it is." To Cooper she said, "Do what your heart tells you. We'll support you no matter what you want to do."

Cooper looked at the chopper that held his girlfriend and I knew the decision was made. "I appreciate all you guys have done for me, Echo, but...I'd rather help people like they do. It's nothing personal."

I wanted to try to convince him otherwise, but Bailey squeezed my shoulder. "Let him go, E. Fair is fair. He's old enough to make those decisions for himself. If it doesn't work out, you can always come to us."

I forced myself to nod.

"I'll make you proud, Echo. Really I will."

"You already do, Coop."

Scion turned to her crew and told them to secure him and prepare for takeoff. Then, she turned back to me, her eyes softening. "I never imagined you were really alive, Charlie. I guess Harmon lied so much, I just stopped believing everything he told me."

"At least he told you *you* had a sister. I never had that luxury."

"Actually, I had a few memories about us. He told me you had died of meningitis and your death sent Trish around the bend. It wasn't until I was older I realized my whole childhood was a pack of lies...I thought you dead, and now...here you are."

"Here I am."

"Maybe someday, we'll fight on the same side."

I nodded and watched as Bailey released the animals. "Anything is possible, but for now, I need to get to know my mother and grandmother and see if that doesn't help me figure out who I am."

She shook her head sadly. "He's such a fucker."

"Harmon?"

She shook her head. "He had you erased."

I nodded. "That's what I thought."

"He took you to a super who erased part of your memory."

"I thought erasers were a myth."

"You've probably never met a hybrid, either. That doesn't mean we don't exist. Few of us live beyond the grafting stages. They don't know why. An eraser is a hybrid as well."

"Can I get them back?"

She tilted her head in thought. The sirens grew louder and it sounded like they had finally made it past whatever roadblock they had created. "When an eraser wipes your memory out, he actually absorbs them himself."

"Whoa." This came from Bailey. "You're telling us some guy is walking around with her memories?"

She shrugged. "I'm just saying it's possible. They were doing a lot of weird shit back then." She looked over at Delta and Connie who were slowly getting to their feet. "We have our cleaners in the chopper. You want—"

I turned and looked at these two women who had risked their lives to help us. "No," I said, shaking my head. "Not them."

She turned to Danica, who had not lowered her gun. "What about Rambo, here?"

"Only if you want your cleaners sent home in body bags," Danica snarled.

My sister had a partial grin that resembled my own. "Yeah, I thought as much."

I motioned for Danica to lower her gun and take Delta and Connie out of earshot. Reluctantly, she did so.

"While I wish we could stay and chat, those cops are getting closer and we need to get the hell out of here."

We stood for a moment, just staring at each other; sisters. Sisters in crime. Sisters in blood. Sisters, at last. And yet, she was nothing more than a stranger to me. My real sister, the one who kept all my secrets, the one who kept harm at bay, the one who had killed a man to protect me, stood by my side now, knowing beyond any doubt where her place was in my heart.

"Do me a favor, will you?" Kristy asked as she started backing up toward the helicopter. "Explain to Trish what really happened. Tell her the reason I can't come home; that I'll never come home. Tell her the last time she spoke with me was when I was six. On my sixth birthday and that I carry that conversation with me everywhere I go. Anyone else she talked to after that was some other girl."

I nodded, feeling the incredible sadness she felt. "Kristy?"

She stopped, opened her mouth to correct me, and then stopped. "Yeah?"

"Why did you bite me?"

She grinned. "You had something I wanted and wouldn't give it to me."

I grinned at the irony. "At least this time you didn't bite me."

She smiled softly. "Almost. Take care of yourself, Charlie." And with that, she and her people jumped into the chopper.

I watched in silence as the chopper blades beat the air once more, kicking up more dust and leaves. Bailey and Danica both put their arms around me. It was harder than I thought it would be, watching her go. To have her right in front of me, only to have her disappear once more.

"You okay, Clark?"

That was a good question. "I guess I'm okay for someone who found her sister, lost her sister; found Cooper, lost Cooper; and found out that my father is the worst kind of scum on the planet."

Danica pulled me closer. "What counts is we're all alive."

"Barely," came Taylor's voice from behind us. She was holding a rag of some sort up to a wound on her shoulder.

"Taylor!" We all surrounded her. She was pale and shaky, but appeared to be all right.

"I don't know what happened. One minute we were screwed, the next, the whole damn wall blew out. Anyway, we didn't get far enough away from the explosions, and I caught a piece of debris. It's no biggie."

"Let me look at that," Bailey said.

Taylor pulled the bloody rag away. There was a five-inch gash in her shoulder that would surely require some stitches.

"We have to get out of here, ladies," Delta said, scooping up all the weapons and stuffing them in the duffel bag.

"We'll take Taylor in our car," Bailey said. "I can dress the wound there."

Taylor grinned, her energy seeping quickly from her. "You some sort of nurse?"

Bailey nodded. "Sorta." She put Taylor's arm around her and half-carried her back to the car. "Come on." Snapping her fingers, she called Buster to her, who waited while she loaded Taylor into our car.

In a fraction of the time it had taken us to get set up, we broke down our base camp, tossing everything quickly into Delta's Durango. She used her cell to call Megan to make sure she was fine. She was. Just panicky. After the Electricus had disabled our headgear, she had to wait and watch as the chopper came down and took the girls from the Genesys lab. She had no idea what happened next.

When we got the cars loaded, we just barely got out of the there before we saw the police and fire trucks as they made their way to the burning embers of what had been a Genesys lab.

Bailey took something out of her bag, sprinkled it on her palm and blew it in Taylor's face. Taylor's head slumped forward. She was out.

"We don't want to have to explain," Bailey said.

I nodded. "She going to be okay?"

"She's lost blood, but this is one tough woman."

"Hospital necessary?"

"I don't think so. I'll get her patched up and she should be fine."

"Looks to me like she needs stitches," Danica offered.

"She does. I don't use stitches. A little sap, a little superglue, and she'll be good to go."

"Ugh. Superglue?"

"Yeah. Superglue, Rambo." Bailey looked over her shoulder at Danica and grinned. "For a second there, I thought for sure you were going to put a bullet in her brain."

Danica looked at me as I drove over hedges and grasses in an attempt to keep up with Delta. "I would have if she wasn't Clark's sister. That bitch was getting on my last nerve."

I gripped the wheel as I saw the Durango go airborne. "Damn."

"Don't get us killed, Clark, really. The danger is over. They're never going to catch us."

The radio crackled and came to life. "How you guys doing back there?"

"Our teeth are rattling out of our heads, if you really want to know."

"Taylor okay?"

"Yeah. She's out," Danica said, looking in the backseat. "Bailey's tending to her now with Buster assisting."

"Good. Does she need a doctor?"

"Nope. Got one right here. We're good to go until we get home." Danica looked at Bailey to make sure that was right, and Bailey nodded. "We'll...uh...explain more then."

"That'd be good," Connie said. "Just one question, though, and then I'll leave you guys to discuss everything that happened back there."

"Go for it."

"Are you one of them?"

Danica smiled. "No, Con. I'm not. I'm good...just not that good." Putting the radio down, she chuckled. "Rambo, my ass."

It was nearly midnight by the time we got back into the city. Taylor had woken up just as we crossed the bridge and sat quietly nursing her bandaged shoulder. She was still pale, and very weak, but was in no pain. Bailey had stopped the bleeding and managed to close the wound with something resembling honey.

We didn't talk much on the drive back, and I was thankful for that. So much had happened and I just couldn't take it all in. I was so relieved everyone was okay, and that we hadn't had to sacrifice anyone for my mistakes. I was relieved to find my sister was alive even though she had suffered unimaginably at the hands of a company wanting to use her and others like her. I thought back to Tip's words and the promises she made to Melika. I would not be able to make such promises. Not now. Not ever. If they brought this battle to my doorstep, I would not hesitate to engage.

"*You there?*" I asked Tip.

"*Of course. You think I would let that go down without keeping tabs on you?*"

"*Oh, so you do break some promises, then?*"

"*Yep. When it comes to your safety, I do. I take it you don't need cleaners.*"

"*No.*"

"*Echo? What about your friends...your Charlie's Angels?*"

I smirked. "*Aren't you funny?*"

"*You can't let them remember any of this.*"

"*They were out for most of it. Look, I know the risks, and I threw the dice. I know what it's like not to have memories, Tip, and I will not do it to them.*"

"*Mel and The Others aren't going to be happy about that.*"

"*Tough shit. My sister was right, Tip; times have changed. Hell, I have changed. We don't need cleaners and that's the end of the discussion.*"

Pause. "*You all right?*"

"*Yeah. No. I don't know. I have a lot to think about.*"

"*What about the kid?*"

"*He went with them.*"

"*Damn. All that and you lost him.*"

"*I can see why they wanted him so badly. He blew out the entire side of a building. He'll make a nice offensive weapon for them.*"

"*You sound like you might admire what the group does.*"

"*I don't agree with the way they go about things, but they serve a purpose.*"

"*Funny, that's what they said about Mel. I'll fill you in about them and their tactics when I get there.*"

"*You're coming back here? Why?*"

"*To make sure you're okay and to get Bailey. There's another collection we need to make.*"

"*So soon? Tip—*"

"*She wants this, Echo, and she needs to be successful.*"

"*How do you know she won't have to fight S.T.O.P. for him or her? How do you know they won't be there every single time you go after someone?*"

"*They're not interested in lower level psi's. They're all about power. Like Cooper's.*"

"*And Cinder's?*"

"*Yeah.*"

I drove in silence for a little way, wondering where she went.

"*Still here. I know how you are, kiddo. You need to process everything that's happened to you, and that's a lot.*"

"*No kidding. I'm feeling a bit overwhelmed at the moment.*"

"*Hey, you did good. You're all in one piece. You got your people out in one piece. Be happy no one got hurt. You'll get it next time.*"

"*There won't be a next time, Tip. I am no collector.*"

"*No, you're not. You are so much more, although now isn't the time to talk about it. You get some rest tonight. I'll be by your place later tomorrow evening. Tell Bailey to be ready. We have a ten o'clock flight out of SFO.*"

"*Will do. And thank you.*"

"*Don't thank me yet, kiddo. You have a lot of explaining to do to Mel and The Others. Not cleaning your friends is going to be a tough one to pass through Congress. If it's any consolation, I'm on your side.*"

I grinned. She always was. "*I appreciate that. I can't wait to see you tomorrow.*"

"*Same here. Get some rest. You deserve it.*"

Looking in the rearview mirror, I saw that Bailey had fallen asleep with her head on Taylor's good shoulder. Buster was snoring so loudly, I was surprised he hadn't woken her up. Taylor's eyes were half-mast, but she was definitely coming to, and Danica...good old Danica, was wide awake and looking straight ahead.

"Some night, eh?"

"You could say that. I was sitting here trying to decide who's crazier: them or us."

"Them, S.T.O.P., or them Connie, Delta and Taylor?"

"The latter."

I nodded. "Too close to call?"

"Undoubtedly. They were like...enjoying all of that shit back there."

"Takes a special breed to do what they've done in their lives."

She nodded, and sighed. "Taylor was something to watch, huh?"

"So were you...Rambo."

"Shut up."

I laughed. "She could have fried you on the spot, Danica. What were you *thinking*?"

"I was thinking she needed to be *very* clear that my little firefly buddy is off-limits to Robin Hood and her merry band of mutants. I just wanted her to be crystal clear how much she was biting off if she ever chose to go there. If she or her pals go after Cinder, I'll spend the rest of my life hunting each and every one of them down. I may be a natural, but if I go ghetto, I may as well be one of you."

This made me smile. "I'm pretty sure she got the message. You know...there are times when I'm not quite sure you're sane."

"Me? *Me?* I'm the sanest one in the whole damn car! If I wasn't so—" Before she could finish, the vidbook beeped and she answered it.

The boys had been worried since they hadn't heard from her, so she gave them a brief rundown before asking them what sort of bonus they'd like. Their answer was that they wanted to make another video game, only they wanted to make it holographic.

"Order whatever equipment you need to make that happen, fellas. You've earned it." Closing the vidbook, she lay her head back on the headrest and sighed. "I have a good life, you know? Although taking care of your back is a twenty-four-seven job. Maybe I should get a raise." She pointed ahead. "What are you going to tell Starsky and Hutch?"

"I can't tell them the truth."

"Don't you think they pretty much already know it?"

"Not sure what they know, and not sure they'd care. Taylor could have been killed...they all could have been killed. You don't just start playing with their minds because they saw things we didn't want them to see."

Danica nodded, but was quiet a moment before saying,

"Weird how you struggled all this time with whether or not to tell Finn, but four women you just met have actually *seen* you in action."

I nodded, feeling this awful feeling in the pit of my stomach. "I'm thinking they're pretty good at keeping secrets."

"No shit. They've clearly got a few of their own. So, you're thinking about telling them who and what you are but still keep Finn in the dark?"

"I guess that says something about my relationship, huh?"

She laid a hand on my shoulder. "You're gonna end it, aren't you?"

I nodded again. "I have to. We're not at a place where I feel like I can tell her, and the truth is, I don't know if we ever will be."

"Yeah. Cut her loose. Make it a clean break. Finn deserves more and so do you. Just don't even *consider* going back to the Big Indian."

"I won't. I think I need to be alone right now. I have so much to process, so much to think about. I have a whole life I need to sort out; a mother to get to know. I told Tip earlier that I've changed. I think...before I drag anyone else into my life, I need to sort it out."

Danica squeezed my shoulder. "Yes, you do."

We drove the rest of the way in silence...well...relatively speaking. Buster sounded like a twin engine plane. As we made our way through the city, I thought about Danica having no compunction about pulling the trigger and killing my sister.

My *sister.*

That wasn't really what she was. Maybe biologically, but that was all. I had gone in search of my family, thinking I would learn something about myself, and I had. I learned I already had an irreplaceable family who loved me and trusted me to do the right thing. I had people who cared for me, taught me, listened to me, and helped me grow into the woman I was becoming. I had a mother, and her name wasn't Trish. I had brothers and uncles, and people who would put the muzzle of a gun against somebody's face if she felt we were being threatened.

I had a family.

Melika had told me I wouldn't know where I was going until I knew where I had been. I guess I kept expecting to come out of my perceived darkness from a childhood I couldn't remember and somehow be transformed.

Kristy was right about one thing: Charlie *was* dead. *My* life began the day I met a tall, spindly black girl who had her nose crammed in a computer book. My life, and who I would eventually become, started the day I beat a kid's head in with my math book for threatening that tall, spindly girl. Echo was born then, and anything that happened prior was immaterial and just not important.

Looking over at Danica, I grinned warmly.

"You gonna go all mushy on me now, aren'tcha, Clark?"

I chuckled. She knew me so well. "Not at all. I just want to say thanks…Rambo."

I could feel her glaring at me. "Pfft." She chuckled. "My pleasure, Clark. It's what we do." She looked in the backseat and shook her head. "So…that bitch was your sister."

"Looks like it."

"I'm thinking I don't care much for her."

"Ya think?"

"Pretty damn powerful with those laser beams blasting out of her eyes. I nearly crapped my pants."

"Yeah, that was a pretty amazing fireworks display."

"Were you…you know…tempted?"

"To?"

"Put on a red cape and leap tall buildings? What she does is pretty cool and sorta right up your alley. There was a moment there when I wondered if maybe you belonged with her."

"Not a chance. I'm no freedom fighter, Dani. I just want to help the supers live as normally as they can. I am not ready to spend my life fighting."

She was quiet a moment before chuckling. "Did you see the look of pure hatred in her eyes when I called her Uncle Fester?"

I started laughing. "I would have busted out a laugh if I hadn't been so flippin' scared. You're lucky she didn't turn you into ashes."

"I wasn't afraid of her. I can out butch any blonde any damn day of the week. The day I can't, you can punch this girl from the 'hood card."

"Out *butch*? Dani, I think you've been hanging around the lesbians too long. Trust me. Rambo trumps Uncle Fester any day."

She grinned. "Maybe you're right, but *I'm* not the one you have to worry about."

I turned to her. "Meaning?"

"You didn't see the small sparks flying between doctor and patient back there?"

"No. Get out!"

She laughed. "You better fine-tune your empathy radio, Clark. You really missed it."

I looked in the mirror and shook my head. "I'll be damned."

As I pulled into a parking spot near Delta's, Danica turned to me. "Clark, you told your sister you didn't know who Charlie was…do you know who Echo is?"

I smiled at the woman who meant more to me than life itself and nodded. "I do now."

"And?"

I stared into her brown eyes, knowing that what I was about to say would change the course of both our lives.

"I'm the woman who is going to replace Melika."

Publications from
Bella Books, Inc.
Women. Books. Even Better Together.
P.O. Box 10543
Tallahassee, FL 32302
Phone: 800-729-4992
www.bellabooks.com

CALM BEFORE THE STORM by Peggy J. Herring. Colonel Marcel Robicheaux doesn't tell and so far no one official has asked, but the amorous pursuit by Jordan McGowen has her worried for both her career and her honor.
978-0-9677753-1-9

THE WILD ONE by Lyn Denison. Rachel Weston is busy keeping home and head together after the death of her husband. Her kids need her and what she doesn't need is the confusion that Quinn Farrelly creates in her body and heart.
978-0-9677753-4-0

LESSONS IN MURDER by Claire McNab. There's a corpse in the school with a neat hole in the head and a Black & Decker drill alongside. Which teacher should Inspector Carol Ashton suspect? Unfortunately, the alluring Sybil Quade is at the top of the list. First in this highly lauded series.
978-1-931513-65-4

WHEN AN ECHO RETURNS by Linda Kay Silva. The bayou where Echo Branson found her sanity has been swept clean by a hurricane—or at least they thought. Then an evil washed up by the storm comes looking for them all, one-by-one. Second in series.
978-1-59493-225-0

DEADLY INTERSECTIONS by Ann Roberts. Everyone is lying, including her own father and her girlfriend. Leaving matters to the professionals is supposed to be easier! Third in series with *PAID IN FULL* and *WHITE OFFERINGS*.
978-1-59493-224-3

SUBSTITUTE FOR LOVE by Karin Kallmaker. No substitutes, ever again! But then Holly's heart, body and soul are captured by Reyna... Reyna with no last name and a secret life that hides a terrible bargain, one written in family blood.
978-1-931513-62-3

MAKING UP FOR LOST TIME by Karin Kallmaker. Take one Next Home Network Star and add one Little White Lie to equal mayhem in little Mendocino and a recipe for sizzling romance. This lighthearted, steamy story is a feast for the senses in a kitchen that is way too hot.
978-1-931513-61-6

2ND FIDDLE by Kate Calloway. Cassidy James's first case left her with a broken heart. At least this new case is fighting the good fight, and she can throw all her passion and energy into it.
978-1-59493-200-7

HUNTING THE WITCH by Ellen Hart. The woman she loves — used to love — offers her help, and Jane Lawless finds it hard to say no. She needs TLC for recent injuries and who better than a doctor? But Julia's jittery demeanor awakens Jane's curiosity. And Jane has never been able to resist a mystery. #9 in series and Lammy-winner.
978-1-59493-206-9

FAÇADES by Alex Marcoux. Everything Anastasia ever wanted — she has it. Sidney is the woman who helped her get it. But keeping it will require a price — the unnamed passion that simmers between them.
978-1-59493-239-7

ELENA UNDONE by Nicole Conn. The risks. The passion. The devastating choices. The ultimate rewards. Nicole Conn rocked the lesbian cinema world with *Claire of the Moon* and has rocked it again with *Elena Undone*. This is the book that tells it all...
978-1-59493-254-0

WHISPERS IN THE WIND by Frankie J. Jones. It began as a camping trip, then a simple hike. Dixon Hayes and Elizabeth Colter uncover an intriguing cave on their hike, changing their world, perhaps irrevocably.
978-1-59493-037-9

WEDDING BELL BLUES by Julia Watts. She'll do anything to save what's left of her family. Anything. It didn't seem like a bad plan...at first. Hailed by readers as Lammy-winner Julia Watts' funniest novel.
978-1-59493-199-4

WILDFIRE by Lynn James. From the moment botanist Devon McKinney meets ranger Elaine Thomas the chemistry is undeniable. Sharing—and protecting—a mountain for the length of their short assignments leads to unexpected passion in this sizzling romance by newcomer Lynn James.
978-1-59493-191-8

LEAVING L.A. by Kate Christie. Eleanor Chapin is on the way to the rest of her life when Tessa Flanagan offers her a lucrative summer job caring for Tessa's daughter Laya. It's only temporary and everyone expects Eleanor to be leaving L.A...
978-1-59493-221-2

SOMETHING TO BELIEVE by Robbi McCoy. When Lauren and Cassie meet on a once-in-a-lifetime river journey through China their feelings are innocent...at first. Ten years later, nothing—and everything—has changed. From Golden Crown winner Robbi McCoy.
978-1-59493-214-4

DEVIL'S ROCK by Gerri Hill. Deputy Andrea Sullivan and Agent Cameron Ross vow to bring a killer to justice. The killer has other plans. Gerri Hill pens another intriguing blend of mystery and romance in this page-turning thriller.
978-1-59493-218-2

SHADOW POINT by Amy Briant. Madison McPeake has just been not-quite fired, told her brother is dead and discovered she has to pick up a five-year old niece she's never met. After she makes it to Shadow Point it seems like someone—or something—doesn't want her to leave. Romance sizzles in this ghost story from Amy Briant.
978-1-59493-216-8

JUKEBOX by Gina Daggett. Debutantes in love. With each other. Two young women chafe at the constraints of parents and society with a friendship that could be more, if they can break free. Gina Daggett is best known as "Lipstick" of the columnist duo Lipstick & Dipstick.
978-1-59493-212-0

BLIND BET by Tracey Richardson. The stakes are high when Ellen Turcotte and Courtney Langford meet at the blackjack tables. Lady Luck has been smiling on Courtney but Ellen is a wild card she may not be able to handle.
978-1-59493-211-3